FINDING HAPPINESS AT HERITAGE VIEW

HELEN ROLFE

Boldwood

First published in 2022. This edition first published in Great Britain in 2022 by Boldwood Books Ltd.

Copyright © Helen Rolfe, 2022

Cover Design by CC Book Design

Cover Photography: Shutterstock

A CIP catalogue record for this book is available from the British Library.

Paperback ISBN 978-1-80415-508-0

Large Print ISBN 978-1-80415-504-2

Hardback ISBN 978-1-80415-503-5

Ebook ISBN 978-1-80415-501-1

Kindle ISBN 978-1-80415-502-8

Audio CD ISBN 978-1-80415-509-7

MP3 CD ISBN 978-1-80415-506-6

Digital audio download ISBN 978-1-80415-500-4

Boldwood Books Ltd
23 Bowerdean Street
London SW6 3TN

For my husband, always x

1

'How did I ever let you talk me into this?' Hazel was sitting in a church hall with her good friend Lucy, pencils poised, but she was having trouble attempting to sketch the naked man seated before them. 'It's all right for you, you're arty. I'm hopeless.'

Lucy didn't laugh, but the corners of her mouth twitched. 'You need to get out more and this is a start. I'm being a good friend. And besides, I knew it would be better than coming on my own. I needed to fill my creative well and I appreciate the support.'

'You didn't tell me it involved nudity,' Hazel whispered. 'You had me thinking we'd be drawing a basket of fruit or an old-fashioned teddy bear.'

Lucy's pencil stopped its action on her paper and she turned to face Hazel, keeping her voice low so they weren't disturbing anyone else. 'To be fair, that *is* what we did three weeks ago. And according to one of the other ladies, last week they drew a crumpled-up paper bag. What would you rather?' She glanced briefly in the model's direction, eyebrows raised, before turning her attention back to her sketch.

Hazel couldn't help but smile. 'I suppose it *is* better than drawing a pile of rubbish.' Although she wouldn't feel self-conscious gawping at a paper bag.

She supposed she'd better make a start. The tutor was doling out general advice and making her way around the group and Hazel would look pretty silly if she didn't at least attempt to do this. And, she supposed, it was fun. It wasn't often – or ever – that she got to sit and stare, without judgement, at a naked man. Perhaps this was the biggest treat she'd get all summer.

'Your first life model?' the tutor, behind her, asked her in a voice Hazel wished didn't carry quite so well. She also wished her easel was a little higher so she could properly hide behind her paper in case the model looked her way.

'Yes,' she muttered, as quiet as she could. 'I'm here with Lucy, really, I'm not much of an artist at all.' She knew the tutor had already complimented Lucy on the start she'd made with her picture.

'There aren't any wrongs with art, it's your interpretation,' she said, as though Hazel's claim not to be an artist was neither here nor there. 'Try to relax your shoulders a bit...' she lowered her voice, '...and you'll need to spend a lot of time actually looking at the model, otherwise how can you hope to draw him?' Not much difference in age to Hazel's thirty-seven years, she didn't seem uncomfortable at all with the nakedness in such close proximity, not even when she spoke to the model as though he was a man in the street, fully clothed, nothing to see here.

The tutor moved on to someone else and Hazel got back to her drawing, although every time she stared at the model, she only did it for a few seconds before she had to look away. The rest of the group didn't seem to have her issues, although perhaps they, as artists, thought of him differently – more of an exhibit than a good-looking man without any clothes. All Hazel seemed capable of fixating on was that the only thing separating the group of six wannabe artists and his very fine naked form was a mere couple of metres and a semi-circle of easels, pieces of paper, and fancy pencils.

'Remember, no straight lines, we need curves,' the teacher vocalised at volume as she continued her rounds, observing, advising.

As she attempted more of her sketch, Hazel wondered whether it wouldn't be so bad if the life model didn't have such a good body, or if he was a few decades older, or perhaps if he was a she.

Lucy leaned over to whisper to her, 'Is this the first man you've seen naked since James?'

Hazel appreciated the interruption. Her sketch was going nowhere fast. 'For your information, yes, it is.'

'He seems to think you'll be naked friends again someday.'

Hazel shrugged. 'The jury's out.'

She and James had been serious, they'd been engaged, but a year ago, Hazel had felt almost as though she was suffocating and she had a hard time separating whether that was because of James and their relationship, or whether it was because she hadn't dealt properly with what had happened three years ago. All she knew was that, twelve months ago, she'd had to tell James that she needed time, she needed space. He was still around, on and off, still in her life as a friend, but she didn't know whether she wanted to go back to what they once were.

Lucy leaned closer to Hazel's drawing and nodded what Hazel thought might be approval. 'It's not bad, considering you said you were terrible.'

'You're being far too kind. Don't think I'll be contacting a gallery to put this on display anytime soon.' All she had was the start, the curve of his shoulder and his torso and around at the bottom, which was where she'd stopped. Thinking about his bum was a step too far, even though she could only really see the rather strong

thigh propped up to conceal certain other bits she was pretty sure
the artists around the other side had a great view of.

'Every now and then, I like to do something out of my comfort
zone,' Lucy explained when she saw Hazel's hesitation to draw any
more, the pencil hovering in her hand.

'Well, this is definitely out of *my* comfort zone,' said Hazel, her
pencil scraping the beginnings of the man's thigh finally and
moving down after she glanced at the muscle and tried to replicate
it on the paper. 'You owe me a drink. Or two.'

Lucy, an artisan blacksmith in Heritage Cove, where they both
lived, usually made things from iron, copper, or other materials in
her workshop, using an old-fashioned forge for some of the beautiful items. But there was no forge inside this church hall situated a
forty-minute drive from the Cove. The only thing heating up
around here were Hazel's cheeks when she caught the model's eye.
For the most part, he made sure he didn't make eye contact with
anyone, but he'd adjusted position as he got comfortable again.

'Do you think the others sat around that side on purpose?'
Hazel wondered, although when one of the artists on the other side
looked her way, she hoped she hadn't spoken too loudly.

'You mean so they see... everything?' Lucy grinned. 'The model
wasn't sitting there when we set up, remember, so it was potluck as
to the angle you got. Don't mind this one too much. Go take a peek.'

'Oh, my goodness, Lucy!' But Hazel was laughing and this time
more than one person in the group looked her way at the disrup-
tion, which made her want to laugh all the more. 'I will do no such
thing. And there's no way I could draw *that*.'

It was more than a relief when they reached the end of the class.
Hazel couldn't wait to get out of there. She joined in with clapping
their appreciation for the model along with everyone else and
busied herself packing up the pencils she'd used, collecting her
bag, rolling her drawing so nobody else could see it, and by the

time she looked up, the model had gone, presumably to find his clothes.

'Ready.' She stood beside Lucy, who was still using the side of her pencil to shade an area on her picture.

'I wanted to ask the tutor a couple of questions.' Lucy pulled a face, sensing Hazel's desire to leave. 'Do you mind?'

'Not at all, but we're in a one-hour spot outside.' She shook off Lucy's rush to pack up. 'It's not a problem, give me your keys and I'll move the car if anyone comes while I'm waiting.'

When Hazel took the keys, she looked closer at Lucy's drawing. 'You're seriously good at this.'

'I loved every minute. It really looks like him, doesn't it?'

Hazel cleared her throat as she brought her mind to the picture rather than her vision of the man who'd just posed for it. 'It really does.'

'If Daniel asks,' said Lucy, 'we drew an eighty-year-old man. I don't want to make him jealous.'

Lucy's boyfriend Daniel didn't strike Hazel as the jealous type at all. He ran the Little Waffle Shack in Heritage Cove and he was all heart, just like his brother Harvey, who was married to another local friend, Melissa. 'I won't lie to him, but he'll take one look at your drawing and know full well that the man is nowhere near old age.'

Hazel left Lucy to talk with the tutor while she headed out of the shadows from the back door to the church hall and into the evening sunshine. Lucy had driven them both over from the Cove and they'd dropped in on her parents first for tea and scones, which was lovely but made Hazel miss her own parents all the more. Her mum and dad, Thomas and Sally, had retired to the West Country. It had been their dream for many years, despite their lives and their business in the Cove. Hazel and her brother Arnold had known the change was coming, they'd both wanted to take over the business since they were younger, but it still took some getting used to. But she was getting there. And she loved her home at Heritage View House which, along with Heritage View Stables, was situated down a lane leading from the village's main street.

Hazel inhaled the rich scent of the brightly coloured rhododendrons on the summer evening air as she reached the end of the path and opened the gate. At least the fresh breeze kept the temperature more bearable after the heatwave that had hit the country last week. It was the one time of the year when Hazel welcomed her early starts at the stables – it was an excuse to get up and get on.

She followed the pavement along, taking out her sunglasses to put on, ready to intercept any traffic warden about to pounce. At the start of July, the weather was gorgeous, and the birds in the trees twittered above her as she walked as though they were as much in support of the season as Hazel was.

She'd almost reached the car when she heard a commotion coming from the other side of the road. With parking fines on her mind, she expected it to be someone fighting their corner and pleading with a traffic warden to be let off with a warning. But it wasn't.

'It's him,' she said under her breath, because looking across the road, she instantly recognised the man who'd just modelled for them, despite him wearing clothes now – jeans that hugged his buttocks, a T-shirt that clung just enough to be able to see the outline of his torso and strong shoulders. His light-brown hair was cut short but had waves in it she could imagine being sketched out by pencil – obviously by someone with more artistic talent than herself.

Hazel had seen the physical details of this man – she couldn't remember his name, even though the tutor had introduced him to the group – but what she hadn't seen inside that church hall was any hint of his personality besides the confidence to sit there in the nude in front of a bunch of strangers. Now, she could see his shoulders were tense as he confronted a group of teenagers a fraction of his age.

Should she call the police?

His anger was evident. Had those teens been hanging around his car, trying to steal it or vandalise it? But if that was the case, surely they would have run off.

It turned her stomach when Hazel saw how scared those teenagers were, frozen to the spot. She'd witnessed that kind of stance before and it had been terrifying. She'd never forget it. The man before her now had a tightness in his expression that she zoned in on: his clenched jaw, the jerky head movements as he said his piece. He got right up in the face of one of the boys to make whatever point he was trying to get across, and Hazel knew if that were her standing before him, she'd be petrified.

Hazel had her hand on her phone, about to call the police, when the boys ran off and the man didn't give chase. She reached Lucy's car, the next one up, unlocked it, and climbed in, sinking down in the seat, praying that the man hadn't spotted her.

She didn't look up until Lucy got back into the car.

'You okay there?' Lucy, in the driver's seat, wound the window down for air.

Hazel sat up straighter, cautiously looking in the wing mirror to check the man had gone. When she saw that he had, she opened her own window. 'You owe me a drink.'

'I haven't forgotten. The Copper Plough?' Lucy looked at her after mentioning their local pub. 'What's wrong?'

'Nothing, just still in shock at what you made me do, that's all,' she laughed, although the laughter was forced. She didn't want to admit that what she'd just seen was a stark reminder of something she'd been trying to forget for a long time. Her way of coping was to stop her thoughts from ever travelling in that direction again. And it worked, kind of.

'Parking police,' Lucy announced and wasted no time pulling out of the space.

Hazel was more than happy to get well away from here in case she saw that man again. Good looking he might be, particularly naked, but behind that exterior was a whole lot of anger and she never wanted to be on the receiving end of that kind of fury again.

* * *

'Tell Barney why you owe me,' Hazel laughed as they stood at the bar in the Copper Plough some thirty minutes later, Lucy paying for the round of drinks with her card. 'Tell him what you had me do.'

Barney, in his seventies and a man who had the community's interests at heart, loved nothing more than a good story. 'I'm all ears.'

'You're making out I tortured you,' Lucy tutted. 'She enjoyed it,' she winked at Barney, before filling him in on exactly where they'd been.

Barney, pint in hand, chuckled away. 'I'll bet you didn't expect that, Hazel.'

'It wouldn't be so bad if I could draw, but I couldn't even stare as I was too embarrassed every time the guy looked up.'

'At least it made for a fun time, you young girls need to get out and about a bit. It can't be all business.'

Lois, love of Barney's life, came over and hooked her arm into his. 'Did I hear something about a naked man?'

'Look what you started,' he grinned to Hazel and Lucy, and off they went to find a table.

'He's right, you know.' Lucy slipped her credit card into her purse. 'It can't all be work. Don't get me wrong, work is a great distraction, I know that as well as anyone, but it's not everything.'

With an eye roll, Hazel followed Lucy outside and into the beer garden. It was way too nice to sit inside, and right at the back they found a spare table. Some of the oldies probably didn't want it because local teacher Linc was playing his guitar and they might not be able to hear one another, but for the girls, the music simply added to the atmosphere.

'Talking of work, how's business?' Hazel enquired of Lucy. 'You always seem to have people popping in and out of the workshop.'

'I get lots of commissions, which I love, because with those I can start from scratch, sketch out what they want.'

'I'm still in love with my wine rack, by the way.' Hazel sipped her beer as the sun sank a little lower in the sky.

'Glad to hear it's being used, good choice by your brother.'

The Christmas before last, Arnold had commissioned Lucy to design and make a gorgeous wine rack which was made by joining horseshoes together and held a couple of wine glasses upright as well as a couple of bottles. Unbeknownst to Arnold, that same Christmas, Hazel had already asked Lucy to make a boot scraper for her brother, and the ornate piece that sat at the door of the office worked perfectly to rid boots of dirt and mud. He'd loved it, although she was sure she used it more than him because she was the one who handled most of the paperwork in the office while he did the majority of the teaching at the riding school. It had always been the intention that brother and sister would both teach and know their way around the office, just as their parents had done. But Hazel had backed away from the former in a big way. The Heritage View Stables were renowned for teaching beginners, and though it was key to their business, it was something Hazel just couldn't manage these days.

They talked about Arnold for a while, but Hazel didn't let on that her brother was growing increasingly frustrated at her refusal to teach more classes. It didn't exactly make for a harmonious, or tenable, family business.

'He's still single,' Hazel smiled at her friend. 'I always thought he'd settle down first out of the two of us and I'd end up being the spinster living in the big old house with her brother and his wife.'

'What happened to the girl he hung around with last summer?' Lucy asked.

'She was nice, clever too,' Hazel replied. 'So clever she decided on a career change and took herself off to university in Edinburgh. She wants to be a vet.'

'Talking of vets, did you hear about the new village vet practice opening up on the same road, up past the florist, any day now?'

Hazel made a face. 'I hadn't heard. Or I had, but I've forgotten.' This was why Lucy, amongst others in the village, was trying to get her out and about more. She spent too much time in her own head with her own problems and, because it was easy to cite the business as a reason to do little other than spend time in the office or busy at the stables, she was missing out on village life.

'You spend a lot of time thinking about work... too much time,' Lucy said.

Hazel didn't deny it, but she also didn't add that it wasn't only thinking about work all the time, it was worrying that she was stuck in a rut. 'Is the new practice opening in the old key-cutting place?'

Lucy shook her head. 'Way too small for a vet's – and I think Valerie from the florist has her eye on that place to expand her shop. There has been some talk amongst the younger girls around the Cove that they might like a nail salon in the village.'

'I'll bet Barney would have something to say about that,' Hazel laughed as the music filled the night air and Linc began to take requests. 'Not much gets past him and I'm pretty sure a nail salon wouldn't.'

'Tilly tried to wind him up, said there were some real plans being drawn up.'

'Trust Tilly to tease him, although given how close they are since Tilly took over her gran's shop and turned it into Tilly's Bits 'n' Pieces, I suppose she's allowed to. And I'll bet he didn't believe her.'

'Exactly. He's far too switched on to have been fooled, don't you worry.'

'So where's the new veterinary practice going to be then, if not in the old key-cutting place?'

Lucy explained that it would be in the run-down, bay-windowed old bungalow that had sold a while back. 'Harvey and Melissa said that if they didn't live in Tumbleweed House, they would've bought the place as a business interest to do up and sell on.'

'They would've done a good job too,' Hazel approved. 'But a new vet locally is convenient and far less of a pain than travelling out of the Cove.'

A new vet in the village would be good for both of them. Lucy had a slate-grey cat called Shadow, who was often seen lying in the sunshine outside her workshop or up towards the Waffle Shack. Hazel and Arnold had a tabby cat who had wandered into the paddock almost a decade ago. Hazel had scooped the cat up in her arms before she got trodden on by one of the horses. When the cat didn't seem to be in any hurry to leave, Hazel's parents had put up posters around the village to say she'd been found, but nobody ever came forward and so, with her one eye and unknown age – the vet had estimated around five years old – and under the new name of Tabitha, the cat had made her forever home at the Heritage View Stables.

Lucy finished her beer. 'Another round? Come on, I owe you after the art class.'

'Please don't remind me.' She'd tried to put that man out of her mind – his amazing body, the curves and muscles she'd been given permission to look at – and she'd definitely tried to block out his temper. 'Next time, please let me draw horses, I'm way more comfortable around those.'

'I could make a very inappropriate joke about body parts right now,' Lucy laughed.

'Did you sneak a peek?'

'Couldn't see from where we were sitting,' she grinned before heading off to get the drinks. 'Next time, perhaps.'

And by the time they'd had a few rounds and Hazel headed home to Heritage View House, she was glad Lucy had dragged her along to something that put her way out of her comfort zone. Because, deep down, Hazel knew she needed it.

2

The morning after the art class, Hazel ventured downstairs shortly after six, happy it was summer and the sun came up nice and early. It helped her to get out of bed when the rest of the village was likely sleeping, with the exception of Jade and Celeste, who ran the Twist and Turn Bakery and kept bakers' hours. She picked up the post from the mat – a single brown envelope that was most likely something financial. She found Arnold in the kitchen, sitting at the farmhouse table as usual, browsing news on the iPad the way he always did, a mug of coffee in front of him, an empty bowl left behind from his cereal.

Hazel set down the envelope and grabbed the sliced bread from the bread bin before locating the butter dish, a knife, and a plate.

'You all right to take the lesson at eleven o'clock?' Arnold finished his last mouthful of coffee.

'I told you I would.' The lesson was more of a supervision session for an adult who had been riding here for many years, a friend of their parents. Hazel would merely give tips and guidance for a series of low jumps in a small circuit that she would set up while the rider and the horse warmed up in the school.

'Don't take your hangover out on me.' At least her snappish tone seemed to amuse her brother. Sometimes he could be too serious and it detracted from the dark-haired good looks passed down from their dad. Hazel and her brother were complete opposites in looks – she had blonde hair, highlighted all the more from the sun, while he had a few greys now he'd reached forty. She had none to speak of, as she liked to remind him. Hazel had blue eyes, Arnold had brown. Her skin turned a golden brown without much effort at all, while he had to be more careful, being slightly fairer. In temperament, however, she liked to think they were pretty similar. They both worked hard, they were both thorough and patient, but while Arnold's way was to meet challenges head on, Hazel tended to hold back when she feared something.

'I'm not hungover,' Hazel told her brother as she dropped two slices of bread into the toaster before pouring herself a mug of coffee. But taking in the amused expression on her brother's face, she admitted, 'All right, a couple of beers turned into a fair few. But we had a nice time.'

He seemed to mellow as he put his bowl and mug in the sink and at the back door pulled on his boots. 'I'm glad you went out, socialised a bit.'

'You make it sound as though I'm a recluse.' She wasn't that bad. It was more a case of being busy, focused. She noticed Arnold hovering at the back door. 'What's wrong?' She'd always be able to read him and he knew it.

'I had to turn down another booking late last night for three siblings who want riding lessons.'

'We can't fit them in?'

He raised his eyebrows – wasn't it obvious? 'Not with only one of us teaching.'

'I teach,' she defended, although she wasn't teaching nearly enough, and her brother was picking up the slack. Their clientele was heavily weighted to the young, inexperienced side, and those were the riders she had a problem with. 'I'll get back to it properly. I will.'

'We're doing well financially but you know I hate turning down business, Hazel. This is our livelihood.'

'I said I'd get back to it,' she repeated. She hated tension with Arnold. They'd never had much growing up, apart from the usual sibling irritations and bickering – whose turn it was to dry up the dishes, who hogged the remote control, which one of them got to sit in the front seat if only one parent was in the car on an outing.

With a sigh that told of his frustration, he headed outside to open up the gates for the hay delivery, which was due any minute now.

'I'll be out soon,' she called after him, a gentleness to her tone.

Heritage View was home, the only home Hazel had ever known or wanted to know, and no matter what happened or the problems she still had, the walls of this house felt safe.

Hazel pushed the back door open fully to allow the breeze to bring inside the freshness of the summer season. The back entrance to Heritage View House led out and around the rear of the property, on past the tack room and to the stable block, which was accessible from two sides, and the office, as well as an indoor riding school. From the front of the house, with its grand door surrounded by ivy and climbing roses, they could see paddocks directly opposite and beside those, the outdoor riding school with further paddocks beyond. All of this land was nestled in Heritage Cove with the main street of the village a short distance away, walkable or rideable, if that was what you chose.

The toast popping up made her jump and from the larder she found the elderflower jam she'd bought locally to spread on her toast after the butter.

As she ate her breakfast, Hazel picked up the brown envelope she'd retrieved from the mat earlier. She realised it was way too soon for the postman and that actually there was no postmark. With a piece of toast between her teeth, she ripped open the envelope and pulled out the piece of paper inside. A Post-it was stuck to the front, which said in curly writing:

Especially for you, enjoy it whenever you need to, love Lucy x.

She almost choked on her toast. In her hand was Lucy's picture of the nude model from yesterday and the way she'd captured him on paper was as though he was sitting here at her kitchen table with her. If Lucy ever decided artisan blacksmithing was no longer for her, she could make a fortune drawing portraits, although Hazel wasn't sure what market there was for nudes.

Hazel had only just got up to take her plate and mug over to the sink when there was a knock at the front door, most likely the actual postman, not Lucy, who must've come by at the crack of dawn to make the delivery.

But it wasn't the postman; it was James. He leaned in and kissed her on the cheek, the way he'd become accustomed to doing since they split up.

She looked at her watch and then back at him. His cheeks were rosy from the fresh start at this early hour. 'It's crazy early.' She spotted his Audi parked behind him, as though it might be too much effort to walk over from the designated parking area outside the main gates to the house and the riding school. Everyone else seemed to manage to park appropriately and it was only deliveries that came up this close, even when the gates were open.

He'd spotted her eyeing the car. 'You're going to ask me to move it, aren't you?'

'You'd better. We're expecting a hay delivery.'

He pointed the remote and the bleep sounded before he

climbed in. One sure way to make him move the car was any threat of it being scratched or covered in debris and a hay delivery satisfied both of those categories.

Hazel hovered at the front door until he jogged back over. 'I've got to go into the office in London,' he explained, as he followed her along the hallway and into the kitchen, where she offered him a cup of coffee. 'Then I have a couple of on-site meetings with clients, so it was an early start this morning. I was passing through, thought I'd stop and check in.' He was dressed smarter than usual, not that he varied much in what he wore. Today he had on charcoal-grey trousers and a light-blue shirt that complimented eyes of almost the same colour and his blond, wavy hair that was always slightly too long. James had been a consultant solicitor specialising in employment law for well over a decade and had the same passion for his job that Hazel had had for hers until something unexpected had knocked her sideways.

'It's kind of you to check in.' Hazel quickly picked up Lucy's sketch and put it beneath the brown envelope on the side as James sat at the table. She didn't really want to answer questions about why she had a hand-drawn picture of a naked man and why she had obviously been looking at it over her breakfast. 'What time is your train?'

'Trying to get rid of me already?'

'You know what mornings are like around here.' She was glad he'd come now and not once she'd got going with the morning routine. As if on cue, the rumble of a truck announced the hay delivery.

When she put a mug of coffee in front of him, he thanked her, blew across the liquid, and braved a sip. 'You seem stressed.'

'No more than usual,' she said, her standard response. 'I'm fine.'

'You always say that. I worry about you.'

'I know you do, I appreciate the concern. But I'm still standing.'

James didn't look too sure. 'I don't want to see you stressed or running yourself into the ground with too much work.'

'If Arnold heard you say that, he'd flip. He's still doing more than his fair share.'

'I'm sure he's coping, don't let him give you a hard time.'

She resisted the urge to leap to Arnold's defence. She shouldn't have bothered mentioning Arnold's workload, as all James saw was the problems she was having. She supposed that was his caring side, the supportive partner role, but it also showed that despite his job and all his worldly experience, when it came to her and her family business, James rarely understood the bigger picture.

'Running your own business is never easy,' he added with another slurp of his coffee.

'I knew that going into it.' All true, but what she hadn't realised was that one event could turn everything upside down when you least expected. She and James had been dating for less than a year when an accident happened at the riding school and well and truly left its mark. James had been there for Hazel through the terrible times and every day since. They'd been engaged when getting married felt like the appropriate next step. Or at least it had until Hazel, confused and all over the place, began to wonder whether she'd clung onto something solid and reliable because everything else was falling apart. She began to be critical of her relationship with James; not about him specifically, but more about what they each wanted in life. And try as she might, she couldn't make their goals align. He wasn't a horse person, not that that mattered, it was good to have different interests, but horses were a major part of her life and when she and Arnold took on the business from their parents, it became even more so. James had never really seemed on board, even though he insisted he was.

'You did know it wouldn't be easy, but did you ever predict it would be this hard?' he asked her now.

And she honestly couldn't answer with anything other than no, so she moved the conversation on to talk about her parents and how they'd settled well into life in the West Country before asking how his parents were and whether they'd given any more thought to retiring from the law practice.

'I can't see them ever giving it up,' James told her as he finished his coffee.

'Funny how careers run in the family, isn't it?'

'It doesn't have to be that way, not if you need a change.' He put a hand over hers and she knew she'd walked right into that one. 'You have options – sell your share, get outside help in.'

But when she simply smiled before looking at her watch again, he picked up on the hint, taking his cup to the sink and rinsing out the dregs. 'I'll get going then, let you get on.'

'Thanks for stopping by.' She knew he did it because he cared, and it was nice to have people on your side. Hazel walked him to the door and when they got there, he pulled her into a hug.

'I'll see you again soon.' He kissed the tip of her nose as though they weren't taking a break from one another at all and added, 'Think about what I've said, Hazel. I don't want this place to break you.'

All she could do was wave him off and then close the door behind him before leaning against the wood. This place *had* almost broken her, but she wanted to fight back, she wanted to push through to the other side, and his words didn't help, even though they came from a good place.

Hazel rushed upstairs to clean her teeth, then back in the kitchen, she pulled on her boots, only just remembering to take the sketch with her when she left the house.

As Hazel hurried past to the office, drawing in hand, Arnold was unloading hay into the barn behind the stable block. She unlocked the office, found one of her notebooks from the shelf above the desk, and slotted the drawing in there. Arnold wouldn't find it there, nobody would – her slightly naughty secret should be safe.

She was still grinning after one last appreciative glance at the drawing before she checked the office voicemail for messages. There was one from a man who was interested in stabling his horse here. Hazel did a little clap. They'd been advertising vacancies at the Heritage View Stables for a while, trying to fill the last remaining spot. With capacity for ten horses, they'd only had eight at the start of the year when one owner moved to Wales and another retired and was able to keep the horse on his own land. One spot had been filled last month but the other had remained vacant. Livery was an important source of income for them, though they made most of their income from the riding school. Arnold would be happy too, especially as the owner had said he would stop by today, so they could get things moving sooner rather than later.

Hazel headed to the stable block to say good morning to the horses, her favourite thing to do. They stabled their horses overnight and it was reassuring to know they were safely tucked away. It was a nicely renovated block, having had a makeover recently, and now, rather than ten separate stables facing each other and blocked in on either side, each stable was separated with bars positioned on the upper portion of the walls. Horses were highly sociable animals and this way they could see one another. It also meant that the stables were well ventilated.

The first task of the day would be to turn out the horses from the stables to the paddocks. Hazel opened up and folded back the main doors to the stable block. She fixed each door out of the way using the sturdy hooks to leave a nice wide entrance all the way down the middle. There were five stables on either side as well as a dedicated wash area and a space opposite that to keep supplies including shampoos, brushes, buckets, wheelbarrows, and a selection of shovels and pitch forks. There was a hay bale there right now; the surplus they hadn't needed for the nets last night but rather than put it back in the barn, they'd left it here for the next top-up.

After she put her basic grooming kit outside the stable block, she called out, 'Good morning, guys and gals,' and started with Sherbert, the liveliest horse of the bunch, and the one who already had her nose poking over the stable door, anxious to get her day started properly. She wasn't daft, none of the horses were, they all knew this was coming the second those stable block doors opened in the mornings. Hazel ran a hand down the Palomino mare's golden nose and felt the horse's breath on her face as she opened up her stable door. 'You always have to be first, don't you?'

She fitted the horse with the halter and led Sherbert out into the morning sunshine, where she fixed the halter loosely to the wall with a rope, close enough so Sherbert couldn't go running off anywhere but with room for movement should the horse want to turn her head. She picked out Sherbert's hooves and gave her a quick brush before leading her over to the paddock, the familiar clippety-clop sound a simple part of life here at Heritage View.

Hazel closed the gate to the paddock. Sherbert had already stretched her long neck towards the ground to nibble at the grass. Hazel repeated the turnout process with every horse until it was time to go back for the last. She greeted Jigsaw, a gelding who had done well to be so patient, his long face looking at her over his stable door as if to ask when it would be his turn. 'Last but not least, Jigsaw,' she smiled before running a hand down from the area between his eyes to the tip of his nose, her cheek against his for a moment. 'You're a handsome boy.'

'I appreciate the compliment,' came a voice from behind her, before she had a chance to open up Jigsaw's stable door.

She turned and came face-to-face with someone who looked oddly familiar. She couldn't quite deduce who the man was, as his body was outlined by the sunshine pouring in, making it hard to look directly at him. 'May I help you?'

He extended a hand as his body moved out of the sunlight. 'I'm Gus, I just spoke to your brother and he pointed me in your direction. I called and left a message about keeping my horse here.' He hesitated. 'Do I have the wrong person? You're not Hazel?'

Hazel had lost the ability to speak. No wonder he seemed familiar. It wasn't that many hours ago that she'd been attempting to draw the outline of his body, except he'd been sitting down and totally naked. Now he wore well-fitted jeans and a white T-shirt, neither of which detracted from the body she knew lay beneath, and she focused on Jigsaw to hide her face from him. It wasn't that she'd seen him naked that was the worst thing, it was that after the class she'd seen him angry, threatening, and it had brought back terrible memories for her of a confrontation that had changed everything. Was this really the sort of man she wanted to have any involvement with, despite him bringing business their way?

'Are you Hazel?' he repeated as she grabbed Jigsaw's halter and undid his stable door.

Jigsaw's ears twitched at the conversation as she slipped his halter over his head before leading him out of the stable. 'I'm Hazel, yes.'

The man, who she now knew as Gus, followed her down the centre of the stable block towards the outside. 'Is now a bad time?' When she said nothing, he sighed. 'I should've called again, given you a time to expect me. It's just, I have things to do later on this morning and I really wanted to sort the stabling today if I can. You *do* have space, don't you?'

Hazel secured the rope to the halter and the halter to the wall, ensuring Jigsaw was comfortable. She had to put this man's behaviour last night out of her mind, this was business, income, their livelihood. 'It's good to meet you. Always a busy time here, but we can still talk. Feel free to wander around while I get Jigsaw groomed and out into the paddock.'

'Thanks, I appreciate it.'

She'd already grabbed the hoof pick and with a little coaxing of her hand running down Jigsaw's hind leg, the horse lifted his foot off the floor so she could get on. She wasn't sorry when Gus went over to look at the outdoor school before taking a peek into the stable block and then moved over towards the paddock while she worked. She wasn't sure she wanted to do this with him as an audience, he made her jittery, which had plenty to do with seeing him naked but a lot to do with his temper too.

Before long, she led Jigsaw over to the paddock so he could join the others.

Gus's brow furrowed as she closed the gate. 'I'm sorry, have we met before?'

Unsure quite what to say, she led the way towards the office, indicating for him to follow, but before they got there, she turned to face him and, in that moment, she saw recognition dawn on his face.

3
_____

Gus wished the guy with the hay who'd introduced himself as Arnold hadn't been busy because it would have been a whole lot easier talking to him rather than this woman who had already seen him naked. It was what his daughter, Abigail, might describe as 'hashtag awkward'.

When Gus was embarrassed, he usually got a compulsion to flee, something he'd really wanted to do last night in that church hall where he'd sat on a hard wooden chair in front of half a dozen people, pencils and sketch pads at the ready. He'd done his best to tell himself that these were people interested in art in a serious way, they weren't there to ogle him or ridicule him. He'd done his best to look confident and hoped the session would go quickly, so he could put his clothes back on and go to meet his daughter, who was in one of the back rooms of the church hall, waiting for him. The sooner the art class was over with, he'd told himself, the better. And as far as he was concerned, no matter how much he owed anyone a favour, he'd never volunteer for anything like this ever again.

'You were at the art class,' he said to Hazel as they reached what he assumed was the office. She stopped and scraped her boots on an ornate boot scraper that looked far too fancy for clumps of dirt and hay. He still couldn't believe his bad luck. He'd modelled once as a huge favour, he'd gone to a class well away from where he used to live and far enough from here in Heritage Cove, the village where he was setting up home, assuming he'd never see any of the amateur artists ever again.

'Yes, I was.' Hazel, now inside the office, held out a hand to indicate the free chair at the side of the desk as she sat in the larger leather one. He went to close the door, but she shook her head. 'It's a lovely day, leave it open.'

Gus's compulsion to flee a situation was almost as great now as it had been at the art class as he sat at an angle to Hazel, who looked equally uncomfortable. He only hoped she didn't judge him on last night and wouldn't see him as anything other than a respectable man, a father, and a horse owner. Because if they couldn't keep their horse here, he wasn't sure what he'd do, and Abigail would be devastated.

Hazel leaned and pulled a folder from the filing cabinet. She didn't seem keen to talk about the art class either, which was more than fine by him.

'You were after a working livery, is that correct?' She opened up the folder and took out a pamphlet, plus what looked like a form, pushing her chair back a little to create a bit more distance between them.

'That is correct.' Weird being formal with someone who had seen your birthday suit already. 'Although could you clarify exactly what "working livery" is? I've had an informal arrangement up until now, but my understanding is that working livery is cheaper than full livery in exchange for you using the horse during lessons.'

'Your understanding is correct.' Her voice wobbled; she seemed nervous but gathered herself quite quickly as she explained. 'We will use your horse for lessons, which keeps their fitness and their schooling abilities up to date. The full list of inclusions we provide here for your horse is in the paperwork but, to give a brief overview, we keep your horse in a stable overnight, we deal with turnout and bringing him in for the night, we feed the horse and we'll take care of grooming needs as and when required. When he first arrives, we'll need to assess him to be totally sure he's suitable for working livery but judging by what you said in your voicemail, I don't see a problem.'

'What if he isn't suitable?'

'Then it's a discussion and we take it from there.'

Denby was a good horse, he'd been ridden by plenty of different people and Gus couldn't see a problem either. And while it would be expensive to pay for full livery if he couldn't be used for lessons, Gus would just have to suck it up and pay the extra cost. He just hoped it wouldn't come to that.

'Let me tell you a bit about us,' she went on. Business-like, she gave him the run-down of the place. 'The Heritage View Stables are a family business, owned and run by me and my brother Arnold, who you just met, and prior to that, our parents. They retired,' she added before he could jump to any conclusions. Probably wise, he already had a fear of somehow making a total idiot of himself again in front of this woman. 'Arnold and I have worked with horses ever since we were kids, we have a lot of experience, both riding and caring for horses and teaching.' Before he had a chance to ask about the teaching, she added, 'What's your horse's name?'

'Denby.'

A small smile spread across her face, and she looked a lot prettier when she lost the frown. 'That's a nice name. And you've recently moved to the village?'

'We have.'

'And where do you currently keep Denby?'

'He's stabled with a good friend and neighbour – the woman who sold him to us, actually – back in the Peak District.'

'That's certainly a beautiful area of the country, but don't worry, there are plenty of special places to ride and walk here on the east coast.'

'I don't doubt it.'

'Most people get in touch long before a house move,' she said, the frown back for a moment. 'Was it sudden? The move, I mean.'

He was a little taken aback by the suspicious undertone, but she had a right to know as much as possible if he was going to be a client. 'It's a job move I've been meaning to make for some time, then the opportunity came up and by lucky chance a place at the local school for my daughter opened up too. Everything apart from Denby's home aligned, including a house to rent.' He shrugged. 'At the end of the day, Denby could stay where he is as long as he needs to, it's just not ideal.'

'So you're looking to get Denby here to Heritage Cove as soon as possible?'

'Yes, otherwise I'll have to answer to my ten-year-old daughter.'

Hazel smiled again, and it hinted that perhaps she understood the pressure he was under to find Denby the perfect home. He really hoped this was it right here, as there weren't exactly many other options and from what he'd seen of the place, he liked it.

'Well, we are ready to take Denby as soon as you need us to.' She sat, pen at the ready to make more notes. 'Tell me a bit about him. I take it you're the registered owner.'

'I am, yes.' Gus felt like he was at a job interview, or Denby's interview, and said on his behalf, 'He's a well-trained gelding – Joan, the previous owner, saw to that – and he's used to being ridden by different people. He's obedient, most of the time. Let me see, he's just over fourteen hands, chestnut with a flaxen mane and tail. Joan was my neighbour, who had him for twelve years before we bought him, and we kept him stabled with her.'

She scribbled away and he waited until at last she looked up and met his gaze briefly before she handed him the pamphlet and the form, which was in fact the contract. 'All the information you need is in there,' she said, indicating the pamphlet. 'And the contract is a draft. It contains specific details of our services, facilities, financials, the care Denby will get and the working arrangements for your horse. Take a look at it and then, if you could forward all of yours and Denby's specific details, I can draw up the final contract for you to sign.'

He glanced over it now. The contract was certainly thorough. There was a section detailing the provision of stabling and grazing, basic feed and hay and bedding, what the responsibilities of each party were.

'If you require anything additional – particular bedding or feed, for example, let me know and I'll add it in to the contract.'

'Will do.'

'The fees are all in there too.' Somewhat reluctantly, she leaned closer so she could point out the relevant section on the paperwork. For someone dressed in jodhpurs and a simple T-shirt, someone who had been around horses long before he arrived this morning, she smelt pretty good, like a heady summer fragrance that made you want to cling onto the day that lay ahead.

'Are they as expected?' she asked when he didn't comment. She'd already moved away again. 'They should be around about what was quoted on the website. I can't remember how old that draft is.' She pulled a face.

He cleared his throat, willing himself to get a grip. It wasn't like he'd never been in the company of an attractive woman before, it was more that this morning, she was unexpected. And he wasn't sure what to make of her demeanour – friendly one minute, wary the next, as though she was trying to work him out. He held up the contract and pamphlet. 'They all look satisfactory to me. I'll take a look at all of this and be in touch with the details – mine and Denby's.'

'Great. Now, I'll need to take a deposit from you today to hold the stable place.'

'Is it your last?' He felt his back pockets one after the other and pulled out his wallet. He flipped it open and slipped the card out to hand over to Hazel.

'It is, almost a full house,' she smiled, grabbing a card machine from behind a stack of papers on top of the filing cabinet.

'You must love your work.'

'I really do.' Something in the way she said it hinted that she might be reminding herself of that rather than telling him, and he punched in his PIN once she'd inserted his card and entered the amount to be paid.

The pamphlet in his hands, after Hazel had stapled his receipt to the front of it, Gus flipped through to find the section about Denby being used for riding lessons. 'My daughter is worried about this bit.'

She glanced over to see which section he was pointing at. 'Please tell her not to be. Rest assured we will fully assess Denby ourselves to make sure he's suitable for riding lessons. And both Arnold and I will decide what age group is appropriate for Denby to be paired with, what level of ability his riders should have. It's an important part of settling him in and I can assure you we are used to doing it. We'll get to know him first, as it's important to us that he's matched with the right riders when they come along.' She pointed to the contract. 'You'll find details in the paperwork of how many hours Denby will be ridden as a maximum and on what days. As you'll see, it's not crazy amounts. And days and times can be adjusted if need be.'

'That sounds reassuring, I'll let Abigail know.' He closed the pamphlet. 'So both you and Arnold teach, is that right?'

'We certainly do. Do you ride?'

'Previously I've had some lessons with Denby's former owner, she's very patient. We went out on a few long rides too, saw a bit of the countryside. It was nice to get to know Denby when we bought him. Couldn't let Abigail have all the fun.'

She seemed to relax at his revelation that he might care about horses almost as much as his daughter did.

He hadn't really thought about learning anything else but found himself telling her, 'I wouldn't mind a few more lessons as a reminder, a familiarisation, if you like. Would you have any space?'

She nodded. 'I think I do. Let me take a look in the diary.' She opened up a big book and reeled off a few different days and time slots. 'When you know your own schedule and once Denby is here, give me a shout.'

'Thank you, I will do.'

'I think Denby will be happy here.' She said it with an air of pride and also with a love for what she did. He could see it in her demeanour, the way she softened as she talked about horses, the way her smile met her eyes. 'Don't forget, as the horse owner, you can pop in as much as you like, you can use the school, indoors or outside, you can take Denby out on a ride. We like people to feel a part of life here at Heritage View.'

He tried to work out whether that was her standard line but even if it was, he could tell she meant it. And he was glad she didn't seem quite as jumpy with him now. When they'd first come into the office and she'd insisted on leaving the door open, he'd had a feeling that they clashed, that this was never going to work. But now he felt confident that it would. 'I was thinking of having Denby come here at the weekend. Joan can bring him as soon as we like.'

'Then let's get the contract in place. I'll need any requests for changes in writing.' She leaned across the desk and he caught a glimpse of her belly button when her T-shirt rode up as she reached for one of the business cards in a container at the back. 'Take this, all my details are on there.'

'Do I deal mostly with you, or your brother?' Please let it be her. Already he quite liked the idea.

'Most likely me, as I'm the one who manages the office, but if you leave a message and Arnold picks it up, you might hear from him too.'

'Great. Would it be all right to take a better look around?'

'Sure, let's do that now.' She gestured for him to leave the office first and once she was outside, she closed the door behind them.

Gus met Arnold briefly as he finished putting away the bales of hay they'd had delivered and Hazel had a short conversation with him, agreeing to tack up a couple of horses when they were brought in from the paddock in a little while. Her brother must be taking a lesson. 'Sometimes the horses in the paddock give him the run around,' she said good-humouredly, 'but hopefully not this morning. He doesn't have much time before the lesson.' She checked her watch.

'I appreciate you doing this when I gave zero warning I would turn up so early.' He'd already taken Abigail to school in time for breakfast club this morning and although he hadn't wanted to let her go into the new environment just yet, he had no choice if he wanted to sort out a place for Denby. Abigail had seemed happy enough with the arrangement, almost enthusiastic to get on with it, but Gus hadn't been. It had taken all his willpower not to look back at his daughter after he closed that classroom door in case she looked so lost and vulnerable that he ran back inside, scooped her up, and took her back to the house. Home schooling had briefly filtered through his mind but so had Joan's voice, telling him he had to let her experience everything other girls her age did.

'It's really not a problem,' Hazel assured him as she led the way to what looked a little like a shed from the outside. 'This is the tack room.' She seemed to try to keep some distance between them, ever the professional, but it was a compact space, so it wasn't easy.

'It's very organised.' Against the walls were saddle racks, each with a saddle and the name of the horse on the wall behind it. It reminded him of Abigail's first day at primary school, when they'd found her coat peg with her name on it. She'd been gutted she had a fish and someone else got a horse, he wasn't sure she'd ever got over it, at least not until she stuck a big sticker of a horse over the poor fish.

'This space is for Denby.' Hazel had her hand on an empty hook ready for Denby's bridle and then moved over to show him the space for the saddle, where his saddle pad and girth would go.

She waited beside him and he moved out of the way when he realised she wanted to get past. 'I'll grab Minstrel's tack while I'm in here,' she explained. 'He's in the lesson this morning.'

'That all looks heavy.' He eyed the saddle, the girth she'd laid across, the bridle she'd looped onto her shoulder and the saddle pad she laid on top of what was in her arms. 'I can help.'

She hesitated but then said, 'Actually, if you wouldn't mind, could you bring out Peony's tack?' She indicated the spots where it was kept.

Gus picked up the bridle from its hook on the wall and looped it over his shoulder the way she had, then found the saddle and the girth from a shelving unit at the end, and the saddle pad from a big wooden organiser. He followed Hazel outside, where they put the tack onto a rack fit for the purpose.

After he'd helped her, Hazel seemed happier to be with him and even stood less than a couple of metres away, less wary of him, perhaps. She took him to see the indoor school, all the while talking about other horses they'd had here who were working livery and how their owners had enjoyed the experience, taking away a lot of the responsibility for them. 'I get what it's like,' she said, 'people have jobs, kids have school, and looking after a horse is a massive commitment.'

'But worth it,' he said.

She briefly considered his words before she led him to the outside school and towards the paddocks. He looked over at the main house too, impressive in its proportions. 'Growing up here must have been a blast. All this space to run around. Imagine the games of Hide and Seek.'

She laughed. 'We did have a few of those games and yes, it was a wonderful place to grow up. Still is.'

'You're still growing up?'

Her cheeks reddened slightly, and he realised it had sounded like flirting when he hadn't meant it to be. 'Something like that,' she said as Arnold came out of the paddock, leading one of the horses.

Hazel took the horse while Arnold went back for another. 'I think you and your daughter will love being here in Heritage Cove.'

'I'm hoping so.'

'It's the sort of place people come to and never want to leave.' She said it while looking at the horse, one hand on his halter, the other running down his long face.

Gus looked over to the paddock, where Arnold was trying to grab another horse, who was playing a bit of a game with him. It was fun to watch.

Hazel had already made a start with grooming the horse she had.

'I assume this is Minstrel?' Gus checked as she finished scraping out the remaining hoof and dropped the pick into the tidy box in exchange for a brush that she began to run across the horse's glossy brown coat.

'It sure is.'

'Cool name.' He approached the horse from the front so his touch didn't take the mare by surprise and once he'd run a hand down her nose, he did the same down her neck, her coat smooth on the side Hazel had just been brushing, clean and gleaming in the sunshine.

'Minstrel, I think you'd be a lovely horse to ride.' When Gus spoke, he felt Hazel watching him, taking in his almost soppy undertones, but she looked away when he met her gaze.

'Minstrel would be good for you to ride in a lesson.' Hazel finished brushing the other side of Minstrel's body. She picked up the saddle pad from the rack and positioned it correctly. And with a smile, she told him, 'I still remember one of the first men I taught, years ago now, was only here because his girlfriend loved horses and he wanted to impress her. He ended up loving riding so much he bought a horse.'

Gus nodded his approval. 'I hope he got the girl.'

'They married soon after,' she grinned.

'Talking of lessons, I need to sign my daughter up before myself, really. She's more important.'

'Actually I'm not sure I do have space.' She cleared her throat. 'Arnold is your man to ask about lessons.'

Arnold? What happened to her teaching?

He let the query go for a moment while she carried on tacking up the horse. Gus tuned in to the far-off whinnying, the sound of hooves as Arnold brought the other horse from grass to concrete, the sigh from Minstrel as she was attended to. He inhaled the freshness of country air that made him feel as though they were in the middle of nowhere and his mind drifted to his daughter and the way horses were not only her passion, but her need. Horses had been Abigail's focus in life when everything around her seemed to be falling apart.

'You're very comfortable around horses, even though you don't ride,' Hazel observed, her voice bringing him back to the present.

'It kind of comes in the job description. I'm a vet.'

Things seemed to click into place for Hazel. 'Ah, then you must be the new vet in the village.'

'Guilty.'

'A lot of people are pretty happy about the new practice, I expect you'll soon have a full client list.'

'Let's hope so. And about those lessons... for Abigail. She can ride, but she needs a refresher and a sense of the area out on a hack. She's also really keen to learn jumping.'

'Like I said, Arnold is your man.' Hazel's response didn't miss a beat. 'He's a great jumper and a brilliant teacher. He's been in several competitions – those rosettes in the office are mostly his.' Gus remembered a line of rosettes pinned up on one wall behind the desk. 'He only stopped competing when we both took on this place and it all got a bit much.'

Gus knew Abigail would appreciate either teacher, but Hazel seemed gentle, kind, and his daughter needed that. She'd been through enough. Not that he knew anything about Arnold, he might well be the better bet out of the two. And he had to wonder why Hazel had been all for it, offering him lessons with her, with nominated days and times, yet now he was asking about Abigail, she was saying she didn't have availability and pushing him towards her brother.

With someone arriving in the parking area where he'd left his car, a horse rider dressed in the full gear, Gus sensed they were way too busy to discuss lessons for anyone right now.

'You finally caught her,' said Gus, when he saw Arnold bringing the other horse in from the paddock.

'She likes to give me the run around, this one.' Arnold secured her halter to the wall with a piece of rope the same way Hazel had done with Minstrel.

The guy was friendly and his sister could be too, which gave Gus a good feeling about the Heritage View Stables. He could see himself, Abigail, and Denby being a real part of all this. That was all he really wanted, a fresh start that brought with it a sense of permanence.

Hazel saw the young boy approaching, and after reminding him not to walk around the back of the horse, she removed Minstrel's harness and put on his bridle, the bit slipping into the mouth with ease before she checked the fitting was comfortable.

'We got a bit behind,' Arnold grumbled as the boy asked if it was almost time. Someone else had just arrived in the car park, presumably the other kid in the lesson. 'Almost ready.'

'Sorry, I expect that's my fault,' Gus apologised as he watched Hazel start the grooming process for Peony. 'You're doing it all over again?' From the information Hazel had given him he knew horses were groomed prior to their morning turnout.

Hazel smiled. 'It's a good idea before a lesson, it makes sure the horse is comfortable, but at least it's quicker this time round.' She ran her hand down the horse's leg to let her know she was going to clean her hooves for her and obediently Peony lifted her foot, eyes closing against the sun and the odd fly.

Arnold came over to Gus and apologised. 'I'm sorry, I wasn't implying I'm behind because you're here today.'

'It's not a problem.' But he didn't want to be in the way. He'd seen enough, time to get on. 'Thank you both for today. And Hazel, I really appreciate you showing me around.'

'See you again soon,' Arnold smiled before telling his sister, 'Be quick, lesson starts in less than five.'

'I know,' she said in a tone that suggested he might have said it a few times already. She was onto the second hoof already.

It had to be hard, running a business with a sibling. Thank goodness there was only him to worry about with his practice. Gus was his own boss with nobody else at the helm. 'I'll leave you to it, then,' he said to Hazel as she flicked more dirt from the hoof and looked briefly at him. 'I'll be in touch, it was good to meet you. Again.'

He walked away. *Again?* Why had he said that? Judging by the look on her face, it had conjured up visions of his naked torso for her as well as him.

But he shook off the embarrassment and climbed back into his car. Things were falling into place and already he had a good feeling about being here in this stunning village on the east coast of England.

4

Satisfied with Denby's soon-to-be home, Gus drove away from the Heritage View Stables, catching one final glimpse of Hazel in his rear-view mirror as she helped a young girl mount Peony. The brother and sister duo, apart from having a bit of tension between them, definitely knew what they were doing when it came to horses, and he was relieved to have nabbed the last stable available. He'd have hated to leave the horse with Joan for any longer than he had to or to keep Denby at stables further away from the village. Abigail liked to see him pretty much every day, often more than once.

He pulled out onto the main street and past the bus stop before making his way along The Street, the road that brought people into the village from one direction and took them out in another. He drove slowly, not only because the speed limit required him to take his time, but because he wanted to take in the quaint feel of the place. Prior to Heritage Cove, he and his daughter had lived in a stunning area of the country, no doubt about it, but their house had been one of only three set back from a main road that brought tourists to the region, and not much had been within walking distance at all. Here was very different, with amenities close by and a seemingly relaxed pace in the heart of the village.

Gus swung into a parking space outside a bakery with a Tudor-style exterior and latticed glass windows. He had time for a little walk around before he headed back to the house they now called home, conveniently situated around the corner from his new veterinary practice, and carried on with some of the unpacking. He needed some more milk and bread anyway, so he'd pick those up as he explored The Street.

Gus had come to Heritage Cove a few times prior to their actual move, but his visits had always been focused on getting the practice ready. He'd met with the project manager, the architect, made sure everyone was on the same page, then he'd sorted out the rental property for him and Abigail. Most of his visits were made when Abigail was still attending school in the Peak District, apart from the day they'd enrolled Abigail in the local school here after a meeting with the headteacher. Abigail had had the opportunity to meet some of her classmates too, something which he'd dreaded but that she took in her stride.

On so many levels, Abigail was your average ten-year-old girl, but after an accident had left severe scarring on one side of her face, she'd gone from a fun-loving kid to someone who thought carefully about everything she did. And he'd gone from a parent who didn't worry unnecessarily to constantly obsessing about whether she was all right. Was she staying safe? Were others taking care of her? Were people paying her unwanted attention and upsetting her?

In the days following the accident and for months afterwards, Gus protected Abigail at all costs. It was what a parent did. If Abigail went with him to the shops and didn't like it, they would leave straight away. If they went for a walk and she thought someone looked at her strangely, they'd turn and go back home. They didn't go to the local display on bonfire night for the two years after the accident because she didn't want to be in a crowd. She wouldn't go shopping with him for a new school uniform or shoes and he'd had to guess the size. She had refused to go to the hairdresser's when her hair was in desperate need of a cut because all that time looking in a mirror with someone else looking in it too and being so close to her scars was too much to cope with. Gus had ended up cutting it himself until Joan had invited Abigail round to hers the day she had her own hairdresser visit. They'd both had their hair done and followed up the activity by making scones together, which they served with jam and cream piled so high Abigail could barely open her jaw wide enough to get the treat inside.

Gus wasn't quite sure what they would've done without Joan, but she'd always been very honest with him and told him that being overprotective of Abigail would do her no favours in the long run. She told him he could still love and protect his daughter without it being too much. But Gus had still found it difficult not to spend the majority of his waking moments after the accident on high alert, waiting for something terrible to happen, and then, even when it didn't, for someone to make a comment or ask too many questions and ruin her day in that way instead. It was exhausting, stressful, and he'd had to learn the entirely new skill of not constantly worrying about what might or might not happen.

Joan had been a close friend through the whole ordeal, and she'd tried to educate him the best she could, telling him Abigail would learn by example, that his behaviours had an effect on his daughter and only he had the power to make them positive or negative behaviours. Joan had even said that of his relationship with Abigail's mother, Julie. Julie and Gus were no longer together, but Julie was still in Abigail's life, something Gus struggled with. Not because he didn't want her and her daughter to have a relationship, but because Julie was unreliable and had a tendency to cancel prearranged visits at the last minute or buy Abigail expensive gifts out of guilt for what happened. When he'd tried to talk to his ex-wife about the presents she showered Abigail with, her only rebuke had been that he'd bought her a horse and you couldn't get much more expensive than that.

Gus locked the car and passed the archway after the bakery that separated it from a tearoom. It pleased him that there were so many eateries around here for him and Abigail to wander to whatever the season – it was something they'd never had before. He'd spotted a sign for a waffle shack too, across a green space behind the bus stop. Abigail loved her waffles.

He came to a small shop called Tilly's Bits 'n' Pieces and after he looked in at the window display of ornate furniture and accessories, he decided to go inside. It wasn't that he didn't want Abigail getting presents, Julie could buy her things whenever she liked, it was just that Julie had missed his point. His point wasn't the gifts or the expense, it was that she was buying them instead of showing up, as an apology. And that was what didn't sit well with him.

As he looked around the shop, he hoped that when he picked Abigail up from school at 3.30 p.m., he'd see a smiling girl, one who'd had a happy day, someone who hadn't faced a barrage of questions about her scars, or worse, ignorant and nasty comments, which he knew she'd had at her last school. There'd been one particular day when she'd claimed to have an awful tummy ache and had stayed off school. She'd admitted to him later on that the real reason she hadn't wanted to go in was because they had French class. At the last lesson, the boy who sat behind her had asked her, in French, why her face was such a mess.

Gus had cradled his crying daughter, letting her get the anger and the upset out of her system. She'd sobbed and told him she hadn't known what the words meant until the girl she sat next to told her. Gus had a good mind to march up to school, find the boy, and demand to know why he was such a prick. But he couldn't do that. And so instead he'd brought up Google translate on his iPad and found a really rude and totally inappropriate insult for the boy, which he said out loud, and at Abigail's puzzlement showed her the English words. 'Dad!' she'd said, wide-eyed, but the shock and the laughter at her dad being so naughty had scared away her tears. He'd told her not to say it out loud but to repeat it in her head if that boy ever said another word. She'd done just that, but she also told Gus that the teacher had found out what the boy had said to her and given him a detention, and since then he hadn't said a word to her, in French or English.

Inside the shop, a woman around Gus's age, dressed in a floaty, floral dress with her hair pinned up, smiled at him from her position over at the till. Gus had no idea what he was looking for. He picked up scented candles but wasn't sure about those. Abigail was a bit young and he suspected she might leave them burning unattended – a drama he would rather avoid. He found cute bookmarks, coasters, pretty scarves that were too old for his daughter, a selection of keyrings.

'Are you looking for anything in particular?' the woman asked after he'd been in there a few minutes. She came over to him. 'I'm Tilly, welcome. This is my shop.'

'Hello, Tilly. I'm Gus and yes, I am looking for something in particular.' He rubbed a hand around the back of his neck. 'It's for my daughter. A little gift, kind of a housewarming present. She's ten and we just moved here. Today is the first day at a new school.'

'Always daunting,' Tilly agreed. 'Well, firstly, welcome to Heritage Cove. I don't suppose you're the new vet?'

'I am,' he laughed.

'Don't be alarmed. I don't mean to make you feel as though everyone will know your business. It's not like that around here, I promise,' she smiled. 'But we're a friendly bunch and a lot of people have been waiting for your appearance.'

'Do you have pets?'

'I don't, not yet. Thinking about a dog, so I might ask you more on that if I need to.'

'Happy to help, any time.'

'Great, now let's find something for your daughter.' She looked around the shop and, indicating the central display, suggested a cushion. 'We have some pretty ones, and girls love scatter cushions. We have plain or here's one with a moon and stars,' she said, pulling out the design and then finding another. 'We have wood-land creatures too.'

'Unless you have a cushion with horses on it, I'm not sure,' he said as politely as he could.

'She's into horses?'

'In a big way,' he laughed. 'We have a horse, I've just come from the Heritage View Stables, where we'll be keeping him.'

'Then I have the perfect gift.' They squeezed down the aisle on the other side of the central display and towards the end, Tilly found what she was looking for. She held up a water bottle with an illustration of a horse and the words 'Born to Ride'.

Gus took the bottle to inspect it. 'She'll love it.'

'It's not a traditional housewarming gift, but she'll be able to take it everywhere – bedroom, lounge, school, to the riding stables.'

'Sold.' He followed her over to the till.

Gus, pleased with his purchase, left Tilly's Bits 'n' Pieces and carried on up the same side of the street, past the convenience store, where he grabbed some bread and more milk. Right at the end of the street, he found a pub. The Copper Plough, its name on the brickwork, had plenty of character and looked steeped in tradi-tion, with iron lamp-posts marking out the path that led to the front door and dark wood around the entrance, which he imagined lined the inside too.

Gus crossed over to walk back up the other side of the street instead, passing the chapel, which had well-tended grass out front and looked to have a cemetery out back, judging by what he could see. He reached a track that ran from The Street but there was no sign to indicate where it led, although it didn't take him long to realise that this must be the way down to the elusive cove itself, the reason this village got its name.

Gus had heard about Heritage Cove via Joan. He'd grown close to her since both of his parents had passed away. And when his marriage disintegrated and Gus still had to hold himself together, Joan had saved his arse more than once with her babysitting services. Without her, he'd have struggled to keep seeing patients and earn a living to support both him and his daughter. Joan had a no-nonsense attitude and felt like an extension of their family, and it was with Joan that Gus had talked about the next step for him and Abigail. For a long while, Gus had wanted to start his own veterinary practice, but he'd never been in a position to before. At first it was the finance and when he was left some money after his dad died, his plans came crashing to a halt when Abigail had her accident. His life had been turned upside down with her injuries and then his marriage breakdown. It hadn't been the time to think of anything else, but he'd reached a point where he knew if he didn't do it soon, he might never do it. And he wanted a change for Abigail too. She was still living in the house where her accident had happened, the house where they'd lived as a family. And so Gus had set about trying to find somewhere suitable to relocate.

Joan had helped with his search, enthusiastic even though it would mean them moving away from her. 'You've been hiding behind me and my horses long enough,' she'd told him. 'You both need some independence, to move forwards, to put your pain behind you.' And he'd nodded before she went on, 'Your priority must be good schools. You want a village setting but with a bit of life for you both.' They'd talked late into many an evening about where to go, looking all over the country. They'd trawled through listings for premises for sale. They'd discounted plenty – too much competition nearby, no good schools in the area, too far from any sign of civilisation, too expensive. And then Joan's daughter, Kaya, had been to visit for the weekend and when she heard what her mother was helping Gus do, she told them both about how much she loved where she'd moved to on England's east coast to teach art. She'd moved to the outskirts of Southwold and had shown Gus photographs of an area that looked so beautiful that Gus had begun to think coastal might be an idea.

He and Joan had turned their online searches to focus on the coast and by narrowing their search, they began to see opportunities. And once the temptation of living by the sea had been dangled, it was hard to go back. Gus knew his daughter would love it too. He made a few enquiries to no avail until he found an old bungalow in a village called Heritage Cove. It was the perfect premises for a new veterinary practice. It had land next to it that he could convert to a small car park, there were enough rooms to make the reception and two practice rooms. The competition was outside of the village and the population in Heritage Cove was large enough that he knew he could make a decent client base there. There were also a couple of properties to rent in the village for him and Abigail, each within a great school catchment area, and slowly everything had begun to fall into place.

This move had been in the making for a while but out in the sunshine now, exploring the new village, Gus found himself smiling. It had been a leap of faith but totally worth it.

Gus crossed over and back to the car. He'd have to check out the track down to the cove another time, but he wanted to get home and at least make a dent in more of the unpacking so the house didn't seem quite so alien when Abigail came home from school. He drove the short distance to his new home and the first thing he did when he got through the door was call Joan to tell her he'd been to the Heritage View Stables and, not only did they have a vacancy for Denby, but it seemed a place where he'd be happy.

'I am glad.' Her relief was evident, because as much as Denby was Gus and Abigail's horse now, she still loved him as much as she always had. 'I will miss him, but I can visit.'

'You'd better,' he told her before they discussed the particulars for Denby and Joan agreed she'd bring him down on Saturday.

'Any more questions, just give me a call,' said Joan.

'I will but I'll email all of this extra information over to Hazel, the owner, and that should be enough for the contract to be drawn up.'

'What's the village like?' Joan asked, now business was out of the way.

He stood in his kitchen, boxes still surrounding him, and smiled before he told her all about the main road that ran through Heritage Cove, the shop he'd found, the eateries within walking distance. 'I think we're going to be happy here.'

'Me too.' He could hear a smile in her voice.

'Now, onto more serious matters. The art class.'

Silence, but only for a moment before he heard a distinct chuckle. 'Kaya said to pass on her thanks again. And she told me that you did wonderfully. You were totally relaxed.' She began to laugh properly now. 'Well, all right, she knew you hated every second of it, but she was ever so grateful.'

It was Kaya who'd organised the class. He'd been a bit shocked when she'd asked him to fill in. 'You've got a great body,' she'd told him, something she could say without him thinking she was interested, given she'd been living with her partner Faye for the last three years. 'Please, I really need to build up a good reputation with these classes,' and she'd sounded so distraught that he'd agreed.

'I'm glad I helped Kaya,' Gus told Joan, 'but I have to say, never again.'

'If it helps, Kaya got lots of positive feedback.'

'I don't even want to think about that.' The part of his body they were providing feedback for didn't really bear thinking about. 'Oh, before I forget, Abigail wanted me to tell you to give Denby a hug from her.'

'He's missing her already. It was hard to say goodbye to the both of you, but I know this is going to be for the best. And I can't wait to see Heritage Cove myself on Saturday.'

'I'll treat you to waffles, a pub lunch, ice-cream, something from the bakery or tearooms, your choice.'

'Looking forward to it. I'll set off nice and early, should be in Heritage Cove by lunchtime.'

He finished the call, and after he'd made a cup of tea, he headed up to Abigail's bedroom. The removal team had been here yesterday to drop everything off and, before Gus had headed out of the village to the art class last night, he'd assembled both his and Abigail's beds, found the kettle, and put away the food he'd picked up at the supermarket en route. But apart from that, he'd done little else. And after the evening had ended so badly when he'd had to yell at those teenagers, he hadn't been able to face anything else when he got in the door apart from settling Abigail down with a mug of cocoa, despite the summer temperatures, and asking her to get her bag ready to start at school.

Gus knew his own room needed sorting, but all in good time. For now, it consisted of a bed and a load of boxes he could just about navigate his way between. In Abigail's room, he was pleased that it already felt better than last night. Now that you could see the turquoise bed covers with a mixture of white and turquoise scatter cushions, this room at least stood out from the rest of the magnolia house. The carpet was thankfully beige, so went with everything, just like the carpet in the other rooms. And he was grateful that the downstairs hallway had wooden floorboards, giving them somewhere to leave their shoes so they didn't walk dirt over the rest of the house.

Abigail had already unpacked the boxes for her desk and had that set up, all the way down to the pen pot on one side. The magnetic board above the desk was already filled with horse paraphernalia, including a magazine article about grooming your horse, a photograph of her sitting on Denby that he'd taken a couple of months ago, an array of rosettes Joan had given her – cherry red, gold, emerald green and royal blue, all won on Denby over the years before he became Abigail's horse. She'd fixed up a photograph of her with Gus on Christmas day at their house by a roaring fire. It'd been taken by Joan before she took Abigail to see Denby so that Abigail could give him his Christmas present – a wooden plaque for his stable door. Gus had the photograph of Abigail standing beside Denby's stable door once the plaque was on there, Abigail smiling and Denby's nose hanging over the door. He'd put that photograph in the lounge on the mantelpiece already.

Gus went to find his toolbox. He and Abigail had agreed the position for her wooden-framed illustration of horse and pony coat colours late last night after he'd used his pipe and cable detector to make sure they wouldn't be doing any damage, and he'd promised he'd put it up today. This being a property that had been rented out a few times before, the owner seemed relaxed about any little additions they wanted to make, as long as Gus cleared it with him first.

He drilled a hole and, with the wall plug inserted, put in the screw before hanging the picture. He stood back before readjusting it once, twice, until he was happy with it, and as he got the final position, his eyes fell to the horse with the beautiful golden coat and white mane and tail and its label, 'Palomino'. It looked a lot like Sherbert at the Heritage View Stables and an image of Hazel came into his head, with her long, blonde hair, and the slight awkwardness between them. He knew that going up to see Denby at the stables was going to be even more pleasurable if she was in charge. He'd have to ask again about the lessons, though; Abigail needed those and he felt sure Hazel would be the best person for the job. They'd been spoiled with Joan on hand to tutor Abigail in anything and everything to do with horses, but lessons here in the village would give Abigail more skills and knowledge, as well as confidence. She could learn to jump as she'd always wanted and go on hacks locally, which would help her get to know the area.

With the picture hanging, he undid another box and unpacked Abigail's *Pony* magazines, of which there were a whole pile. He plonked those neatly on top of the lower chest of drawers of the two in Abigail's bedroom. She could move them if she wanted, but at least this way she'd come home and see familiarity with all her things around her. The next box he came to was full of her clothes, but she could deal with those. He went and found the box of hangers and brought a good stack of them up to his daughter's bedroom, leaving them on the bed for her. It would be a distraction if nothing else, if she'd had a terrible time at school. He'd spent all day doing his best to push that thought from his mind, choosing to focus on the positives and trying not to worry.

From another small box, Gus pulled out the plaque from Denby's stable that Joan had given Abigail, telling her he would need it for his new home, and set it on Abigail's desk, propped up at the back so she could see it and know she and her horse would soon be reunited. He took out a cushion from yet another box – this one had an amusing depiction of a horse's anatomy with arrows pointing to parts such as the tail, which was known as the 'fly swatter', and the bum, which was 'fertiliser dispenser'. He unpacked one of Denby's old horseshoes and placed it on top of the taller chest of drawers, next to which he put another framed photograph of his daughter with her horse, this one his personal favourite because she'd been helping Joan to bathe Denby and she was soaked from head to toe. It seemed Denby had been hesitant to get wet that day and so Abigail had stood in front of the horse and told him it was okay, the water wouldn't hurt, and promptly turned the hose on herself. That day was the most he'd heard her laugh since her accident and he'd laughed hard too, although he noticed Joan shedding a tear at the little girl re-emerging from the shell she'd squeezed herself into.

With only a couple of hours before school pick-up, Gus made a sandwich before he tackled more of the boxes in the kitchen, putting away pots and pans, more plates, glasses, cups and all the small things that together mounted up. It was beginning to feel more like home.

By the time Gus was due to collect Abigail, he'd mastered the art of distraction and hadn't worried too much about his daughter. But now his heart pounded harder as he passed the school gate and found a place to pull up. They'd agreed this was where he would wait, and he was a good fifteen minutes before the bell, so there was no danger of her missing him. She'd been going to school for years and pick-up had never felt so tense as it did today. Even after the accident and her return to school, this was different. Back then, she had a small group of friends who knew what happened, who carried on with her as normal. But here, it felt like he'd thrown her into a lion's den.

When he finally saw Abigail approaching in his wing mirror, she didn't look distraught, although she didn't look happy either.

She flung open the car door. 'When's Denby coming?' Ah, of course. Denby was on her mind.

'Hi, Dad, I had a lovely day, thank you,' he joked, relieved that at least there were no tears.

She didn't respond to his sarcasm. And when he asked about her day, she shrugged, 'It was good.' And she smiled at him as though it were no big deal. Gus noticed she'd taken her hair out of its bobble. He hoped it wasn't because she wanted to hide behind the curtain of light brown locks the way she'd sometimes done in the past to stop people seeing so much of the scarring. But he wasn't going to comment.

'When's Denby coming?' she persisted.

'One thing at a time. Now open the glove compartment, there's a little gift in there for you.'

She pulled it open and took out the water bottle and broke into a smile before she leaned over for a cuddle that lasted long enough for Gus to realise she'd missed him today. He kissed her on the cheek and she pulled away like most girls of her age would, the way she had done in the early days with her injuries as she remembered the scars were there, the scars Gus had got used to and were now a part of her. If it was just the two of them, or they were with Joan and Denby, then he was a lot calmer and less overprotective, but as soon as other people came into the mix, Gus panicked, and he hated the way some strangers reacted to his daughter. It was as though they'd never seen a person who was slightly different, as though they couldn't see past the marks on her face and their curiosity, their impulsiveness to ask her what happened led to questions that they didn't stop to think she might not appreciate.

Gus gave Abigail another hug and kiss and told her they were from Joan. He checked his mirrors, glanced over his shoulder, and pulled away from the kerb. 'I called her to tell her that Denby has a home at Heritage View Stables as of this weekend.'

Now his daughter looked happy. 'He's coming at the weekend?'

When he nodded, still admiring her bottle, she went on, 'Do you think they'll let me put up his plaque?'

'I don't see why not.'

'Can we go there now?' She sipped from the icy cold water he'd already put in the bottle for her. 'To the stables.'

He turned into another street. 'They're busy up there, but we could pay a quick visit.' Hazel had implied that owners could pop in whenever they liked.

'I can't wait to see where Denby is going to live.'

Gus turned onto the main street and drove through the village, turning off before the bend near a beautiful-looking inn. They followed the lane all the way down to another one that led up to the entrance of Heritage View House and Stables.

Abigail was aghast. 'Someone lives here?' She took in the big residence, all the green space around, the horses in the paddocks.

'The owners live here. And Denby will be one of ten horses, so he'll have company.'

'He'll have friends,' she smiled. 'I like that.'

He parked up in the car parking area and they walked in through the gates. Gus spotted Hazel before she saw him. She was in the outdoor school taking a lesson, instructing a woman on horseback as she turned the horse and again had it trot over poles lined up on the floor and then went over a jump made by poles crossed in the middle. Hazel and the woman were engrossed in what they were doing, and Hazel didn't notice him and Abigail until after she'd tugged her blonde hair from its ponytail and run both hands through it. She opened up the gate to the school for the woman to ride out on her horse, onto the concrete area, which seemed to be where the tacking up and dismounting happened, as was the case this morning.

Hazel came over to them as she put her hair neatly back into its band. 'Hello again.' Her eyes immediately wandered to Abigail. 'You must be Denby's other owner.'

'This is Abigail,' said Gus, one arm around his daughter's shoulders.

'It's good to meet you, Abigail.' Hazel waved a hand in front of her face. 'Excuse me, I'm really hot, would you mind if I went and got a drink and sorted Lorna out?'

She must mean the woman who'd already dismounted and secured the horse outside. 'Of course, we won't take up too much of your time, Abigail was just curious and wanted to have a look at the place.'

'As every good horse owner should be.' She smiled at his daughter, her expression not giving away whether she'd registered the scars that made one side of Abigail's face so different from the other.

This woman was beautiful, no doubt about it, and he watched her head over to the rider to say a few words and then go in another direction, presumably to get that drink.

'Dad,' came Abigail's voice with a sense of urgency, and when he turned, she was looking up at him. 'You're staring at that lady.'

'I'm not,' he denied. Although it was true.

'You were, and you know I hate it when people stare.'

'You're quite right, Abigail.' He pulled her closer in a playful headlock, ruffling her hair. 'I'm very rude.'

'She's very pretty,' Abigail said when he let her go.

'She's coming back,' he shushed his daughter.

'That's better.' Hazel had a bottle of water in her hand. 'I'll need to put Milton over there out in the paddock but then I could show Abigail where Denby will be sleeping.'

Gus and Abigail leaned against the fence to the paddock while Hazel put Milton out to graze. Her love for all the horses was evident. Just like Joan she talked to them, she fussed over them, the same way Abigail did whenever she got the chance.

Starting with the stable block, Gus got his second tour of the day. He hadn't expected it, he'd merely thought Abigail would see Denby's new home but would have to wait until a better time to really look around. Hazel showed them the tack room next, the smell of leather and horses all mingled into one in the small space. It reminded Gus of how close he'd had to get to Hazel when they'd been in here this morning.

'Did you get all the information I sent you?' Gus asked.

'I haven't checked my emails yet, but I will do.'

Abigail tugged at his hand and when he leant closer and she asked him a question, he told her to ask Hazel.

'Ask away,' Hazel encouraged.

'Denby has a name plaque for his stable.'

Hazel smiled, a strand of blonde hair falling forwards over her cheek until she pushed it away. 'And you're wondering whether I'd use it here?' Abigail nodded. 'Of course. Bring it at the weekend and we'll put it on his stable door for you.'

Hazel had a lesson soon but enough time to show them the hay barn, the indoor school and they circled back around to the outside school. Hazel looked past them and said, 'That's my four o'clock, always early.'

'Early is better than late,' smiled Gus, more than happy that Hazel was so friendly. He'd worry a lot less if he knew Abigail's riding teacher was someone she gelled with. Already the pair of them had chatted about Denby and the horses here as they explored the indoor school. 'Before we leave you to it, I wanted to ask again about lessons. I know you said Arnold was a great teacher, but I wondered...' He tilted his head in Abigail's direction, not wanting to sound like he was begging or to make his daughter uncomfortable. 'Are you sure you don't have any availability?'

Her reaction was as though he'd thrown a glass of water over her. Up until now she'd been open, friendly, but now she seemed skittish, tripping over her words. 'I... I don't have many vacancies.'

'We can do any day, can't we Abigail? We're flexible with times, too. And perhaps a few private sessions before group lessons might be a good idea.'

'That certainly works for a lot of riders no matter their level. I'm sorry, I have to go get Pebbles.' Abigail began to giggle, and Hazel fell into her friendlier persona. 'It's a great name, isn't it? He's grey, just like the pebbles on the beach. But he also likes to run away when he knows he has a lesson, so it's probably not a bad thing his rider is early, it'll give me a chance to catch him.' Her anecdote had Abigail laughing some more.

Before Hazel could head into the paddock, Gus persisted. 'Would you reconsider about the lessons? When I asked earlier, you initially said you had a few possible time slots.'

She opened her mouth and nothing came out at first. 'I misunderstood.'

'Misunderstood that I was asking for lessons?' He'd never seen anyone look so flustered at what really was a simple question. 'Why tell me you were available when you're not?' He felt his frustration rise. He didn't mind that they didn't have any lesson availability, but he did mind being lied to.

'I apologise.' Her cheeks coloured. 'I really am very sorry, but it is Arnold who you will need to speak to.' And before he could argue the case once more, she lifted the latch to the gate and stepped from concrete onto grass.

He'd have to accept it, then. It was what it was. But rather than enjoy watching her run around the paddock after Pebbles, he'd lost a bit of admiration for this woman. He was getting very mixed messages about having lessons here. One minute, it sounded as though she had free slots, the next, she didn't. He wasn't sure quite

what to make of it. Surely it wasn't that she felt awkward around
Abigail. Perhaps that was it, maybe she wasn't sure how to handle
Abigail in a group class if other riders asked questions or weren't
very nice. He'd seen the same reaction before when Abigail was
teased at a dance class and the teacher clearly had no idea how to
handle it. Abigail hadn't been that into her dancing anyway, it was
something her mum had signed her up for, and it had been a good
excuse to pull her away from those lessons for good.

'We'll sort some riding lessons for you,' he told Abigail. He was
disappointed. He'd had a good feeling about Hazel, but this left a
hollow feeling in his gut. And yet she'd been really friendly and
kind to Abigail until he started on about her availability to teach
again.

'And we can visit Denby whenever we like?' Abigail asked.

'Yes, I promise.' That part was at least in the contract. 'And
Denby gets to have his plaque on his stable door.'

'I don't want anyone else riding him, Dad.'

He sighed as they set off towards the car. 'We talked about this,
remember?' In fact, they'd talked at length. 'When Denby was with
Joan, we got a bargain, she was very generous to us with her time
and her charges for his keep. But now Denby is our responsibility
and this is a really nice home for him. We wouldn't be able to afford
it without allowing him to be ridden. And remember he'll have
horse friends here, that's nice for him. And he's nice and close to us
here in the village.'

'What if someone is mean to him?'

He crouched down on his haunches and took her hands in his.
'Hazel assures me that they won't be and that it'll either be her or
Arnold teaching. They'll keep him safe. And look, don't all the
horses seem happy?' He nodded towards the paddock.

She began to laugh. 'Pebbles looks happy.'

He couldn't help his smile either because, over in the paddock,

Hazel had almost touched the grey horse, who indeed waited for her to try to grab his halter before he turned and sped off in another direction, stopping a little distance away. 'Wonder how long he'll do that for?' It was a game Gus suspected he could watch for quite some time if he wasn't so confused as to why she was giving mixed messages.

* * *

Back at their newly rented home, the two-up, two-down with the postage stamp garden out front and courtyard out back, Gus unlocked the door and let Abigail go in first, hollering after her, 'Shoes off!' before she took any dirt upstairs to her bedroom. 'Are you hungry? How about some crumpets?'

'Yes, please,' she grunted, her shoelace having formed a big knot where she'd tried to pull it one end and done something to upset it. She ended up prising the shoe off at the heel and leaving the lace as it was, and today he wouldn't complain about her treading down the backs of her shoes.

In the kitchen, which was beginning to look reasonably organised, he popped a couple of crumpets into the toaster and took out a tub of strawberry yogurt, her favourite. He left it with a spoon at the table and once he'd buttered the crumpets, he called to her from the bottom of the stairs.

A knock at the front door came as he was calling a second reminder up the stairs that had Abigail at last coming down. She'd be in horse heaven up there with all her things around her.

Gus answered the door and smiled at the grey-haired man on the other side. 'Hello.'

'I hope it's all right for me to call on you,' the man said. 'I wanted to welcome you to the Cove. Locals call the village "the Cove" rather than Heritage Cove – lazy buggers we all are.' The man, who Gus estimated was in his seventies, chuckled. 'Allow me to introduce myself, I'm Barney.' He held out the hand that wasn't holding a basket and Gus met the greeting with a handshake.

'I'm Gus. Good to meet you. You live nearby?'

He waved a hand in the approximate direction of The Street and the pub. 'Around the bend, as you head away from The Street, I have a home with a big barn on the land.'

'I've seen it,' Gus smiled. 'Lovely property, all that space.'

'Thank you.' He held up the basket in his hand. 'Now, some say it with flowers or chocolates but my welcome to the village comes in the form of eggs – the yolk type, not chocolate,' he added, passing the basket with at least a dozen eggs inside to Gus. 'They're freshly laid by the chickens I keep.'

'Come inside,' Gus encouraged. 'Although you'll have to forgive the mess, we only arrived in the Cove last night.' He grinned at his local colloquialism as Barney came into the house and followed him along the hallway and straight into the kitchen. It was polite to ask the man in but also, Gus wanted to make sure Abigail didn't run off to her bedroom with her food, he wanted her to talk to him some more. Shutting herself away had been a habit after the accident and one he and Joan had worked hard to break. He knew it was habitual for tweens and then teens, but he knew Abigail would benefit from not falling into that mould too soon.

Abigail looked up at the stranger and managed a hello.

'This is my daughter, Abigail,' said Gus.

Barney didn't hesitate, he went over to the table and held out his hand to formally introduce himself. 'Delighted to meet you.' When Abigail returned the gesture, even though a big focus was on her crumpets, Barney asked, 'Do you like eggs?'

Abigail peered into the basket her dad showed her. 'Are they a housewarming present?'

Barney chuckled. 'It's a little odd, isn't it?' He put a hand to his forehead. 'Oh no, don't tell me you have an egg allergy.'

'No allergies here.' Gus put his mind at ease. 'And we love eggs, don't we, Abigail? Poached eggs are Abigail's favourite.'

'Are they now? Well, I happen to know these make very good poached eggs. Freshly laid this morning, too.'

'You have chickens?' Abigail asked. 'At your house?'

'I most certainly do. They have a coop that's more of a palace, to be honest, they're well looked after, and this is the reward.'

Abigail's eyes widened. 'We could make pancakes.'

'They'll make perfect pancakes too,' Barney declared. 'And if you need lemons, you'll get those at the convenience store down the road.'

'Pancakes it is, then,' said Gus. 'We'll have them after dinner tonight.'

'Did you start school today?' Barney spotted Abigail was still wearing her dark grey skirt with a white blouse and a striped tie.

'Dad didn't want me to have too long off for summer.' She said it with a frown. 'We get six weeks off school anyway, he said.'

Gus leapt in to defend himself. 'It wasn't that I didn't want you to have a really long holiday. It's more that I thought it would be nice for you to know some other kids before the school holidays, that was the reason behind it.'

'Very wise,' Barney agreed. 'But you'll soon get to know people, everyone is friendly here and there are lots of kids from the school who live fairly close, you'll make friends in no time, I'm sure.' He looked to Gus. 'Now, do vets look at chickens?'

'We most certainly do. Do you have any concerns?'

'Not right now, but it's good to know you're local.'

'How many chickens do you have?' He liked to get an idea about his clients and he sensed Barney wasn't going to be one of those who stayed with the vet they'd found elsewhere if he could get the same service on his doorstep. He was knocking on a stranger's door with a basket of eggs, so this man was all about community spirit, as far as Gus could see.

'We have fifteen at the moment, enough for us to manage. Luckily we have plenty of room.'

'They'll need that,' Gus agreed. 'Do you have any homework?' he asked Abigail who'd already got up to put her plate and spoon into the dishwasher and dispose of the yogurt pot.

She grumbled. 'Yes, maths.'

Barney sucked air in between his teeth. 'Never my forte.'

Gus didn't want to nag his daughter too much, he'd let her have some time in her room, do some unpacking and then he'd mention the homework again after dinner. Maybe before pancakes and then she'd have an incentive to do it before they made them together.

'When will you be up and running?' Barney asked.

'The vet practice? Any day now.' Gus transferred the eggs from the basket into a big decorative bowl that sat perfectly at the edge of the bench along from the cooktop. 'I wanted to settle Abigail into school and sort this place out first.'

Barney dipped his head. 'And on that note, I'll leave you to it, I'm sure you've got lots to do.' He led the way back towards the front door. 'Before I forget...' He pulled a card from his pocket and passed it to Gus. 'That's a business card for Sandy, whose parents own the Heritage Inn. She works at the inn, but she's also a childminder and very well thought of, lovely girl, gets my vote. Plenty of folks around here use her services – she looks after Valerie's little one – Valerie runs the florist. She's always looking after Terry and Nola's grand-kids, so you can ask them too.'

Gus smiled and took the card. 'Thank you. I appreciate it.' Because as much as it was a big step to leave a stranger looking after Abigail, she was old enough now that he wasn't as worried. And without Joan, he might well need someone to call on. 'And thank you for the eggs too, it's a really lovely and novel way to make us feel welcome.'

'It was my pleasure. I'll see you again soon, I hope.'

'I don't doubt it.'

And when Gus closed the door behind him, he felt something inside him mellow. Abigail had got through her first day, Denby had a home and was on his way. He had a feeling that things were heading in the right direction.

heading in the right direction.

5

Hazel had had a busy week. They'd had a lot of rain in the last two
days, which meant a couple of the horses had frolicked in the
muddy paddocks, having a grand old time, giving them a bit of
extra work with more bathing required and more time-consuming
grooming. But she couldn't begrudge them their fun; her horses
were happy and that in turn made her happy.

Hazel cleaned her teeth and then pulled on her beige jodhpurs
along with a navy T-shirt and a pair of socks. She brushed her hair
and tied it into its customary low plait that started at the nape of
her neck and finished at her waist. She was in her bedroom at
Heritage View House and Saturday was always the morning Arnold
got up and dealt with the start of the day tasks, helped by their
stable hand, while she had an extra hour to herself – she repeated
the favour on a Sunday morning – and after a cooked breakfast
consisting of eggs, tomatoes, mushrooms, and toast, as well as an
accompanying mug of tea, she'd come up to get ready before
heading to the stables to take her horse Cinnamon out on a long
ride through the countryside.

Cinnamon had been Hazel's thirtieth birthday present and when he arrived, he was broken but only just beginning training, so he wasn't quite used to following commands. Hazel and her dad had worked hard with him, and Hazel had of course been in love with the chestnut roan gelding from the start. He had an even temperament and a funny habit of being inquisitive when they were out on a hack. It seemed he wanted to know about everything, whether it was a passer-by or another rider or something lying on the ground. Cinnamon was a beauty, too, with a smooth coat and tail that in the right light had a wonderful reddish colour.

As Hazel came downstairs, her heart sank a little as James peered in from the other side of the glass. She opened the door and, despite her frustration, she adopted a smile. 'Welcome back.' He'd been so good to her. She should appreciate him checking in on her, even if it was unannounced, but instead she was frustrated. She knew he was trying to find solutions for her, but they usually involved taking a further step away from the riding school, and that was the opposite of what she wanted. 'How was London?' she asked him, avoiding a more serious conversation, as she led the way into the kitchen. He knew she tended to go out the back way after she got everything she needed.

'Great. I stayed on a bit longer and had a few drinks last night but came back on the last train. Thought I'd take you for lunch as it's your day off.'

'Morning off,' she corrected him. It was never the entire day, he knew that.

She ducked into the utility room and found the riding hat she wanted from its hook and her boots as well as a body protector and hi-vis vest. The room was full of all their extra gear – boots, jackets, hi-vis vests, body protectors, extra hats, waterproofs. Thankfully it was an enormous space – it needed to be, because it also housed a washing machine and tumble dryer as well as two airers, which they used constantly because neither of them had time to keep hanging out washing or bringing it in. Inevitably any washing stayed in position on the airers for days until another load went in and they needed to take things upstairs to make space. A business as well as a household to run was demanding, and they weren't quite on top of it, but Hazel didn't stress about it. If the stables were operational and they were making money, that was the main focus. Dirty clothes, or indeed clean ones, could always wait.

'So... lunch?' he asked again. 'An early one, then you can get back to work.'

By the back door, she pushed one foot into its waiting boot and then stood on one leg to do the other. 'It's really kind of you, James, but we've got a new arrival today so it's going to be even busier than usual.'

'It's a full house?'

'At last,' she smiled. He knew how keen they'd been to fill the last available spot at the stables.

'You know you could take on more help here.'

'No need.'

'I doubt Arnold would agree with you.'

'What's that supposed to mean?'

'You're not teaching much, you could get someone in to at least do that.'

'It's an option.' She just didn't want to do it. She saw it as admitting defeat. If she gave in and got another teacher, she might never get back to the riding instructor she'd once been.

'A valid option,' James urged. She'd heard the suggestion from him before, more than once. 'Then we could spend some time together. I know you wanted space and I've given you that, but don't you want to get back to normal?'

'I'm not sure it's that easy.' She'd never said that to him before and she wasn't even sure what she meant by the words that were out before she could really think about what she was saying. All Hazel knew was that she didn't know what normal was. Normal would've been her accepting Abigail as a riding pupil, saying of course she'd teach her. Normal would've been not contradicting herself and looking totally unprofessional when one minute she'd told Gus she could teach him, giving him a list of times and days she was available, and the next she'd advised him that he'd have to ask Arnold about lessons for Abigail. It made her look as though she was hiding something, which of course she was. She didn't want other people to know how she feared teaching so much sometimes that she wanted to crawl up to her bed, pull the duvet over her head, and sleep the worries away.

James stepped closer. 'It can be that easy if you stop fighting it.'

The way he wrapped his arms around her told her he assumed she was struggling with how to put things between them back to normal. But that felt like the least of her worries. Most of Hazel's doubts were concerned with the stables and how she was going to get back to the person she'd once been, full of enthusiasm and confidence in her own abilities. Unless you had a physical injury that he could see, James was the type of person who assumed there wasn't a real problem. He didn't believe in stress, thought it an excuse for people to take time off and be lazy. He wasn't totally lacking heart, she wouldn't have stayed with him for so long if he was, but he had always had trouble seeing the bigger picture. And Hazel had done her best to explain her feelings to him before. She'd told him her fears, her worries, and he'd done the same as he was doing now, he'd come closer and pulled her to him, told her it was all going to be fine and that he'd support her whatever happened. It wasn't bad for him to do those things, but none of it helped when he wasn't listening to her.

James chanced a kiss on her lips, lightly. 'I'm all in if that's what you want, you know I am.' He kissed her one more time. 'Think about it.'

He might not get it, not properly, but he'd always been there as a shoulder to cry on, urging her to take care of herself and admit she needed help. She just knew he didn't see what a mess she was emotionally. And perhaps that was what he chose, perhaps he thought it the best approach.

Hazel picked up her riding hat, body protector, and hi-vis and as James left her to it, she headed first to the office to replace the lessons booking folder that she'd been looking at last night to try to find a slot to fit in Gus's daughter. Arnold had watched her searching in vain for a space when he came into the kitchen.

Tiredness in his voice, he said, 'Told you, I'm fully booked, turning down requests left, right, and centre.'

She'd been about to say she was sure it wasn't left, right, and centre, but sensing his tone, she kept quiet. 'Are you sure there isn't any availability?'

'There's plenty, if you teach. Our business relies on teaching younger riders, they make up the bulk of our clientele. You know that. It's not feasible long-term to only teach older riders or those who can already ride.'

She blew out her cheeks. 'We've been through this. I know I need to sort myself out. And I will. I'm just... I'm not ready.'

He sat opposite her then, dinner long since finished and the dishwasher chugging away. 'So get ready, Hazel. Go talk to someone about it, I don't care who, but business is going to suffer if we're not careful. What would happen if I was injured one day and couldn't teach?'

'Unlikely,' she replied.

'It could happen. And if it did, would we drop regulars who'd likely take their business elsewhere? Would we be happy to employ another riding teacher who we don't know all that well, who we would have to rely on to uphold our reputation?'

She put her head in her hands. 'I want to, Arnold.'

Her brother had picked up the bottle of wine from the side and was pouring himself a glass. 'Put a timeline on it, then. Set a date when you'll be back, and in between now and then, get some help.'

He'd left it at that and had taken his glass of wine into the other room, leaving Hazel feeling wretched that they were having words about it more and more these days.

Now, before she reached the office, Hazel set down all her things so she could give Tabitha a fuss. The cat had found a patch in the sun around the back of the stables. In the winter, she was more likely to curl up on the end of Hazel's bed during the night but in the summer, like everyone else, she liked to make the most of the outside. And Heritage View Stables and House were a great place for a cat, she'd chosen well, with so much room to roam and all the attention from visiting riders, as well as Hazel and Arnold.

Hazel gave Tabitha one more rub beneath her chin as the cat, eyes closed, tilted her face towards the sunshine. With a gentle breeze flapping the sleeves of her T-shirt, Hazel picked up her things and let herself into the office. She put the folder back at the end of the desk where it always sat – it held details of riders in every lesson, their emergency contact details you hoped you never had to use, a little bit about them sometimes. Some kids were more suited to different horses, some didn't mind the livelier equines, others would only cope with a more placid animal. At least Abigail would ride Denby, her own horse, so perhaps that would make it easier.

But no, thinking that way, Hazel still couldn't do it. She couldn't hold the responsibility of a kid in her hands, she just couldn't. And worse, if things didn't go Abigail's way in a lesson, if Gus didn't like the way she was teaching, she did not want to be on the receiving end of another parent's anger. She'd heard him roar before too, she remembered it well after the art class, and although she'd quite enjoyed his company when she'd met him here at the stables and had even begun to like him, she wasn't prepared to take the chance.

Thoughts of Gus had Hazel sneaking a look at Lucy's drawing of him and she felt her cheeks colour, even though she was on her own. His temper was nowhere to be seen on this sheet of paper, he was just a beautiful man, an attractive male around her age who was only looking to do the best by his daughter. And she hated that she couldn't help him do that. Because Arnold was right; he had no room to fit Abigail into his current schedule. He was also right that if something happened to him, they'd be in trouble. They'd lose money faster than a bucket with a hole would lose water if they didn't run many lessons. And finding a teacher last minute was never desirable. It wasn't something to rush, the right fit was too important.

But now, she reminded herself, it was a Saturday morning. She took a deep breath as she slipped the drawing back inside her notebook and slotted it onto the shelf. It was her morning, time for just her. Everything else she'd worry about later.

She collected Cinnamon's tack and set it on the hooks and racks outside the stable block before she went to collect her horse from the paddock where he'd been grazing, moving about a bit after a night in the stable. 'You ready for a ride? The sun is shining, it's a beautiful day.' She pulled a small bag from her pocket and took out a few slices of pear as a treat and when she held it flat in her hand, his lips tickled her palm.

The treat finished, Hazel led Cinnamon over towards the stable block and secured his halter so he didn't wander off. She cleaned his hooves, gave his coat a brush all the way down his neck and shoulders, across his back and buttocks, making sure there was no dirt caught anywhere, particularly in the area where the saddle pad would go. Brushing him also gave her a chance to make sure he wasn't sore anywhere and it had the added bonus of warming up his muscles. Once her horse was brushed, she reached up to position the saddle pad with its top towards the withers. The stirrups were rolled up on the saddle as she put that on Cinnamon's back and adjusted it to sit properly before fitting the girth and taking the strap under his belly to the other side to buckle up and keep the saddle in place. She fussed him around the ears and the top of his face, the way he liked it.

Cinnamon had a habit of putting his head up whenever she tried to put the bridle on. He didn't always do it with the halter, especially when it was turnout time, but it was as though, when he knew he was going to be ridden, he liked to play this game. She managed to get the top of the bridle over his ears with a little bit of pressure, the bit slotted comfortably into his mouth and he gave her the same amused look he usually gave her to say he was unimpressed that she'd won without too much trouble. 'You're a funny old thing,' she told him, 'but I love you.' She pulled out his forelock from beneath the browband and double-checked all the straps were comfortable for him.

'Almost ready,' she told her horse as she shrugged on her body protector and hi-vis, put on her hat and fastened the chin strap before waving across to Arnold and the stable hand to say she was off. She called out that she'd be back in plenty of time for Denby, then mounted up and rode away from the stables and towards the gates that led onto the lane. Before long, the familiar rhythm of hooves tapped against the tarmac as they followed their familiar Saturday morning route and the slower pace let Cinnamon warm his muscles and get his joints moving some more.

Hazel was pleased the weather seemed to be cooperating this morning as the sun barely ducked behind a single cloud. The lanes leading towards Heritage View were reasonably quiet today, which made it a far more pleasant ride and any cars that did pass, as well as a tractor, were considerate and gave them a wide berth with no tooting of horns. When Hazel had first got Cinnamon, the horn tooting had been his pet hate – most horses didn't like it, but Cinnamon really loathed it, and whenever it happened, he would take longer than some of the other horses to settle. He'd got better, but she still dreaded it happening. Hazel had once tried to get James into horse riding but when the horse he was on didn't cope too well with a car that passed way too close, he'd told her he'd rather stick to cycling because bikes didn't have feelings, they didn't spook.

Hazel reached the end of the lane that led up to the main road and turned left from The Street and around the bend past the Heritage Inn. The owners, Giles and Tracy, were outside washing the front windows and called out their hellos and summation of the morning. A little way further, Hazel and Cinnamon crossed over and came to a gate that would take them away from the roads and alongside stunning country landscapes with arable land and pasture. She dismounted and opened up the big gate, led Cinnamon through and closed it behind them before mounting up again, ready for the bridleways and wide spaces that they both favoured. In the spring, this area welcomed you with a breath-taking display of bluebells, but for now, it was green as far as the eye could see. Animals grazed in the distance and Hazel swatted a fly that insisted on buzzing near her face. A tractor went up a slope, the country house that stood on the brow of the hill overlooked them all, and a squirrel darted across, scurrying out of the way of the horse's hooves as Cinnamon plodded happily on.

Riding in a group along this way was always fun, the company was nice, but there was something about being only you and your horse with nothing but nature for company that was particularly special and calmed the soul. Cinnamon trotted along the bridleway then slowed as they came to another gate that crossed another path.

Through that one, and they had plenty of space to break into a gentle canter.

They soon adopted a more leisurely pace, the trees to one side providing patches of shade that Hazel welcomed. There was a path, just wide enough for a couple of people side by side, that led to The Street in Heritage Cove, another path that headed up to the country house she'd seen as they rode past, and one that went straight on and would eventually curve around to take the widest route back towards the village.

Hazel and Cinnamon carried straight on and slowed as they saw dog walkers in the distance. With a pat to her horse's neck and some encouraging words, they both simply enjoyed the freedom, the release, being out here today.

She hadn't realised at first, but the dog walkers were village locals, Melissa and Harvey, who had married last Christmas up at the local Christmas tree farm. Winnie, their Labrador, was off the lead with nobody else around, but seeing Hazel, Melissa called Winnie to her, and she obediently sat as they came to a stop. The dog's tail wagged on the ground as she looked up at Cinnamon. Cinnamon seemed mildly curious, his ears twitching this way and that at the different sounds of the new voices, looking interestedly at the dog who, looked back at him with similar scrutiny.

'Gorgeous morning,' Melissa smiled, her arm linked in Harvey's, her other hand on Winnie's head, probably to make sure she didn't get any ideas about annoying Cinnamon. 'We'll let you both pass, or Winnie here might decide she wants to try playing with Cinnamon.'

'Thank you, I'm not sure Cinnamon here would be in the mood for a game.' Sometimes random dogs weren't on the lead when she was out on a ride and came over to Cinnamon, thinking he would appreciate it. Most of the time, Cinnamon probably thought it was a case of him being the bigger one, nothing to worry about here, but sometimes dogs could be a nuisance and he'd get annoyed. Owners weren't always considerate either, uttering phrases such as *oh, he's only playing, oh, he's fine, he's gentle*, but most of the time they were like Harvey and Melissa and had an ounce of common sense. 'I don't usually see you two out on a Saturday morning, you picked a good day for it.'

'We're getting out while we can,' said Harvey. 'Another busy renovation job starting later today.'

With a hint of amusement in her voice, Melissa changed topic entirely. 'I heard about the art class.'

Hazel felt her cheeks colour. 'I had no idea what Lucy was getting me into.'

Harvey clearly didn't know about it at all and so Melissa gave a brief summary. 'We're trying to get Hazel to think of pleasure as well as business,' she added after her explanation. 'I suggested speed dating to Lucy, but she said that was ridiculous and you'd never go for it.'

'You're right, I wouldn't.'

'That sounds like hell,' Harvey told Hazel in support, Winnie at his feet now demanding he pay her some attention like Hazel was doing with Cinnamon as they talked, rubbing her horse's neck to compliment him on his patience.

'I thought Lucy would come up with something dull,' Melissa admitted, 'and I thought I was right when she said she was taking you to an art class.'

It certainly hadn't been dull, Hazel mused.

'It takes a certain kind of courage to be able to sit there with no clothes on,' said Harvey. 'Imagine being stared at and having people trying to draw every inch of you.'

'Not going to volunteer for me to have another go?' Hazel teased. It might take a certain amount of courage, but the artists had drawn Gus from a visual level, they hadn't tapped into what was inside, what she'd seen after the class.

'No chance,' Harvey answered without hesitation before looking at Melissa, 'and, much as I love you, don't go getting any ideas.'

'Hey, your naked form is for my eyes only,' she assured him, linking her arm through his as Hazel prepared for the off by tugging gently at the reins to ease Cinnamon back to facing the way they were going. 'But I want to hear more about this male model when we're next at the pub, Hazel. I mean it,' she called after them as Hazel and Cinnamon walked on.

Hazel just raised a hand to wave goodbye and laughed. But it didn't stop her thinking of the sketch contained in her notebook in her office, for her to enjoy when she wanted, and when she thought about it, it was hard to believe Gus had been as angry as he was that night. She'd certainly picked up no hint of his temper since then, but you couldn't always read a person's character just like that. All the parents who came with their kids to the riding school were polite enough, nice enough, encouraging, but she'd seen another side of a few when things didn't go exactly the way they expected. Hazel had found people's unpredictability increasingly hard to deal with and she knew that was her biggest hurdle, one she needed to deal with, just as Arnold had reminded her last night.

After passing through one more gate, they were onto a narrower pathway that emerged onto the back roads, which would lead down to the bend that took you out at the opposite end of the village or took you to the pub and The Street.

Hazel passed the florist, greeting Valerie, who was unloading a van full of deliveries with exquisite pink, white, and red colours in blooms Hazel knew would smell just like summer.

A few doors away, the sign for the new veterinary practice came into view. Positioned out front of what had been an old run-down bungalow until recently, the sign had a sky-blue background with white looping wording that said 'Heritage Cove Veterinary Practice' and in three corners of the sign were silhouettes of animals – one was a dog, the other a cat and the third was made up of three smaller animals she couldn't really see. She pulled on the reins to slow Cinnamon right down so she could better focus.

'One's a guinea-pig, the other a rabbit and the third, a hamster.' Gus had come around the side of the building.

If she'd known he was outside, she wouldn't have slowed. But she said good morning; he was a client, and she wanted things to remain amicable between them despite her awkwardness every time she thought of either his temper or the way she'd contradicted herself about lessons.

Gus stepped closer, slowly, and ran a hand down Cinnamon's nose after Hazel nodded her approval. 'He always likes a fuss,' she told Gus. 'And he's worked hard this morning.'

'Good ride?'

'Excellent, thank you.' She began to smile when Cinnamon's nose headed towards Gus's other hand. The horse's nostrils twitched with interest. 'You got something there?' He had his hand behind his back, so no doubt there was food involved, judging by Cinnamon's reaction.

Gus reluctantly showed the apple, half-eaten. 'I was enjoying this, but it looks like if I'm not careful someone else might finish it.'

'Yep, be careful.'

Gus smiled at her, at Cinnamon. 'May I?'

'Go for it, if you don't mind losing your morning snack.' She loved the way he was with horses and when he smiled, it was hard to believe he could ever be angry with anyone.

Gus had barely offered it to the horse before Cinnamon snaffled it from his open hand. 'The sign looks good,' she told him, unsure what else to talk about.

'I'm happy with it.' He went over and plucked what looked like a flyer from the Perspex container on one side of the sign.

She took the colourful piece of paper from him. It had bullet points telling people what to expect at the practice, the animals he treated, contact numbers, services he offered and social media symbols to show how to find more information. The practice was starting off in modern times and a social media presence made sense. They'd done the same with the stables and Hazel kept content updated – plenty of riders had found them through those channels.

'I know you have an equine vet,' he said, 'and I don't generally deal with horses, but I can always be called on in an emergency if needed.'

'Good to know, thank you.' She folded the flyer and pushed it into one of the pockets on her hi-vis. 'We have Tabitha too, so it'll be easier to bring her here if we need a vet rather than going farther afield.'

'I saw a cat milling around when I was last at your place. She looked happy enough in amongst all those horses.'

'She is, just need her to keep her one remaining eye. She gets around well enough, but if she lost the other?'

'Well, let's hope that never happens, but I'm sure she'd amaze you by how much she uses her other senses to stay safe.' The way he talked showed he was sensitive, thoughtful, and she appreciated it. 'What happened to her eye?'

Hazel shrugged as Cinnamon moved his head around, clearly getting impatient now he'd finished the apple and there wasn't much else on offer. 'I've no idea, she found us rather than the other way around. She's part of the stables now.'

'I'm sure she is.'

'Talking of the stables, I'd better get back. This is my free morning, only one I get all week.'

'We all need time for ourselves.'

The concern on his lips was touching, but the only reaction was to laugh because Cinnamon had gone back to nuzzling at Gus's top as though he might have another treat hidden somewhere.

'I guess we'll see you later on,' said Gus, who didn't mind the horse's attentions at all. When she looked confused, he added, 'Denby's arriving today.'

'Right, yes. Don't worry, hadn't forgotten. In fact, Cinnamon here will be his neighbour, won't you, Cinnamon?'

'Good to know.' He gave Cinnamon a final rub on his neck. 'While we're on the subject of Denby, I wanted to ask again about riding lessons for Abigail. I'm a bit confused.'

And that was her fault. 'I'm sorry, I've been a bit all over the place. I'm trying to have Arnold find some free time in his schedule. We'll work something out.'

He hesitated before he met her gaze. 'Is Abigail the problem?'

'Abigail?'

'It's just that you had sessions free and then you suddenly didn't. And the only thing I can think of is that it's specifically to do with Abigail.'

And now it was worse. He thought she didn't want his daughter, that perhaps she didn't like Abigail. And that wasn't the case at all. It made her sad that he might in any way think she was a terrible person for refusing to teach, when one minute, she told him she could, the next, she changed her mind. But she'd done well to protect the reputation of the stables and part of that had been carrying on around other people as though nothing were out of the ordinary. Nobody in the village seemed to know the dire straits she was in, which they might do if she and Arnold suddenly brought in another teacher, a stranger to the village. Gossip might trickle out that she wasn't teaching much at all and so might the reasons why. And no rider wanted to know their potential teacher had lost their nerve, not with horses, but with them.

Hazel smiled at Gus and said the only thing she could think of under the circumstances. 'I promise you it's not personal to Abigail. She really is a lovely girl. I'll talk with Arnold again.' She had to stand her ground. She'd already confused him by saying they had vacancies when she'd assumed he might be the one wanting lessons, she didn't want to do it all over again.

'She's pretty competent and she'll listen to instruction. She knows how to behave.' Before she could reply, he added, 'I thought you might reconsider. She's more confident with women than men, I think females are generally more understanding and patient. Not always, but you two got on when you met. At least, I thought you did, anyway.' He was tripping over his words a little; it would be cute if the subject matter wasn't so painful for Hazel. 'Like I said, we'd be really flexible, fit in with your schedule, weekend, evening, early before school if needs be. Whenever you have the time.'

Gus still hadn't finished, he still wasn't letting her go, as he told her, 'Abigail has had a few knocks along the way with one thing or another. Horse riding is the one thing that's constant, the one thing she trusts and has confidence with. Funny how she can be so confident in that but not much else.' He was almost speaking to himself now, or Cinnamon, Hazel wasn't sure.

But Hazel got it, that lack of confidence in some areas and not in others. Because that was exactly how she felt. She knew what Abigail must have gone through, what she might still be going through.

And yet, what could she say? Sorry, I can't teach her because I lack confidence in keeping kids safe? And how could she, with a confidence problem, possibly support someone else who had similar issues? Arnold was a much better bet – good with any age or ability, patient but firm, and had the ability to crack a joke, some-

times at his own expense, to keep everyone on an even keel. Or
perhaps she could apologise and say sorry I can't teach Abigail
because I saw the way you went off at those teenagers the other
night and having been on the receiving end of an angry parent once
before when a father came at me with a pitch fork, fury etched into
every part of his being; I'd crumble if anything like that ever
happened again. That man had destroyed a part of her that she'd
never fully got back.

'Think about it,' he suggested, his brow furrowing as though he
needed to ask her more questions.

She wondered – if she told him the truth, would he understand?

'Dad!' A voice sounded before Hazel could encourage
Cinnamon to walk on.

'Out here,' he called over his shoulder.

Abigail came running around from out back and immediately
beamed a smile at Hazel before she turned her attention to the
horse. 'Which one is he?'

'This is Cinnamon.'

Abigail kept her voice soft. 'Hello, Cinnamon.' She stepped
slowly towards him. His head moved slightly, his ears registering
her voice and his nose seeking out this new arrival. 'Can I touch
him?'

'Of course,' said Hazel, 'and I appreciate you asking.' Many
didn't and Cinnamon, while he usually responded well, could get a
bit annoyed too. But Abigail was doing everything right, she made
her movements gradual, she reached out for his shoulder first and
stroked his coat before she got closer to his face. Hazel couldn't
even hear half of what she was saying but she did pick up the name
Denby. It seemed the little girl was telling Hazel's horse all about
the latest stable mate he would meet later today.

'Where did you ride?' Abigail asked, way more confident than
she'd been at the stables. Perhaps this was what Gus meant,

maybe her confidence ebbed and flowed according to new situations.

'We have some wonderful countryside and bridleways nearby, so mostly off-road.' Abigail began to laugh when Cinnamon jerked his nose upwards away from her hand so he could explore the sound of a lawnmower that had started in the distance. 'He's inquisitive, sometimes a little too much, but mostly he's a good horse.'

Abigail waited for Cinnamon to lower his head, knowing he'd get more fuss, and she obliged straight away.

When Hazel had first seen the scars on Abigail's face, she hadn't been shocked, but she had wondered what had happened. Going by what Gus was saying, she'd been through something, but whether he was referring to what happened or to her parents not being together, or to a school move, or to all those things together, she wasn't sure. It made her want to ask him more, to sit with him and talk at length about his daughter, a girl she really did like. Hazel wondered briefly whether something had happened to Abigail under Gus's care, but as Abigail and Gus laughed about Cinnamon chomping down his apple when Gus's tummy rumbled loudly, she knew that if it had, it would've been a dreadful accident. And then she berated herself because she knew only too well how easy it was to lay blame at someone's feet. And if you were that person, it didn't matter whether it was your fault or not, it still felt like you were on trial, and it made you doubt yourself.

'I'd better get going,' said Hazel. 'But I look forward to meeting Denby later on.'

They both said goodbye, Gus holding her gaze a little longer than was comfortable and Abigail looking more enamoured with the horse than with Hazel.

Hazel tapped her heels gently against Cinnamon so that he walked on. As they made their way down the street, Hazel could sense she was being watched. It was like when you passed someone you really liked and you knew they were watching you walk away, which made you wonder whether you'd even be able to put one foot in front of the other until you were out of sight so you didn't make a fool of yourself.

Hazel's shoulders didn't relax until she was back on The Street, safely away from Gus and his daughter, past the pub, and on her way home.

6

That afternoon, Gus pulled into the parking area outside the gates to Heritage View and, on foot, he and Abigail ventured towards where they could see Hazel outside the stable block. She hadn't spotted them yet, she was bent over, picking out a horse's hooves, and Gus did his best not to admire her lean figure in jodhpurs and a T-shirt that hugged the rest of her shape. He'd noticed her toned arms and upright posture earlier when she stopped to talk to him on the street and part of him had felt amused that she'd seen him in a lot fewer clothes already, so he shouldn't feel too guilty.

Gus got his mind back on track when she turned around and saw them, even though he had a feeling he could watch Hazel all day. She'd told him earlier that her refusal to teach Abigail wasn't a personal thing against his daughter, but he was struggling with what to believe. It broke his heart a little to even consider that someone who didn't really know his daughter all that well might see her as different. Or was he being paranoid? Was he looking for things that weren't there? He knew he'd done that when the accident first happened, assuming everyone was staring and about to say something inappropriate. Joan had had a quiet word with him and told him Abigail would learn from example. If he reacted badly, she'd do the same, and so he'd dug deep to try to teach Abigail coping skills. But it wasn't always easy when his protective guard went up.

Watching Abigail now, and Hazel for that matter, the two seemed to have a natural rapport, already discussing the horse Hazel was grooming: its habits, its foibles. Abigail was fitting in easily and he should be happy about that because it wasn't necessarily a given for anyone, let alone a girl who'd had a tough time over the last few years.

It had been mostly smooth sailing with school so far too, with Abigail making friends easily enough and even having a couple of girls in her class asking to meet up this morning at the local ice-creamery. Unfortunately, Abigail's request had triggered an argument because yes, of course she could go, but she didn't like it one bit that he wanted to take her there and meet her afterwards.

'I thought you said we moved here so you wouldn't have to drive me everywhere,' she'd said to him, sitting at the kitchen table eating her toast.

She had a point. But she was also being rude. 'Don't talk to me like that, and you're ten, not fifteen.'

'So I have another five years before I can get an ice-cream with my friends?' Her bottom lip had trembled the way it always did when she got wound up.

'That's not what I'm saying.' They had plenty of time before Denby's arrival and meeting up with friends was what he'd wanted; after all, that was the whole reason for having her start school before the summer holidays. And it would give Abigail something to do other than checking her watch every five minutes, counting down the hours until her horse got here.

Gus pulled out the chair next to his daughter. 'It's not that I don't want you to have friends or freedom,' he told her as they sat in the kitchen that almost looked normal now there weren't so many boxes littered around. He'd even managed to get a shopping delivery late last night and fill the cupboards with all the extras you forgot you needed along the way – salt and pepper, vinegar, flour, stock cubes, Worcestershire sauce, pasta. Next on the to-do list had to be sorting his own bedroom, or the boxes he stepped around to get into bed would be in danger of feeling like a part of the fixtures and fittings, and he'd never do it.

'Then why won't you let me go there on my own? It isn't far.'

'No, it isn't.' His mind shot back to the night of the art class, the way those kids had been talking to her because she was different. His fists clenched whenever he thought about it, and they were doing the same thing now. 'I worry about you.'

'Because of my face.' Tears coursed down her cheeks now.

His heart broke that that was the first thing she put it down to. He pulled her to him and held on tight. Joan had told Gus that sooner or later, he had to let her have some independence, and it was part of the reason she'd been okay with them heading this way. Joan would miss them, but she knew it was time Gus and his daughter moved forwards together without hiding behind the routine they'd all too easily fallen into, Abigail only going to and from the stables, home and school, not having any extra-curricular interests that got her meeting other people, not even a riding stables where she was with kids her own age. And, Jean observed, Gus had done the same thing since his marriage ended. He'd closed himself off unless it was being available for Abigail and, while that was admirable, she'd told him, he had to think of himself as well. He deserved happiness as much as his daughter. But it wasn't easy to remember that or act on it. Not when he wanted to be here for Abigail 110 per cent.

Gus put his fingers beneath her chin and tilted her face up towards his. 'Your face is beautiful.' He kissed her cheek. 'You are beautiful both inside and out. You are a remarkable young lady with a bright future ahead of her. It's a parent's job to worry about their child, we can't help it. I worry about everything, from whether you've cleaned your teeth properly to whether you look both ways when you cross the road.' He couldn't bear the thought of mean people targeting his daughter, but at the same time, he couldn't bear it that he might be the cause of her upset if she assumed the only thing he worried about was her differences.

He let out a breath. 'You know what, you're right. You couldn't go anywhere without me where we used to live, and now we are here in a new place, a beautiful little village, you need a bit more independence.' She looked at him hopefully as he smiled. 'Do you have enough money?'

'I can go, really?' She sniffed away a tear. 'Can I walk on my own?'

He wasn't sure where he got the strength from to say yes, but he treasured the way she flung her arms around him and the smile on her face in full beam, despite the scar tugging at one side of her lip and not letting it go up all the way. 'But I'm picking you up so we can go and meet Denby. We can't be late.'

'We won't be.'

'And you have the phone with you at all times, call or text me if you need me.'

'I will, Dad.'

And after he gave her the allotted time she'd need to be ready, he listened as she told him all about Sonia and Jilly, the girls in her class, how Sonia had joined the choir and Jilly did gymnastics.

At the door to the house, his heart broke just a little as he watched his little girl go, sparkly purse over one shoulder, to the end of the path and turn left to make her way into the village. It was safe, he'd seen plenty of kids doing it and it reassured him that she had a phone with her in case of emergencies. It was the reason he'd bought it for her, so she could message or call him whenever she needed.

Gus couldn't rest at home with Abigail out of the house in the village and after he'd checked his phone umpteen times, he jumped into the car long before he needed to for Denby's arrival. He parked up by the tearooms on The Street. He wouldn't do this every time, but he just wanted to make sure Abigail had got to the ice-creamery okay, and after a quick dash across the road, where he surreptitiously checked she was indeed inside with a couple of girls her age, he went back over and into the tearooms.

While Gus enjoyed the French toast he'd ordered, he checked his phone another couple of times, made sure he hadn't accidentally put it on silent.

'A watched pot never boils,' said a voice over his shoulder. The polite lady who had served him at the counter introduced herself as Etna, the owner, and her kitchen sidekick floated past, announcing she was Patricia, it was good to meet him, but she had a few more people to serve before she could say a proper hello.

'A watched pot?' he asked Etna, who wore a sunshine-yellow, linen top and light make-up.

Clearly hot from the heat of the kitchen, she briefly patted her grey hair. 'You're staring at your phone like it should ring any second.'

'Oh, that.' Guilty.

'Do you want it to ring?'

He broke out in a smile. 'Honestly? No, I really don't.'

'Then let's hope it doesn't. Although if it's a new client then that's a good thing?'

'You know who I am?' But then he laughed. 'Of course you do.'

'Everyone knows who you are, and I'm glad we finally meet. How are you settling in?'

'We're doing well, school has been good for my daughter Abigail too. She's with friends today, at the ice-creamery.'

'Kids work fast, don't they?'

He chuckled. 'They sure do.' He hoped to make some friends of his own but accepted it would take time. He wondered how easy it would be in a village community like this one, but if the people he'd met so far were anything to go by, it would be fine.

Etna took his empty plate and left him to it with assurance he should holler if he needed anything else. When it was almost time for Abigail to come out of the ice-creamery, he went back to the car so that he was ready. It was rewarding to see her smiling and hear her talking about the other girls and ice-cream all the way to Heritage View Stables.

Watching his daughter with Hazel at the stables now, he knew that letting her go to the ice-creamery this morning without him had been a step in the right direction. He hadn't liked it, but she needed it.

'Are you excited about seeing Denby?' Hazel asked Abigail as she finished picking out the horse's hooves.

Abigail nodded. She'd been clutching Denby's stable door sign against her ever since they got out of the car and Gus tilted his head to urge her to share it with Hazel.

Hazel cottoned on. 'What do we have here?'

Abigail turned the sign around. 'It's for Denby's stable door.'

'Ah, yes, this will claim his stable, I'll be sure to put it up.'

All the formalities had been covered, the contracts signed, now all they needed was Denby.

Gus admired the dapple-grey horse standing patiently for Hazel to continue. 'Which one is this?'

'This here is Franklin. He's my dad's horse, really, but Dad knows this is where he belongs.'

'How do you choose the names?' Abigail asked as Hazel picked up a grooming brush and began to work on Franklin's coat, all the way down his shoulder and his belly, her hand smoothing his coat alternating with the swish of the brush.

'Most of the names were chosen by our parents, but we did get some say. I suppose you have to think of the colour, the coat pattern, the personality. Franklin here is strong and bold, steady, so the name Franklin kind of fits. Something like Twinkle probably wouldn't.'

Abigail giggled. 'That would be silly.'

'I expect Franklin would think it silly too,' Gus joked.

Hazel grinned back at him. 'He certainly would.' She seemed happy to keep chatting and added, 'He's our oldest, wisest horse.'

'Why didn't your dad take Franklin with him to his new house?' Abigail wanted to know.

'He didn't think it fair on Franklin. Franklin loves it here with all his horse buddies. And my dad still rides him when he comes back this way. They're good friends.'

Gus wondered how much was hiding behind Hazel's smile, because there had to be something. She couldn't be this sure of herself one minute and the next, giving him mixed messages that made him wonder why she wouldn't teach his daughter. He watched as a strand of golden hair came out of her plait and grazed the side of her face and the top of her chest. But his gaze didn't linger long because in the distance he could see a horse box making its way from the lane and down the long driveway towards the house and the gates.

Abigail turned at the sound of an approaching vehicle. 'Denby! He's here!' She yelled out the discovery before running towards the main gate to greet Joan and Denby with her frantic waving, as though they might drive on past if she didn't flag them down.

'I apologise.' Gus frowned at Hazel. 'She knows not to yell when she's near horses.'

'I get it, she's excited. And this one doesn't spook easy – as well as being strong and bold, he's calm too, doesn't let much bother him, do you, Franklin?' She ran the brush across his body again. 'He'll be ridden by Bobby in the next riding lesson and then in the group lesson after that, by someone with very little experience. We need a horse like Franklin to do the best job in that situation, don't we, boy? He doesn't get in a flap or panic.' She pulled the excess horsehair out of the brush and discarded it at the side of the paddock before dropping the brush back into the kit.

'He's all ready to be saddled up,' she told Arnold as he came over with what looked like all the tack for the horse.

'Cheers, sis. I'll leave you to welcome the new recruit.' He nodded a hello to Gus. 'Send Bobby over as soon as you can.'

'Will do,' said Hazel. 'I'm sorry, Gus, I'll be with you all in a few minutes, let me get the rider sorted first.' Hazel excused herself as Gus noticed another car had pulled into the car park beyond and she went off to meet the rider.

Gus saw Joan try to pick Abigail up and twirl her around off the ground, but it was getting harder and harder the taller Abigail got. And Abigail was too impatient anyway, she wanted to get to Denby as soon as possible.

'She could barely sleep last night, knowing he was coming,' Gus laughed as he went over to kiss Joan on the cheek and pull her into a big bear hug.

Joan had Abigail stand back with Gus while she safely brought Denby from the horsebox and down the ramp. She'd paused at the top to give Denby a chance to glance around at his surroundings, but he seemed happy enough.

Abigail had some cut-up chunks of carrot to give Denby as a treat and he munched happily on those and let her fuss around him.

'How did you find driving that beast?' he asked Joan, looking at the vehicle she'd arrived in. 'Not the horse, I mean the horsebox.'

'I've driven it before and I don't mind it so much, although some of the lanes around here are a challenge if you meet someone coming the other way.' She took in his smile after she removed Denby's tail guard and then made her way around him, taking off his leg protectors.

Once Joan had attached a lead rope to Denby's leather head collar and given Abigail the nod, Abigail led him around the concrete area to get him moving again. Gus suspected it also gave the horse the chance to check out his new home, smell the country air, acknowledge that this was a change for him.

Joan retrieved all of Denby's tack from the horse box with Gus's help and between them they set it on a nearby rack beside the paddock.

Joan smiled. 'I must say, from the little I've seen of the area so far, and what I've heard and seen online, this village, the stables and this part of the country suits you both down to the ground.'

'I'm hoping so. And we've not been here long at all, but already...'

'Already it's a fresh start for you both.' She looked over at his daughter. 'And she's happy. I can see that for myself already. Oh, I know a lot of that is to do with Denby, but I can see this was a good thing for you both.' She looked at Gus. 'She'll have a chance to really blossom here.'

Joan thought of Abigail as a granddaughter. Even before the accident, before Gus's marriage ended, the pair had been close. Abigail had often called on their neighbour after school. The pair had flipped through horse magazines together, and Joan had been the one to teach Abigail the basics of riding and introduce her to the long hours of care a horse required.

'My house is far too quiet without her,' Joan sighed.

'I'm sure it is. But you'll be visiting, won't you?'

'Don't you worry.' She rolled up her shirt sleeves, one after the other. 'I'll be back.' She didn't miss Gus's gaze travelling to Hazel, who was dealing with a couple of riders. 'Is that the owner?'

'That's Hazel. And her brother Arnold is a co-owner here.'

'She looks friendly, I'll bet Abigail will like having her as a teacher.' When he didn't say anything, Joan asked, 'You are booking her in, aren't you? I think it's a good idea somewhere new, it'll help her confidence no end, get her out on some hacks, and she'll soon get to know the countryside. It's either that or you run alongside her.' When she realised he didn't share her amusement at the suggestion, she asked, 'What's the issue?'

'I'm trying to get the lessons, there's not much availability... not with Hazel, anyway.'

'Do I sense a problem?'

Hazel was looking their way, so he didn't really want to get into it right now. 'I'm not sure why, but she seems resistant to teaching Abigail. She says it's not personal but...' He shrugged. 'It feels that way to me.'

Joan thought about it as Hazel began walking over to them after checking a young rider's hat fitted correctly. 'People are rarely that easy to read, Gus. I like to think I'm a good judge of character and I've a good feeling about this one.'

He lowered his voice. 'How can you say that? All you know is she's blonde, pretty, and has a beautiful smile.' Hazel had almost reached them and he helped Joan close up the back of the horsebox.

'She's pretty, all right.' With a laugh Joan added, before they were interrupted, 'If there's a reluctance there, there'll be a good reason for it, you mark my words.'

He put an arm around her shoulders and hugged her tight.

'You're a wise woman. And thank you, Joan. Not just for today: for everything.'

She briefly smiled and then admonished him for being soppy and jokingly pushed away his attentions before she introduced herself to Hazel. 'It's wonderful to meet you, I've heard all about Heritage View. And I must say, the surrounding countryside is stunning.' She had a hand above her eyes, shielding them from the sun so she could see further into the distance.

'Thank you, we love it too. And Denby will be happy here. He's got plenty of company and we take good care of all of our horses.' Hazel, alongside Gus and Joan, watched Abigail. 'I understand Denby was your horse once upon a time and so I know his happiness is important to you too. We have a Facebook page for the stables.'

'Oh, I'm not on anything like that.'

Hazel nodded but smiled again. 'You should go on just for the updates. I'm always posting pictures of the horses, out for a hack, in their stable, in the paddocks. You'll be able to see for yourself what kind of place this is.'

Gus caught Hazel's eye and mouthed a *thank you*. Because as much as Joan was trying to be stiff upper lip about this, he knew how hard it was for her to have Denby leave her stables after so many years. Gus had often wondered whether Joan would have even sold Denby had Abigail not needed something to bring her back to the world she sometimes hated. Joan had insisted that Denby was trained, he was ready to move on and needed a younger rider, but Gus wasn't so easily fooled.

Gus looked over at Abigail as she led Denby over to check out at the paddock. She had the biggest smile on her face, and it was more than he could have hoped for.

'Joan, would you like me to show you around the place?' Hazel asked. 'You don't have to rush off, do you?'

'I'd love that, thank you. And I might just think about that Facebook thingy.'

'Do,' Hazel laughed, 'it'll be worth it just for the updates. But if not, I'm happy to email a few photos to you now and then.'

Joan and Hazel started toward the outside school, where a private lesson was underway, and Gus went over to Abigail and Denby. He reached out and ran a hand along Denby's neck and up around his forelock and ears the way he liked it. 'It's good to see you again.'

'You missed him?' Abigail grinned.

'Of course I did. You're part of the family, aren't you?' The horse regarded him with deep brown eyes and what Gus hoped was fondness.

Gus ran back to the car to grab the grooming kit and Abigail set to work grooming Denby while he leaned on the fence by the paddock and watched her. She was like a little professional these days. After the accident, Abigail had spent many a day with Joan and the horses – it was therapy for everything she was going through. She'd eventually taken over much of Denby's care when he became theirs. Joan had even let Abigail attend the veterinary appointments for her horse. Gus had written a letter to the school to request a day of absence twice, although they hadn't been happy. The third and fourth times, he hadn't bothered to ask because he sensed the answer would be no. It pained him that they couldn't see what a learning experience this was for a kid – it was teaching her to put an animal first, to take responsibility, she was learning about an equine vet's job, she was talking with other people outside of school and home, all of it potentially giving her confidence and coping skills for the real world. But schools answered to the government, he got it, there were rules. It was just that when it came to Abigail, he knew her better than they did, and so he let her take the day off and made up a mysterious bug for those days instead.

'His hooves all clean?' he called over. He'd had his forearms against the wood, the sun on his back, the horse closest to him whinnying and tossing his head happily as though saying hello to Gus before he turned and dipped his neck again to graze.

'I got a few bits out,' she called back, which was code for Joan's work being so good she couldn't find much, but she liked to give Denby the royal treatment anyway, for which Denby seemed content. His coat was glistening beneath the sunshine, his ears moving as he took in the new sounds around him as well as Abigail's familiar soothing voice as she moved on to brushing him.

When Denby's head jerked around to see what the new surrounds were, Gus saw Abigail realise it was getting busier at the stables and he clocked the look of worry flicker on her face. He could see from where he was that another two, no, three cars had pulled up one after the other in the car park and he fought the urge to run to Abigail's side. He wanted to let his daughter handle this on her own, the way she'd coped with school so far and the visit to the ice-creamery. But as the two young boys making their way over jostled noisily, followed by a harassed mother barking instructions which they appeared to ignore, it was harder for him to stay over here, out of the way.

One of the noisy boys was jumping up to see if he could get a view inside the horse box. 'Is there one in there?' he asked his companion.

'Can't see,' said the other boy, doing his best to jump as high. They both looked about Abigail's age and Gus wondered whether they were at her school.

Three girls were also making their way over towards the yard, having disembarked from the remaining two vehicles. By now, one of the boys had begun to attempt to climb up the back of the horse box and Gus was ready to go over, but the mother yanked her son back.

'It smells of horse poop,' the boy declared as he reluctantly gave up.

'If there'd been a horse in there, you might've been kicked in the head or anything,' the woman explained. 'Where's your common sense? You can't mess around when it comes to horses,' the necessary lecture went on, 'I told you that when you asked for lessons.' She briefly flipped a smile Gus's way and then, the second she saw Arnold, it was as though she passed him a baton – or more like tossed it through the air – and she was off, leaving her boys in his capable hands.

Arnold told the boys to wait by the gate leading into the outside school and he reiterated they weren't to move until he gave them the go-ahead.

'Those two are a handful,' Arnold told Gus through gritted teeth as he smiled and waved at the mother, who was already clambering into her car.

Gus looked over at the boys, who were irritating each other but not leaving their designated waiting spot. 'They seem to listen to you.'

'They know I won't put up with their messing around.' He frowned. 'They're in the next lesson, not my favourite group, but they'll get there.' He nodded to Denby. 'He's a fine horse. I look forward to having some time with him later.' And when the three girls came over, as well as a parent who was lurking and wanting to watch the lesson today, Arnold left Gus to it. The stable hand who apparently worked here on a casual basis doing the menial tasks had led another horse out to join Franklin, who was patiently waiting for his next rider now he was tacked up.

Gus watched his daughter. As those kids had got closer to them, she'd moved to the other side of Denby where she couldn't be seen. She was brushing him but gone was her look of contentment; instead, the hunch of her shoulders suggested she'd only relax when those kids were in their lesson and she wasn't in danger of being approached. She hadn't been that way at all since they'd arrived in the village, but seeing it now, he realised it was a reaction that came and went and likely always would. It was up to him to help her through it, to make enough fuss to show he cared but not so much it freaked her out. He knew he'd done that after the art class by yelling at those kids and afterwards he'd berated himself and his appalling behaviour for possibly setting back the progress his daughter had worked so hard to attain.

When Hazel and Joan had finished their tour and came round to join them, Gus could tell Joan was more than impressed with Heritage View. 'You like it?' he asked anyway.

'Like it? I love it, thank you, Hazel. And I got to meet Arnold,' she told Gus. 'I didn't realise he was so good at jumping, used to compete a lot. Now he seems to have found his calling.' They all looked over to the riding school, where horses and riders were getting themselves organised.

'Arnold said he'll spend some time with Denby later,' said Gus, thinking Joan might appreciate how much this pair viewed all these horses at their stables as equally important.

Hazel chuckled. 'Arnold likes to give new arrivals a good once-over and get to know them. He likes to talk to them, man-to-man.' She said it in a mock-gruff voice that made Abigail giggle and showed Gus her fun side.

At least the kids' arrival seemed to have been put to the back of his daughter's mind now they were safely behind the fenced-off school. He wondered how she managed it so well in the classroom, although perhaps she did that because he wasn't there to look at her with concern, for her to pick up on his worries as well as hers.

'I'm going to miss him.' Joan was gazing at Denby affectionately and her thoughts stopped Gus from wallowing in self-pity or shame, whatever it was he was feeling.

'Visit any time you like,' Hazel assured her. 'Honestly, it's no problem at all.'

Joan nodded her thanks. 'I'd better get this great big horse box out of your way.'

'Whenever you're ready,' Hazel smiled. 'Now, I'd better go find a hammer and a few nails to fix Denby's sign on his stable door.'

'Thanks, Hazel,' said Gus, smiling after her.

'Hazel is just as nice as she looks,' Joan wasted no time telling him the second she was out of earshot. Abigail had heard where she was going and, leaving Denby with Joan and Gus, she followed after Hazel to see Denby's new stable christened with the sign.

Joan stroked the side of Denby's face, leaning her cheek against his. 'You like her too, don't you?' And then she winked at Gus.

'She seems very good with horses, that's what I'm after. Do *not* go getting any ideas.'

'Me?' She laughed loudly. 'As if.'

Abigail soon came running back, after they heard a little bit of banging that had Denby's attention. 'I need to take him to see his stable.'

Gus shared an amused look with Joan. Denby was probably more than ready to head over to the paddock and meet some new friends and nibble on the grass for the rest of the day. But Abigail had other ideas and led him into the stable block where she showed him the sign in situ, and his stable, which was clean, had a water trough to one side, plenty of shavings on the floor, and bars allowing him to see out of both sides. Hazel went through some of their turnout process with him and Joan to put them both at ease and Abigail even showed Denby where he'd be having a bath when he needed it.

They emerged from the stable block with Abigail leading Denby and they couldn't have timed it any worse because Arnold's lesson had just finished, and the boys didn't seem any calmer. Now they were a bit closer, Gus could tell they were most likely a good couple of years younger than his daughter and young enough to not have a filter when it came to asking questions about Abigail's scars. Mind you, some adults didn't seem to have a filter and sometimes, worse, they talked about his daughter as though she wasn't there, asking questions, expressing understanding or what they thought was understanding.

One of the boys came hurtling towards Abigail, practically skidding to a halt. She kept her body close to Denby, her face almost pressed against his shoulder.

'Is this horse new?' the boy asked. 'Can I ride him?' he asked nobody in particular.

'I don't think we want to torment Denby, do we?' Hazel muttered beneath her breath as Arnold came over and told the boys that their parents were waiting. He was just as good at ushering them away at the end of the lesson as he was at getting them going at the start.

The girls and their mother were far more sedate leaving, and apart from a cursory glance their way, they were less interested in any newcomers. As Arnold went over to help the stable hand remove tack from the horses and have them turned out, Hazel suggested, 'Abigail, why don't we let Denby have some time in the paddock?'

Joan squeezed Abigail's hand. 'That sounds like a marvellous idea.'

And while the girls dealt with Denby, Gus went over to where Arnold was wiping down the tack he'd taken off each horse and put over a rack for the time being.

'Would you like some help?' Gus offered. He wanted to sound Arnold out about the lessons.

Arnold passed him a saddle, which he dumped in his arms and

then hooked a bridle over his shoulder. 'Bet you wish you'd never asked.'

Gus laughed. 'Might as well use me rather than have me standing there observing.'

They took the tack around to the tack room and inside, Gus found the right places for the tack. With a smile, he looked at Denby's name on a hand-written sign and his chocolate-brown saddle in place, his bridle on a different hook.

'Lucy's Blacksmithing does excellent signs.' Arnold's voice sounded from behind him. He indicated Franklin's saddle spot and an iron square engraved with the horse's name in fancy twisty lettering as he put the saddle back in place. 'She's local.'

'I've seen her workshop from the outside, just not had a chance to go inside yet.'

'You should, she makes some wonderful things.' Arnold put the bridle back, as well as the saddle pad. 'That boot scraper by the office was Lucy's work – we have a funky wine rack she made too. She'll make signs if you like, and we'll put them up for you. We like to make owners feel at home here.'

'Abigail has a birthday coming up, it's the sort of gift she'd appreciate.'

'I know horse lovers, and Abigail definitely fits the profile.'

The stable hand was busy outside, cleaning another horse's tack with a wet sponge, and Arnold requested he clean another set after that one, before he and Gus walked back around to the front of the stables.

'I wanted to ask again about lessons,' Gus started. 'I know from Hazel how busy you are and I know a regular spot for a private lesson might be a bit much to ask, but I really think Abigail needs it, if only to settle in.'

'I get it,' Arnold agreed, retrieving a pitchfork from inside the stable block. He rested his hands on top of the fork as they talked, pausing in his day for the newcomer. 'It's just we're really booked up. Most days are as crazy as today. I've only got forty minutes until I've got another group of four,' he said to illustrate the point. 'Sometimes we have cancellations, that might be a good bet.'

'Group lessons are definitely what we'd like in the end, but I think for a while she might need some one-on-one.'

'Is she settling in all right?'

It touched him that Arnold showed concern on a personal level. 'We're getting there quicker than I thought we might, actually.'

'I wish I could be more help, I will get in touch with a free slot if any come up, I promise you that. But I don't think there'll be much before the school holidays, when Abigail will presumably be free during the day.'

'She will be. No plans for a holiday, you know, the business, a new home.'

'You don't need to tell me. Having your own business doesn't allow for much downtime.' Arnold readjusted his arms on top of the pitchfork, his dark hair and fairer skin opposite to his sister's characteristics, with a tanned complexion and blonde hair. 'I was kind of hoping Hazel might offer to teach.' With Gus a bit taken aback by the remark, Arnold appeared to realise he'd been a bit too honest. 'I apologise, that was unprofessional of me. Never mix business with a sibling.'

'Not likely,' Gus laughed, 'my sister is a massage therapist.'

Arnold appreciated the joke but apologised again. 'I shouldn't have made that comment. So please do ignore it.' He sighed. 'I feel bad because who doesn't have an extra hour once a week? I must sound like a total arse to you. Especially when Denby will be used by the riding school for lessons.'

'Hey, no judgement.' Gus was beginning to wish he hadn't pushed it. 'There are limits on your time. And Denby is here as working livery, we know that.'

'I'll get Abigail in as soon as I can. But in the meantime, make as much use of the school as you need to when it's free. If I'm teaching outside, use the indoor school. If I'm inside, go outside.'

'Will do.'

Their conversation was interrupted with a roar from an engine pulling up outside the house next to the horsebox.

'Why can't he use the damn car park?' Arnold grumbled.

'Who is it?'

'James. Hazel's... ex-boyfriend, although he'd like to drop the ex part.'

'And she wouldn't?'

Arnold shrugged. 'I've said enough already. I'd better get on, sort the school and clean up for the next lesson.'

Gus went over to Abigail and Joan and reminded them that a lunch at the pub was on the cards, but he couldn't help turning back to watch Hazel. Arnold was right – this man, James, seemed very much interested and although he didn't know Hazel very well, from where he was standing, Gus could tell that she wasn't.

7

Denby was settling in well at the stables and so far, Arnold had been around when Gus and his daughter visited. They seemed to show up at around four o'clock on the dot, but Hazel hadn't seen much of them since she'd found herself doing the accounts and chasing up orders – hay was needed, a new saddle they'd had on order for Peony was delayed, and then she was in talks with the equine vet to arrange various vaccinations. And each time she'd been in the office, Hazel had sneaked a look at the drawing Lucy had given her, showing Gus in all his glory. And the more she saw the man out and about, the more she realised how well Lucy had done with her drawing. She'd long since got rid of her own efforts, which would never have had the same effect, one that made her pulse race a little, the heat rise to her chest.

Hazel had loved meeting Joan at the weekend and greeting Denby. He was a magnificent horse, generally obedient, and had found his place here easily. Hazel had ridden him twice, Arnold once, both able to agree which riders would be the most suitable for him and vice versa. It was always important to match horse and rider. The last thing you wanted was a rider on a horse who was too

lively for them or a rider who grew frustrated if they were ready for
jumps and cantering and had been assigned an older horse who
didn't go into those things with gusto.

The only downside of Denby's arrival that day had been James
turning up. She didn't usually mind too much, but it was clear she
was incredibly busy, the way she'd told him she would be, and he'd
wrapped her in a hug that she didn't wholly appreciate when it was
in front of a client. She'd definitely seen Arnold cast daggers their
way with James's car parked where he'd been asked not to. And
Hazel had appreciated him turning up even less when he informed
her of why he was there.

'That the new horse?' he'd asked, looking Denby's way.

Hazel had stepped back from the fence and left Joan, Gus, and
Abigail to have time together. 'That's the new horse.'

'Handsome fella.'

'You're not wrong there.'

'You ridden him yet?'

She nodded to the horsebox with a chuckle. 'He's just got here,
don't want to scare him off.' She caught Gus looking their way.

'Not up to you to show them around,' said James, wearing jeans
rather than suit trousers given it was a weekend, but a designer
label T-shirt to go with them, its emblem to one side of his chest. He
tutted at the clump of mud or possibly horse poop caught up on his
shoe.

'It kind of is,' she said, trying to keep the hint of annoyance from
her voice. 'Use the boot scraper inside the stable block.' He sometimes used the fence and it annoyed her immensely because they
frequently hung saddles or other pieces of tack there as they got
horses ready and the last thing you wanted on your saddle straps or
reins was a clump of mud or anything more sinister that you'd then
have to clean off before you could get going with what you
intended.

Once he'd scraped away the dirt the way she'd suggested, he asked her what time she finished today. 'Come on, Hazel,' he urged when she said not until late. 'I know you think I'm hassling you, but I have someone I'd like you to meet. That's why I turned up without calling you.'

'Who is it?'

'Someone from college who I've been in touch with for a few months. He's been in charge of a riding stables in Cornwall and just moved back this way.'

'He's a friend?'

James tilted his head this way and that. 'Kind of, but more than that, he's someone you can talk to about taking on here. Come on, Hazel, I bet you're turning down people for lessons without you teaching.'

'The idea is to get me back to it, not get someone else to take over. Haven't we been through this?' She thought they had, and she'd been clear then too.

'It's a good solution temporarily.'

'And I've told you, it's not what I want. It's not what Arnold wants.'

'So you'd rather lose business?'

'James, just because you get to advise people in your line of work, it doesn't mean you need to do it with me.'

'Someone has to.' But he sighed. 'I'm sorry if you think I keep going on about it. But as far as I can see, you're not doing anything to get back to teaching and sooner or later, something will have to change. You admitted that yourself and I can see the strain you're under and the toll it's taking on Arnold.' With a smile, he added, 'Those filthy looks he gives me definitely hint that he's had enough.'

'He's frustrated that he always has to remind you of where to park, James.'

'I know, I'm sorry. I forgot, again. But parking aside, think about it. Taking someone on here – not just anyone but someone reliable – might be a solution, even only in the interim. Or maybe you'll like him so much it'll be long-term. You don't know unless you try.' He raked a hand through his hair. 'I'm just trying to help you out here.'

'I know.' And it was her own fault. She had moaned to him more than once that she was feeling more stressed lately, and because she didn't elaborate, she couldn't blame him for thinking he'd found the ideal solution. Maybe she was being pig-headed; perhaps if she got in some extra help rather than having this whole business rest upon her and Arnold's shoulders, it might just be the way through to the other side. She could take time for herself, work through her issues, and then be able to move forwards to get things back to the way they were before.

'You could do the other thing I suggested,' James said.

She only had to glare at him to tell him the answer was no. 'I'm not selling a part of a family business. A business I love, that is a part of me, that I will never ever leave.'

'I think you're making a mistake. You need to see the bigger picture.'

He was infuriating. It was him who couldn't see anything other than immediate solutions.

James had left her to it after that and she'd had to forget about what he thought was helpful advice. She'd told him time and time again how much she missed the confidence she'd once had as a teacher. She wanted to pull her weight, she wanted the Heritage View Stables to maintain the reputation it had built over the years with her parents at the helm and now her and Arnold.

Today, Hazel was actually teaching three female riders, all adults, all experienced and responsible: the perfect scenario. She'd already got Jigsaw, Pebbles, and Peony in from the paddock and all three horses were secured at the fence, groomed, and ready for tacking up when the women arrived together.

'I love you three,' said Hazel as each woman took charge of tacking up their assigned horse. 'You all know what you're doing.' Saddles and bridles were on and the trio mounted up to walk around to the school.

The women were a generation ahead of Hazel and it was hard to imagine having all that history, to share all those ups and downs along the way. It was different within a family. Parents and siblings shared it all, or at least you hoped they would and that they would help, but friends were in a whole other realm. Lucy and Melissa in particular had focused their attentions on getting Hazel out and about a bit more, and watching these women, Hazel realised how much she'd needed them on her side. She'd dated James for so long and then focused on him or the business that there'd been little time for anything else. Just basic fun with people around your own age; not love interests – friends.

Hazel hadn't told Melissa or Lucy about what had happened to her years ago. She hadn't told them about her experience with that man, the way he'd confronted her and she'd been terrified at what he might do to her. Being pinned up against a wall by a man wielding a pitchfork had been something she'd only talked about with her parents, Arnold, and James. She hadn't wanted a single thing to become local gossip and impact the riding stables she was so intensely proud of. That included not letting people know about a young rider being injured, her lack of confidence or belief in her ability to teach. As far as the village knew, it was business as usual at the Heritage View Stables and always had been.

As the women warmed the horses and themselves up walking around the school, Hazel thought about Abigail, Gus, and Joan. They seemed much like a family, even though they weren't in the usual sense. As she'd shown Joan around the stables, she'd almost touched upon the topic of Abigail's mother because she wondered where she was in this picture. But Joan had kept the conversation

on horses, whether intentionally or not, and besides, it was none of
Hazel's business.

'Are we ready to try some low jumps today, ladies?' Hazel asked,
smiling at each of them.

They all chorused their agreement and while they worked
around her, Hazel began to line up trot poles in the centre of the
school at intervals for horse and rider to go over. Once the horse
had got used to those, she'd make a small jump out of two poles
crossed at a low level.

The trot poles were a doddle and Hazel enthusiastically assembled the jump. Sherbert, despite his fizz and enthusiasm, avoided
the jump no less than four times, sidestepping it at the last minute.
'He needs to know what you want him to do, and if you're hesitant,
he'll pick up on that, Maura,' she told the rider.

Maura nodded. She looked the most nervous of the three
women, but she was very competent. A fifth attempt had the same
result but on the sixth, Sherbert went over the little jump and got a
cheer from Hazel.

It was Jigsaw's turn to refuse the jump next, despite having done
it a few times, but his rider Jacqueline soon had him try it again and
again until he did it properly.

As she dismounted and thanked Sherbert for the ride, Maura
asked Hazel, 'Will we have you for our next lesson too?'

'Definitely, you're my regulars now.'

'Shame, your brother is nice to look at,' Maura laughed, looking
over in Arnold's direction as he emerged from the indoor school,
where he'd been teaching a one-on-one with a girl of five who was
learning young. Hazel had wanted to steer well clear of that particular lesson.

'And I'm not?' Hazel laughed.

'You're a stunner,' Maura announced, 'but not my type.'

Hazel was still grinning about their conversation as the ladies carried on removing saddles and bridles, and shunted back and forth to the tack room as Hazel turned each horse out. Last but not least, she put Sherbert out in the paddock closest to the house. Cinnamon was in the farther paddock today, which was intentional, as Sherbert had done his best to irritate Cinnamon yesterday. It was a bit like school, separating the troublemakers or putting some horses in the front row or the back depending on their personality. Tomorrow they'd probably be the best of friends.

She went back to the outside school, dismantled the jump, and put the trot poles at the edge of the school near the fence. Her stomach growled – she'd not had time to stop for a morning snack today she'd been so busy turning out the horses, mucking out, cleaning the horse's feed and water buckets, sweeping the yard. She'd also carried out a routine inspection of all their fencing around Heritage View, keeping an eye out for anything that might hurt a horse like a protruding nail or a broken panel that could see the horse try to push through and investigate what was on the other side.

Hazel ran back to the house, grabbed a piece of bread to eat dry, and then it was time to take delivery of the new hay nets from a different supplier, which would hopefully be more durable. She hung two of the new hay nets in the stable block ready for Cinnamon and Minstrel, whose hay nets were on their last legs, she picked up any dung from the outdoor riding school and raked it over so it was ready for the next lesson, and then she headed to the office. She returned a few missed calls, including two new enquiries about beginners' lessons for kids in the under twelve age group – she didn't even want to tell Arnold about those.

When she'd finished the business side, she returned her dad's call. It always gave her an injection of pride, sitting at the desk in the office as she made the call, in charge, in control, continuing their parents' legacy by making the business a success.

'Hazel,' his voice boomed across the miles from the West Country, 'how is my favourite daughter?'

'I'm your only daughter, Dad.' He always asked the same question, but she appreciated it every time.

Hazel recounted her day so far, told him all the fencing was in good repair, including the section at the back which had been fixed after a big storm last year that saw the kitchen roof and a stable damaged, not that you'd know either of those things had ever been a problem now. They talked about Hazel's last lesson and how she felt the women had progressed, they talked about the waffle shack that her dad had fallen in love with and wished they had something similar nearby. And they talked about James too, when Hazel told her dad he'd stopped by.

'It's good he's still supporting you.'

'You know James, he's always been there.'

'He certainly has.' Her dad had always approved of James, but there was a hesitancy in his tone Hazel wasn't sure she wanted to question. 'You sound as though you enjoyed your teaching today.'

'They're all very competent and a lot of fun. I think they'll progress well with the jumping over the next few weeks.' It was satisfying to see, taking someone from one stage to the next. It was something she missed about teaching children, particularly those hesitant about horses. She liked watching how they evolved, how they managed their fears and began to love the animal. When they learned how to react in various situations, confidence came and eventually a joy and passion Hazel knew was priceless.

'And Arnold sounded like he was busy when I spoke to him last night,' said Thomas. 'You were asleep by then.'

'He's taken on the bulk of the teaching.' She wasn't sure whether to say it but chose to add, 'He's frustrated we're turning down bookings. I had another enquiry earlier, I daren't tell him.'

'He'll understand, for a while.'

'Oh Dad, I never thought I'd avoid it for so long.'

'If you don't feel ready then you don't feel ready.' The sympathy was there in her dad's voice, the way it always had been. 'If you rush back and don't take time to deal with what happened, it might well do more harm than good.'

'Were you a counsellor in another life?' She swished away a fly that had come in to join her.

'I'm not sure I'd have the patience, only got it with you kids because you're mine and I love you.'

'I'm working on getting back, Dad.' And she honestly was. 'James knows someone with experience who could come and work here for a while.' Her information was met with a silence. 'Dad, you still there?'

'Of course. It's something to think about, I suppose. How does Arnold feel about it?'

'I haven't mentioned it.'

'You're in this business together,' said Thomas. 'I'm happy to guide you both but at the same time, you don't have to make decisions because I approve. And I'm sure James has your best interests at heart, but he doesn't know the riding business the way you and your brother do. What you both need right now, you and Arnold, is to have one another's backs in whatever way you both see fit. That's what business partners do.'

'I know, Dad. I'll talk to him.' Before James dropped a clanger and caught her off-guard. 'I'm still staying on top of all the finances, and that part Arnold is happy about. It does make it easier having one of us placing orders, staying on top of supplies and inventory.'

'Always worked that way with me and your mother too,' Thomas replied. 'But if the driver of income is the lessons for young riders...'

'I know. I need to get back to it properly. Arnold suggested I have a timeline so rather than saying I'll do it sometime soon, have a date, a goal.'

'Sounds like a plan.'

'Maybe.' Perhaps having a date would give her a focus, help her to process her feelings and her fears and get back to teaching.

Before the confrontation that had rocked Hazel to her core, she'd never shied away from teaching anyone at all. In fact, she'd revelled in it; it was one of her favourite parts of stable ownership. There was once a time when she would've leapt at the chance to teach young kids, when she would've taken someone like Abigail under her wing the moment she heard the young girl sometimes lacked confidence or that she was keen to learn jumping. But as it was, Abigail reminded her a lot of herself – there and present and enthused one minute, and the next? She retreated into melancholy and didn't know how to handle a situation. Hazel had noticed it the day Denby arrived, when those kids in the lesson asked Abigail questions. She'd gone from confident and excited to unsure and tentative, her voice quietening. And she hadn't missed Gus's stance, as though he might go over there at any second and have a word with them but was trying his best not to. At first, it made her think back to the scene she'd witnessed after the art class and she wondered suddenly if Gus's anger that day had had anything to do with Abigail. Perhaps he had been trying to protect her.

Arnold made her jump when he poked his head around the door and when he saw she was on the phone, he came over to the desk and the filing cabinet to look for something.

'Hang on, Dad. I need to find something for Arnold.' The last thing Hazel wanted was Arnold rifling through the paperwork. He didn't know where half of the invoices and records were kept for a start, and she had an order to things. 'What are you looking for?'

'I ordered a new saddle for Peony, wondered when it was

coming. Hey, Dad,' he called out, slightly frustrated that his sister was putting a stop to what he was trying to do.

'I'll find it, you talk to Dad. It's quicker this way,' she assured her brother.

While Hazel opened cabinets and files to locate the correct piece of paper, Arnold talked to Thomas. They discussed her dad's latest hack in the West Country and Arnold assured Thomas that one day he'd make it down there and they could ride together. He probably wanted to add he'd do it when his sister pulled herself together a bit, but he was too nice a brother to say it out loud.

Hazel found the paperwork. 'I'll call them once I've finished with Dad.' She took the call back once Arnold said goodbye.

'Sounds as though you two really do have a system,' Thomas encouraged.

'He'd have spent ages looking for it, it was better I do it.' And there was another reason. She and her dad had kept something from Arnold and Sally, something she didn't want Arnold to stumble upon now, after all this time. It pained Hazel that for accounting purposes she had to hold on to everything for years. She was always living in fear of the tax office doing a random inspection and having them find that a handful of invoices weren't exactly authentic, after Thomas had fabricated them to cover up money he'd used along the way.

Thomas had made a mistake. That was what it had been, and he'd moved on from it, promising never again. When Thomas had an accident while he and Sally were still in the handover phase for the business, passing on as much of their knowledge to their kids as they could before they went to the West Country for good and let Arnold and Hazel run Heritage View Stables, Hazel had taken on a lot of the accountancy work and she'd had to confront her dad about some invoicing and payments that didn't make any sense. He was forced to admit that he'd been gambling with eye-watering amounts. He'd begged Hazel not to tell Sally or Arnold. He'd promised he wasn't doing it any more, that he never would again. And she'd never told a soul.

Hazel told their dad all about the latest arrival at the stables. 'He's a beautiful horse and we'll be using him in the riding school, which is handy. His name is Denby—'

'Like the plates. It's the name of your mother's latest addition to the kitchen – new kitchen meant she wanted to upgrade the crockery, so she's been collecting a shade of green which has a fancy name and has bought everything from pasta bowls, coffee cups and plates to a sugar bowl and teapot.' He sounded amused. 'You wait until I tell your mum this new horse has the same name as her crockery.'

'You sound happy, Dad. You don't miss Heritage View?'

'Always. But it was time to pass it to you and Arnold.'

Thomas's accident had made him realise he wanted to retire while he still had the energy to do other things like travel – they'd been to Europe a few times already and to Africa on safari – and renovate an old cottage from scratch. And while he still loved horses and they rode at least once a week, Hazel could tell that without the business to deal with, he'd found a contentment he hadn't realised he'd been looking for.

After she hung up, Hazel chased the saddle order and went to find Arnold, who had just finished cleaning up the indoor riding school, ready for the next session. A half-filled wheelbarrow at his feet, he leaned the pitchfork against the wall and grumbled that there was no bread left in the kitchen, that he was so hungry he'd pass out in a minute.

'Go get something from the bakery,' she suggested. 'I'll dump that on the compost pile if you like.' Beyond the stables, office, and hay barn, they had another small partitioned half-open shed that had sections for the composting process and daily they'd dump manure and waste onto the pile. Compost management was a time commitment, but it also saved money in the long run.

Arnold looked at his watch. 'I can't really. I've got a quick turn-around with another lesson in less than half an hour. You can go if you like, get a walk in.'

'Really?'

'I'm not that much of an arse. I want you to teach, I'll moan about it again some time, but for now all I really want is one of Celeste's roast beef and horseradish cream baps and an ice-cold can of Coke.'

'Ah, an ulterior motive. I'll go with it, and thanks, I could use the walk.'

She didn't have to wonder whether her dad had mentioned something because Arnold told her, 'I know I'm hard on you but it's only because I care.' Somehow her dad had managed it so discreetly during their conversation that she hadn't picked up on it.

She put her arms around him. 'Love you.'

'Don't get all soppy on me.'

Perhaps now was a good time to bring up James's suggestion. 'Talking of moving forwards, James says he has someone who might be really well suited to working here for a while, until I get back on my feet.'

Arnold had picked up the pitchfork but clanged it down on the concrete. 'Does he now?'

'He's trying to help.'

'Trying to control, more like.'

'He knows I'm struggling and he knows you are too.' When Arnold eased off on the accusations, she said, 'Something to think about.'

'I'm not really sure it is.' His defences were back up. 'I don't want a stranger here working and up until now, I didn't think you did either.'

She didn't, not really, but things were becoming more desperate. 'We have stable hands who help out.' The justification might help if the only solution was to take on an instructor.

'That's one thing, it's on a very casual basis and basically for the grunt work. They're not interested in how we run the place, they don't try to change things.'

'No, they don't.' And it was for those reasons she didn't want an outsider either.

'I want to run this place with my sister,' he went on. 'What's so wrong with that?'

'Nothing. It's what I want too, it always has been.'

'Don't agree to anything, Hazel. Not until you've had a chance to sort through how you feel. And I can take more weight on my shoulders for a while, it won't be forever, right?'

'Right.' She managed a smile.

'Now, where are we on that beef bap and cold drink?'

She picked up the handles of the wheelbarrow. 'I'll get rid of this and then I'll head into the village and get those for you.'

'Cheers, sis.'

But as she heaved the wheelbarrow and its weight all the way from the school to the purpose-built compost shed, she knew that his shoulders wouldn't take the weight much longer. And she hadn't even told him about the other enquiry into lessons.

* * *

The weather had been gorgeous all day and the sun was still shining. Still in navy jodhpurs but with a fresh lilac T-shirt – she hadn't felt she could embrace the village and the bakery in the T-shirt that had signs of manure on it after she dumped the latest load for Arnold – and her sunglasses nestled in her blonde hair, Hazel walked from Heritage View House all the way through the country lanes and emerged onto The Street, waving to Zara from the ice-creamery, who was putting up the umbrella at one of the round tables out front for a customer as Hazel crossed over to go to the Twist and Turn Bakery.

'I need bread,' she told Celeste who greeted her with a warm smile, 'but Arnold is after way more than my usual two wholemeal loaves.'

'Don't tell me, the beef and horseradish cream bap.'

'He's predictable, isn't he?'

'Love it when people adopt a favourite.' Celeste, tall and willowy, with a clear porcelain complexion, had already found a bap and started to make up the order. 'What can I get for you?'

'I'll have the same, saves thinking about it.'

'Things that busy?'

'Always,' smiled Hazel, heading over to the fridge to pull out two cold cans.

'Thick or thin?' Celeste's sister Jade called out from the back.

'Thick, please,' Hazel hollered.

Jade soon came out with two loaves sliced, bagged and ready to go. 'There you are.'

'You're back at work already,' Hazel grinned. 'Nothing like a family business to cut short maternity leave.'

'Maternity leave? What's that?' smiled Jade, who had the same willowy build as her sister, which didn't show much sign of having just had a baby. 'Good job I love it here.'

'How's Phoebe?' Hazel asked, thanking Celeste for the roast beef baps she'd put on top of the counter, both wrapped in a little paper bag with the bakery's logo on front. 'I saw Linc out walking with the pram last week – he didn't want to stop, though, in case the baby woke up.'

'She's gorgeous, I'm totally in love with her and despite the lack of sleep for us both, Phoebe can do no wrong in her daddy's eyes.

He's embracing paternity leave and with the summer rush almost upon us, it works out well, as he's almost into the long school summer holidays, so he's happy to swap teaching for full-time parenting.'

Hazel left the sisters to it and with everything stowed in the reusable bag she'd brought with her, she set off for home. Turning out of the bakery, she walked into a chest she knew the look of beneath the T-shirt. 'I'm sorry, I really should look where I'm going,' she stammered, embarrassed at the body contact but not entirely regretting it.

'No need to apologise,' said Gus. 'I was rushing to get in there and grab some lunch.' He didn't seem in much of a hurry to move away from her either.

'Busy at the practice already?' She wondered if his heart was beating as hard as hers. The way he was looking at her, his eyes falling to her mouth as she spoke, suggested it might be.

'I'm getting there.' And with a sexy smile, he told her, 'I don't like to shut up shop when I don't have a receptionist, it doesn't look very professional.'

'No, I don't suppose it does.' And when she thought she might fluff anything she tried to say, she held her bag aloft and blurted out, 'I can recommend the roast beef and horseradish bap.'

'That sounds good.'

'Arnold's favourite.'

He still showed no signs of rushing off and she wondered how long they could stay here for before someone noticed this was more than a casual passing, that maybe there might be something more than a business arrangement between them.

'The Cove is great for food,' he approved. 'Yesterday I had a full English at Etna's, the day before it was casserole in the pub, I'm still enjoying the novelty of so many places to eat within walking distance.'

'For a small village, we do well on that front,' she smiled, willing him not to mention lessons again. She liked it when it was just the two of them, when they weren't talking about anything that made her feel stressed.

'Will I see you later on?' he asked, as he leaned against the wall beside the bakery's entrance, apparently with no intention to get moving just yet, despite the enticing aroma snaking out from the Twist and Turn Bakery.

'Later?'

He grinned at her confusion and she felt as though maybe he'd worked her out, that he could tell she liked him. 'Yeah, you know, at the stables, where we keep a horse and I might just bump into you.'

'Yes, of course. You'll see me. I'll be around.'

As she walked off, she felt jittery, the same way she had the other day when she rode off into the distance after she saw him outside his new practice, as though she couldn't relax until he was out of sight. Because she still hadn't heard the bell above the bakery door tinkle to let her know he'd gone inside.

8

Hazel read James's text but ignored it. He was persistent, she'd give him that, but she had no time to reply now, no time to consider a polite response to the reminder he knew someone who might be interested in a job at the stables. A job that only existed in his imagination. She'd eaten her lunch in the comfort of the kitchen – Arnold had shovelled his in standing outside before greeting his next riding student – and now it was on to turning the compost in the section pile in the purpose-built shed, then she'd muck out the last stable neither of them had done yet, put down extra shavings in the stables that had been cleaned and aired, and she had a private lesson scheduled.

Hazel fanned her T-shirt when finally, after the lesson and the tack had been wiped down and put away, she found her bottle of water from the office and downed nearly all of it on her way around to the stable block. Her phone had pinged several times and each time she'd ignored it when she saw it was James. She didn't want to be nagged any more about her next step.

'Have you seen Denby?' Arnold asked her as he led Milton from the paddock and towards the outside of the stable block, ready to tack up. For a minute, it sounded like Denby was missing. 'Go take a look. I've brought him in to the closest paddock.'

Hazel wandered over to where Denby was grazing and couldn't see what Arnold was getting at until she climbed over the fence and went around to the other side of the horse. 'Denby... it hasn't rained in days. Did you find the only patch of mud?' His whole left side was caked in mud that he must've rolled in – there was one area at the far side of the paddock that often accumulated water. Most of the horses were uninterested but it seemed that Denby's new surrounds had evoked his curiosity at what it might feel like. Perhaps it had felt good in the summer heat.

When she saw Gus's car pull into the car park, she climbed back over the fence. With Arnold about to take a lesson, she waited for him and his daughter to come over. 'Did you go for the beef bap?' she asked Gus, uneasy beneath his gaze already and not wanting to stumble over her words.

'I did, and I think I'll be having it again.'

She looked at Abigail. 'Your Denby has been up to mischief.'

Any wariness from Abigail disappeared and was instead replaced by amusement. 'What's he done?'

'Come with me.' She led the young girl into the paddock.

Abigail began to smile when she saw his coat. 'Denby, you naughty thing. You're so dirty.'

'He needs a bath,' said Hazel.

'Does that mean I can't go out riding? Dad?'

Hazel looked to Abigail. 'We could bath him together if you like, then you could come back later on to ride him, once he's nice and dry. It's still light for hours yet, you've plenty of time.'

'Can we, Dad?'

'Sure we can.' Gus seemed more than happy with the arrangement.

The little girl beamed with the kind of smile Hazel had previously seen on kids who'd accomplished something they had been trying for a long while, whether it was getting their horse into a canter and being comfortable in the saddle, or taking a series of trotting poles and jumps in the riding school, going full circle for the first time. There was nothing like it.

'Are you sure she won't be in the way?' Gus asked, taking Hazel by surprise. His question suggested he still thought her refusal to teach Abigail was personal and it saddened her beyond belief that either of them might think of her as anything other than approachable and friendly.

'Not at all,' she told him. 'I appreciate the help. Most owners who board their horses like the riding and do the grooming but are happy to let us take charge of giving their horse a good bath. Usually they're pushed for time as it is, with jobs, kids, elderly relatives to care for. Kids who love horses usually want to be a part of the action.'

Hazel explained the order of things to Abigail as she led Denby from the paddock into the wash area inside the stable block. Abigail absorbed all the new information and shared what usually happened at bath time with her horse.

'He hates the water in his eyes and ears,' Abigail explained as she cleaned out the horse's hooves.

'A lot of horses do. I'll put some shampoo on my hands for his face and that way I can rub it in, avoiding the eyes, that'll keep him happy. Then we just quickly and gently rinse that away.'

Once Denby's hooves were done, Abigail found a brush to begin getting rid of as much of the dirt from her horse's coat as possible before any water or shampoo was involved. And while Abigail brushed, Hazel filled a bucket with water to which she added a special shampoo and dropped in a sponge ready to use.

'We'll also take it slowly with the water,' Hazel explained. 'We'll begin at his feet, get him used to the temperature and see how he reacts.'

'Joan does that too,' Abigail smiled, moving the brush further down Denby's belly.

'It's a good method.' Hazel was aware Gus was watching her as well as his daughter. He was leaning against the wall across from the wash area, giving them plenty of space. The horse's ears swished back and forth, listening to his name on Abigail's lips and the conversation between all of them in the stable block.

Hazel did her best to concentrate on the task at hand. She picked up the hose and checked the temperature of the water coming out of it, but Gus's eyes following her the whole time reminded her that she still had a very clear sketch of him tucked away in her office that she could look at any time she wanted. It was hard to think of him as the same man she'd seen so angry after the art class, the way he'd got close to those teenagers to make his point. She hadn't needed to hear the words that night, his body language and threatening demeanour had said it all, and so had the faces of those teens. And yet every time he was here, he was like a whole other person – sensitive, kind, someone she enjoyed having around.

'Someone really wants to get hold of you,' Gus said when the phone she'd slotted onto the shelf beside him buzzed again.

Hazel didn't say anything, just carried on with the task. 'Now, we don't want to give Denby a shock,' she told Abigail. 'I'm sure you know all this, but I'll go through it the way I do bath time, is that all right?' With everything within reach, including the sponge and bucket of water, she said, 'Let's get his feet wet and make sure the temperature is all right for him. Cinnamon likes to dance a bit when I bathe him.'

'Denby does that.'

'Yeah?' Hazel grinned. 'I'll watch my toes, then.'

'Dad always says he has two left feet,' said Abigail, gently beginning to wet Denby's feet with water from the hose Hazel had handed her.

'Your dad or Denby?' Hazel grinned, looking in Gus's direction. He was watching her anyway, so she might as well involve him in the discussion.

'Hey, I'm not that bad,' he called over, 'although it's many years since I danced.' When he tilted his head towards her phone as it pinged again, she wished she'd turned it off.

When Denby was used to the water, Abigail got involved, lathering up the sponge and washing his coat, moving on to his legs as Hazel lifted the bucket to within easy reach. And before they attempted to clean the horse's face, Hazel showed Abigail the way she liked to hold the hose so the horse could play with it against his lips and try to drink.

Abigail laughed so hard she almost stood in the bucket of water. And once Hazel had finished that game, she flicked the hose over in Gus's direction, which made his daughter laugh all the more.

'Hey,' he said good-humouredly, his arm raised to banish the water coming at him.

Abigail took the hose and cheekily wet her dad a bit more, causing Hazel to put a hand across her mouth. 'You're in trouble now,' she said to Abigail, her conspirator.

But Gus took it well and was laughing, backing out of the stable block and fanning his T-shirt, and when Denby softly whinnied, they knew he was enjoying the game as much as anyone else.

When Hazel saw a glimpse of Gus's strong torso and bare stomach, as he lifted his damp T-shirt away while standing in a patch of sunlight, she knew she had to get her attention back on track. But she couldn't stop the smile that spread across her face, glad Gus couldn't see her now.

Hazel showed Abigail a good way to wash Denby's tail by standing to one side of him and putting the tail into a bucket of soapy water and lifting the bucket so it was fully submerged. 'He'll have a clean tail and you've kept yourself well away from his back legs,' she advised as she felt Gus's presence again.

'And his bottom,' said Abigail and she agitated the tail in the bucket to get it well washed. 'He sometimes farts and I do not want to be standing there when he does that.'

The sound of Gus's laughter had Hazel sharing another moment with him as much as his daughter, and it warmed her right through.

Between the two workers, it wasn't long before Denby showed no sign of ever having rolled in the mud. His belly was clean, his legs, his shoulders, back, and face. They mopped off excess water from his coat and Hazel stood back with Gus as Abigail finished the job by combing Denby's mane and tail after a good spray with the detangler Hazel found from her own kit.

'What time can we go out?' Abigail wanted to know.

'You heard Hazel, Denby needs to be dry,' Gus called back, ducking his head towards Hazel to add, 'She knows that, she's just keen to go riding.'

'I was the same way as a kid, still am these days,' she smiled and when she felt him watching her, she added, 'When you come back, feel free to take him down the drive to the lane and beyond, or make use of the inside school – Arnold will take his lesson outside.'

'What if he rolls again and gets muddy?' Abigail asked.

'We'll put him in the closest paddock,' said Hazel. Abigail's question had at least broken some of the tension Hazel felt. She loved Gus's company, but it was awkward when she realised how much she was beginning to fall for him. 'He can graze while he dries and there are no muddy spots for him to explore this time, so don't you worry.'

Abigail seemed happy with that and when Hazel caught a waft of Gus's woody aftershave as he hovered close, she suddenly hoped she didn't smell too horsey, which was quite ridiculous – they were standing in a stable block, she'd spent all day around the animals and shovelling manure. She almost began to laugh at the absurdity of it all. Once again, she ignored her phone and this time switched it to silent.

'Someone you're avoiding?' Gus wanted to know.

'Just busy, that's all. No time to stop, not when I have beautiful horses to bathe.' She went over to Denby to admire the job Abigail had done with his mane and tail. 'We can plait it another time if you like.'

'Yes, please,' Abigail beamed. 'Can I go and get his tack?'

'Good idea. Pop it on the rack at the end of the stable block and then it'll be ready.'

'Thank you for all of this,' Gus smiled when Abigail headed to the tack room and Hazel led Denby outside into the sunshine. When his arm brushed against hers as they walked, a jolt of electricity had her flustered.

'It's all an adventure at her age,' she managed, 'even the stuff that's less fun, although for a lot of kids, they lose interest after the adventure passes.'

'Not Abigail,' he said before she could.

'You know, I think you're right there.' She took Denby over to the paddock and by the time she closed the gate and left him to his grazing, Abigail had retrieved the tack and was busy putting it all onto the rack ready for when her horse was dry enough to ride.

'Right, young lady,' said Gus to his daughter, 'what would you like to do now? We'll need to give Denby a good hour or so to dry off.'

'Why don't you take a look around Heritage View?' Hazel suggested. 'If you walk past the outdoor school,' she said, indicating the way with an outstretched hand, 'just keep going all the way to the very end, past another paddock and eventually you'll reach the edge of the land. From there, you should be able to spot the cove itself.'

'What do you think?' Gus asked his daughter.

'I'd rather hang around here,' said Abigail.

'Take a walk, see the Cove,' Hazel encouraged, 'or you'll only get frustrated Denby isn't drying any faster. By the time you come back here, I should be finished in the house – in the interests of eating before midnight, I have to get some sort of dinner in the oven – then you can help me check the water troughs, we can refill hay nets in the stables ready for the horses when they're brought in tonight. That's another job on my list.'

Gus gave her an appreciative look as Abigail happily went off, leading the way, her tiny form in a T-shirt and light brown jodhpurs dwarfed next to her dad, big, strong and capable.

Hazel went around the back of the house, took off her boots and, leaving the back door open for fresh air, washed her hands and forearms and made a start preparing dinner. She and Arnold had taken turns for a long time, although she'd started to do most of it with him teaching so much, and tonight it would be a shepherd's pie. Whenever she made anything like this, she always made enough for at least six to eight portions that they could freeze and save doing the job from scratch another night.

With one eye out for Gus and Abigail to return, she peeled potatoes, chopped onions, crushed garlic, and pulled thyme from the plant she grew on the windowsill in the utility room. Before long, the meaty mixture was filling the kitchen with a homely aroma, the potatoes were boiling away, and she had the oven dish prepared and ready.

Hazel ignored her phone again when she saw James's name flash up. She suspected he was put out or confused because usually she answered him even if it was to say she was busy, she'd have to call back.

Hazel assembled the dish with the mixture at the bottom and fluffy mashed potato on top and slotted it into the oven before peeking out of the lounge window at the front of the house to see Abigail and Gus heading back this way. She'd been keeping a look out for them as they'd taken longer than she'd thought they would, perhaps impressed with the wide-open space at the perimeter of the land that people rarely saw. Hacks were usually taken off the other way, towards the village and the countryside beyond, or in the opposite direction down the lanes. Riding lessons were never held anywhere other than the indoor or outdoor schools, but Hazel had always loved it whenever she got the chance to take a walk the way Gus and his daughter had been. It reminded her of how secluded they were here, how peaceful Heritage View really was, despite the busyness they often faced.

Hazel went out the back door and pushed her feet into her boots, crossing paths with Tabitha, who wouldn't let her go without having a cuddle first. She gave the cat a fuss and made her way around to the front of the house, ready to grab Abigail to check the water and then haul hay for the stables.

'What did you think of the view?' she asked Abigail, who had started to walk down the side of the house, presumably looking for her.

'I couldn't see much until Dad lifted me up on his shoulders.'

She began to laugh. 'You're way too big for that, aren't you?'

'Dad's strong,' Abigail said simply, and Hazel's thoughts went straight to the sketch hidden away in her office.

Hazel was smiling as she came around to the front, but not when she saw James and someone she didn't recognise walking up from the car park to her right. She cursed under her breath, careful not to let Abigail overhear, because she was pretty sure this was going to be the guy James had told her about, the help at the stables she hadn't actually agreed to having.

Abigail went over to her dad, who was waiting at the fence by the paddock now Denby had come over to say hello to him.

'James, I can't really talk now, plenty more to do today yet.' Hazel smiled briefly at the man he was with, who politely nodded her way.

'I've been calling you all day. Tate wanted to say hello, no pressure, just thought the introduction might help.'

She smiled at Tate. She didn't have it in her to be rude. 'It's nice to meet you but I really do have a lot to do, which is kind of why I didn't answer my phone.' She saw the muscle in James's jaw twitch, the way it did if things weren't quite going his way. Usually she found it endearing, today she just found it annoying.

'Can we get the hay?' Abigail called over.

Hazel held her hand up to Abigail. 'Almost ready.' She could feel Gus watching her too.

'Bit young for a stable hand,' James smiled. 'Tate here is stronger and wiser, I can assure you.'

'James says you might be looking for help.' Tate led the conversation. 'No pressure, but I have a lot of experience.' He pulled his wallet from his back pocket, took out a business card and handed it to her, far more professional in his approach than James who had just turned up even when she hadn't said she was interested in his suggestion. 'Let me know if you want to talk, I can see we've got you at a busy time.'

Hazel hated that she felt so rude, especially if she and Arnold decided they did need the extra help for a while. She turned to the newcomer. 'I will keep your details, talk with my brother, take it from there.'

'Appreciate it,' said Tate.

'I need to go fill hay bales now and water troughs.' She nodded to Tate and James before heading over to Abigail, but not before James leant in to kiss her on the cheek and told her he'd see her soon.

'Ready to do the hay?' she asked Abigail.

'Can I carry a whole bale?' Abigail led the way around to the hay barn.

'I'd like to see that,' Hazel chuckled, finally looking at Gus, who hadn't said a word about her visitor. 'They're rather big and cumbersome.'

'She'll give it a good go.' Hazel wasn't watching James leave, but she could tell Gus was.

When they reached the hay barn, Abigail made several attempts at lifting up a bale on her own, impressing Hazel with her determination, but reluctantly agreed to let Hazel help in the end.

At the stable block, they cut off the twine and Hazel passed Abigail a pair of durable gloves to wear. 'You'll hurt your hands otherwise. Wait...' Abigail was ready to start pulling out hay. 'We'll get the nets first.' She had them go stable to stable and bring back the nets and then brought in an empty round plastic bin.

'Do we put the hay in there?' Abigail asked.

Gus stood back and let them get on with it as Hazel shook her head. 'We put the net into the bin like so. I'll do the first one.' She put it in and hooked its edges over the plastic. 'Now we fill it. Just a small amount at first,' she explained before Abigail tried to shove too much packed-down hay in at once, 'and separate it out as it goes in. That's the way. You've got the hang of it already.'

They did each hay net the same way and went back for another bale as Hazel had known they would. By the time they'd finished and hung them all, with Gus lifting Abigail to do a few of them in the stables, Hazel told Abigail that Denby should be plenty dry enough by now and ready to tack up.

'I think she's already feeling like Denby is at home here,' said

Gus as they all emerged from the stable block, Abigail leading the way over to the paddock to get her horse.

'I'm glad, that's what we like for anyone who keeps their horse here. I hope it's making her feel at home in the Cove too.'

'I really think it might be. I worried she'd miss Joan in particular, and she does, of course, but with Denby settled somewhere as beautiful as here, it helps.'

'Joan seems lovely. You'll miss her too, won't you?'

'You've no idea.' And with a sigh, he admitted, 'Abigail had a bad accident, that's how she got the scarring on her face.' It was the first reference he'd made to something horrible happening in their past and Hazel realised he was beginning to trust her.

'When it happened, Joan was there for us all,' Gus went on. 'She was the support we needed when Abigail's mum left too, when I was in a bit of a mess.' His apparent reluctance to admit the final part and his vulnerability showed yet another side to him, as though he was peeling off a layer at a time and no more.

'Single parenting has to be hard.' Hazel wasn't sure what to do with his admission either.

'Not for the faint-hearted,' he whispered with a smile she didn't have to see on his lips to know it was there. She felt his breath on her neck as he stepped in front of her to help his daughter with the gate to the paddock so she could bring Denby out.

'So, boyfriend?' Gus asked as Abigail led Denby over towards the stable block and the awaiting tack.

Hazel was confused at first. 'Oh, you mean James. No. I mean, he was. Not now.'

'Does he know that?'

'He'd like it to be different.' They watched Abigail position Denby's saddle pad and Hazel lifted the saddle on for her while she fixed on the girth. 'Do you need me to help with the bridle, Abigail?'

'I can do it.' She had it all in hand.

But Hazel didn't and with a panicked gasp, she realised the dinner was still in the oven. She'd meant to set a time on her phone. 'Crap!' She covered her mouth. 'Sorry,' although Abigail was giggling, and Gus wasn't far behind. 'Dinner's in the oven, excuse me!' she yelled back as she ran off, around to the back of the house and in through the door, pulling out the shepherd's pie, which looked as though she'd caught it just in time.

She set the dinner on the top of the stove and, oven gloves still on, closed her eyes and leaned her hands on the edges of the cooker.

This man kept taking her by surprise by showing his kinder, approachable side and more than that, she was getting used to having Abigail around so much. She was good with kids. How had she forgotten how good it could be, how natural it felt? And although she was still not ready to teach anyone too young or inexperienced, perhaps Abigail could be the kid who changed it all for her.

Should she dare to dream that this could be the leap she needed to make and get back to teaching young riders, a part of running Heritage View Stables that she really loved?

9

With Denby finally dry, a process sped up by the season, Gus and Abigail made use of the outdoor riding school at Heritage View while Arnold was taking a lesson in the indoor school and Hazel had gone into the house to rescue their dinner.

'Can't we go out to the village and some of the bridleways?' Abigail asked again as she completed yet another lap around the school on Denby, this time trotting in the opposite direction. 'I'll go slowly, you don't have to worry about keeping up.'

Gus had occasionally joined Abigail and Joan on a hack but mostly it had been just the two of them and sometimes they'd be gone for hours. Here in the village, until Abigail had lessons and had others to go out with, it was down to him to run alongside if she wanted to go outside of Heritage View. And as much as Abigail said she'd go slow, if he took her to the bridleways, she'd want to go a bit faster, and he wasn't sure he was ready to either try to keep up or to watch her go at speed when they didn't know the area.

'We'll get you out and about soon,' he assured his daughter. 'Just not quite yet.'

'Did you ask about lessons again?'

'I did. And we're working on it.' He didn't miss the momentary slump in her shoulders until Denby snorted, a sign of contentment, and she mellowed. Here she was out in the sunshine, on horseback, and that in itself was pretty good.

Some parents were paranoid about their kids learning something as dangerous as horse riding; they were terrified their kid would fall off, that they would get trampled on or the horse would bolt. And while Gus might have had all those fears once, since Abigail's accident and the way her world had shattered, seeing her absorb herself in her love of horses and in particular Denby, and the way she healed with her involvement and her passion, had put a stop to any doubt he might ever have had when it came to her riding. And leaning against the fence now, he also knew that despite any challenges they still had to come, this move to a new village, a new pace of life, was a good thing.

Watching his daughter, he wished yet again that Hazel would agree to the lessons for her. She was so good with Abigail, he'd seen it when they washed Denby, the patience she had, never mind the fun, and then the way she let Abigail help her with filling the hay nets, even though she probably could've done it quicker alone. Hazel had a kind nature, it was one of the things he most admired about her. But maybe he needed to adopt a little patience because perhaps Joan was right, there had to be a valid reason why Hazel wouldn't teach his daughter.

He smiled to himself, wondering how much of Joan's understanding about Hazel's character was down to her getting ideas about the local vet and the pretty stable owner getting together. It seemed a common theme. When Gus had bumped into Barney yesterday at the tearooms, Barney had tried to give him more of a run-down of the locals, as though regular reminders were the best way to learn about the village and its people. When he'd got to Hazel, Barney hadn't mentioned anything out of the ordinary, just that she was kind and generous with her time and that she rarely did anything that didn't involve horses. But he also sneaked in a mention that she was single, and Gus had tried not to laugh because he felt sure that this wouldn't be the first time the old man had tried to fix someone up. And when Etna, owner of the tearooms, had overheard their conversation, she'd said to Barney, 'Let the young man find love himself, it's not your job.' He'd denied that was what he was doing, of course.

Abigail grew impatient in the outdoor school and when Hazel came over to tell them she had a group lesson in thirty minutes, Gus reluctantly agreed to take his daughter and Denby further away from the stables.

'On one condition,' he told Abigail as he closed the gate to the school behind her and Denby. 'I use a lead rope.'

'Da-ad. I'm not a baby.'

'Just humour me, would you? We don't know the lanes, we don't know the village.'

'A lead rope is an excellent idea,' Hazel agreed, hooking a strand of blonde hair around her ear when it insisted on blowing against her cheek. 'It means you get a feel for the roads near here, the level of traffic, which is pretty much the same most days. Denby needs to get used to it too, get his confidence.'

Magic. It was as though anyone reiterating the rules, as long as it wasn't him, worked. And Abigail agreed, with the caveat that they wouldn't do this all the time.

It was coming up to seven o'clock as Gus, Abigail, and Denby walked away from the stables, down the long drive, then all the way up the lane towards The Street. It was a beautiful evening and easy to forget the time with it being summer. In the winter, it grew dark so early that there was no chance of your day going on longer than it should, but that wasn't true of this season, and it made Gus glad his veterinary practice was in the early stages, that he'd planned their move this way so that he could get both himself and Abigail settled before the long school holidays and before his business picked up.

Denby attracted a few admirers, including a group of children waiting near the bus stop who came over to see the horse. Denby appeared to enjoy the attention for a while, with Gus supervising, making sure none of them walked around the back of the animal, that none of them said anything to upset his daughter. He watched Abigail, whose chest was filled with pride at so much interest in her horse. She answered questions, told the children about Denby, and then they walked on a little further before turning back.

Gus was thankful that every car that passed them on the way back to the stables did so considerately, and when they reached the long driveway leading up to Heritage View, he took off the lead rope to let Abigail trot on ahead. She had Denby slow to a walk when she reached the house and Gus noticed Hazel come flying out of the front door with a bulky green holdall in her hands.

She did not look happy.

Gus quickened his pace. 'What's going on?' he asked when he got closer.

'It's Cinnamon, he's hurt.' She rushed towards the area outside the stable block where the horse was with Arnold, who was trying to keep the animal calm. 'It's his leg.'

Gus could see that but what he could also see was Abigail, still on horseback, having ridden closer to where Arnold was with Cinnamon, looking unsure, scared, as she took in the blood on Cinnamon's leg. Gus took hold of Denby's bridle in case he got spooked by a horse in distress.

'Cinnamon...' Abigail whimpered as the horse, agitated outside the stable block, tossed his head as Arnold and Hazel tried to calm him. 'Can't you do something, Dad?'

'Why don't you dismount here, take off Denby's tack, and get his halter, put him out into the paddock with his friends. And I expect they've already called the equine vet. If not, I'll help, how does that sound?'

It placated his daughter and she dismounted on the side of her horse that meant she could no longer see the drama, although he expected she could still hear the clattering of hooves as the horse moved around, trying to prevent anyone from getting near his leg.

With Denby's tack removed and his halter on, he gave a contented snort and Abigail led him over to the paddock while Gus got the gate. 'He's thirsty,' said Abigail as they watched him go straight over to the trough of water.

'He worked hard today.' Gus had a hand on his daughter's back as she climbed up one rung on the fence so she could better see her horse.

'He's happy here.'

'He is.' But when he turned, he could tell another horse was very much the opposite of happy. He hadn't wanted to overstep with Cinnamon, not unless he was asked, and neither Hazel nor Arnold had asked him to take a look. But he couldn't just stand here as though nothing was going on, not when the horse was still so upset and there was no sign of any help on its way. 'Abigail, would you wait here while I see what I can do?'

She nodded. 'I'll watch Denby.'

'Good girl.'

He headed over to Hazel. 'That leg looks nasty.' She didn't say anything, she was upset, worried. She put her cheek against Cinnamon's, still using soothing words to calm him now he'd at least let her get closer. 'Did you call your equine vet?'

'We've been calling him constantly but he's out on another emergency. He'll be with us when he can.' She looked at the blood pooled on the concrete and then closed her eyes. 'I've got a first aid kit, but Cinnamon is too agitated for me to use it.'

'May I take a look at him? I don't specialise in horses, but I know enough, and like every good doctor, I have my bag in the car. I can go get it, if you like. I know my way around my own kit better than yours, save your supplies. And Cinnamon needs you to calm him first anyway.'

Her face said it all before she added the words, 'Yes, please.'

Gus went to grab his bag and with Abigail, who'd slipped her hand into his as he walked past the paddock, went over to Cinnamon. Abigail stood well back and with a bit of soothing and coaxing, Gus managed to get a look at the leg. 'What happened?' he asked Hazel and her brother as he gradually put his hand near the wounded patch but not quite on it yet.

'We think he cut it on the fence behind the trough in the farthest paddock,' Hazel explained. 'I checked the fences but right behind the trough was a damaged part I hadn't seen. I check regularly but somehow missed a spot.'

'Easy to do,' Arnold told her. 'We've a lot of fencing.'

'It's likely that it weakened in the storms a while ago and finally came apart. Cinnamon must have turned too close to the trough and the fence, or perhaps backed up into it, who knows.'

Arnold carried on. 'I spotted it when I turned out the horses following the lesson and went to fill the troughs again. That's when I found Cinnamon.'

Hazel moved over to Abigail, who had started to cry. She put her hands on her shoulders reassuringly, told her that Cinnamon was going to be okay. She was rambling, doing it for Abigail, and for that Gus was grateful.

'Is he going to die?' Abigail's voice shook.

Hazel leapt in with a 'no' before he could. She crouched down on her haunches after turning her body and Abigail's so that his daughter was looking at her, not the injured horse and the blood.

'He isn't going to die. He's just hurt, that's all. Your dad is taking a look at him.'

'But he's upset.' Gus could hear the wobble in his daughter's voice, and was torn between Cinnamon and going over to comfort Abigail.

When Gus saw out of the corner of his eye that Hazel was hugging Abigail to her, he focused all of his attention on Cinnamon. He pressed his fingertips to the bleeding area and maintained pressure, the bleeding slowing quickly. It appeared to only be a very minor wound, but he cleaned it first and then wrapped it, using gauze and a bandage. He didn't have his portable ultrasound scanner in the car, but he advised Arnold to have the equine vet ensure there was no worse damage. He could check himself, but to be on the safe side, their regular specialist in horse care should have a look.

'I'm sure it's only minor,' he said again to Hazel, who had taken Abigail over to Peony – the horse had come to investigate what might be going on.

Hazel was shaking and without hesitating, Gus put an arm around her. 'He's going to be fine, you did everything right.'

'Did I?' The shake of her head suggested she very much doubted it.

He'd taken his arm away but put his hand on her shoulder. 'You calmed Cinnamon exactly the way you should have, you had a first aid kit at the ready and if I hadn't turned up, you would've eventually been able to inspect the wound yourself.'

'You really think so?'

He smiled. 'You don't?'

She was nodding now. 'I suppose I would have done.'

'Calming an animal down is sometimes the hardest part of all and you had no problem taking charge of that with Arnold.'

She put her hand against her chest as though reminding herself to breathe. 'Thank you for being so kind. I feel silly now, panicking, creating such a drama.'

'It was a lot of blood and often looks worse than it is. And the way a horse reacts, the way any animal reacts, can cause you to worry ten times more.' It wasn't that different with kids either.

Abigail's tears had gone now she'd heard that Cinnamon was going to be all right and she was laughing as Peony sighed, nostrils flaring slightly at first and then the air escaping onto Abigail's arm as she petted the horse.

'I can go back to my practice and get my portable ultrasound if you'd like me to take a closer look at Cinnamon,' Gus said to Hazel. He might as well offer, let her decide, rather than making assumptions. 'I can make sure the little bit of swelling isn't hiding anything more sinister, although I'm sure it's not.'

'I'm sure it's fine to wait for our vet – although now I feel rude, unappreciative.'

'Not at all. Joan was always the same. People generally are – they have someone they trust, and they stick with them.'

At that moment, a truck rumbled its way towards the house and parking area and out climbed a man with a tweed cap on his head. 'The equine vet?' Gus guessed before beckoning to Abigail. 'Come on you, bath and bedtime, school tomorrow.'

His daughter groaned. 'A little bit longer, please.'

'Come on,' he repeated and to Hazel, 'She'd sleep here if she could.'

'I would've done at her age, too. I actually did try to sleep in the stables once, both Arnold and I thought it would be an adventure, until Mum caught us.' When Abigail came over, Hazel told her, 'You know, it's almost bedtime for the horses as well. I'm just hoping they don't run away from me tonight or bedtime will take ages.'

'Running away seems to be a popular game for your horses,' Gus laughed.

'Actually, it does,' Hazel mused, waving to the vet who was with Arnold and Cinnamon. 'And some of them,' she told Abigail, 'get a double act going. Cinnamon and Jigsaw are the worst for that. I'll go to grab the halter of one and he'll jerk to the side out of my reach, I'll turn to grab the other horse instead but it's as though they have a secret code and have planned the game in advance.'

'Denby might like that game.'

Hazel wagged her finger jokingly. 'Don't go giving him any tips.' She nodded to Franklin, who'd come closer by now. 'Franklin here is the easiest to get in if it's windy and raining. He doesn't mind the drizzle or a light breeze, all the horses are content in those conditions, but much more and Franklin will hover around the gate if there's a decent patch of grass to graze on so that he's the first to be seen to.'

Abigail smiled. She always liked hearing about horses' different personalities. 'Can I say goodbye to Cinnamon?' she asked.

Gus was about to say no but Hazel took Abigail by the hand. 'Of course, I need to get over there anyway.' And she led her over to her horse and to where the equine vet was starting his examination. Abigail didn't touch the horse, but Gus could hear her saying goodbye, telling him that he'd be all right. And when he heard her say, 'Don't worry, you're not broken,' his heart constricted. After her accident, when she was in hospital and panicking about what had happened to her, about how her face might never look quite the same, Joan had said the same to her. Joan had told her that she was still the very same little girl inside and that could never change.

When Abigail went to put Denby's tack away, Hazel apologised to Gus. 'I'm sorry this was the end to your ride today.'

'Honestly, it's not a problem. And thank you for what you did with Abigail just now. She was scared, you made her feel better.'

'She talked to me while we were by the paddock.' Hazel seemed unsure whether to go on until Gus's expression must have let her know it was okay. 'She told me she remembers how much it hurt when she had an accident, that there was a lot of blood. She said she didn't want Cinnamon to feel the way she had.'

He took a deep breath in and let it out slowly. 'Yeah, that sounds like my daughter.'

'She's a wonderful girl.' And when Abigail emerged from the side of the stable block, Hazel asked, 'What do I owe you for today?'

'No charge at all. It's just a few bandages and I was here anyway.'

She shook her head. 'I'm still a little embarrassed at how much I panicked. I saw the blood. And Cinnamon, well, he's mine, he's been with me a long while and...'

'He's fine.' He almost put his arm around her again and let her lean against him the way she had before. And he almost added that what she could do for him instead of pay him was to give Abigail a few lessons.

But for now, her smile and the relief and the way she'd looked after his daughter, with the care and attention that came naturally, would be enough.

10

Hazel didn't ride Cinnamon when Saturday came around. The equine vet, Stan, said it would be fine to, but she wanted to go on a long ride, and she couldn't bear the thought that he might suffer, so this time she took Sherbert, who was a bit livelier. They had a good ride along the bridleway on past Heritage Cove and ventured down to the beach for a good canter. The rain had come last night and this morning the beach was practically deserted, the tide well out, allowing them a clear path along near the water's edge.

The salty air against her face felt like a spritz of energy as she enjoyed the speed, the freedom, pulling Sherbert to a slow canter, trot, then walk when they spotted people in the distance. She looked behind them. 'Never mind, Sherbert, we can go fast all the way back if you like. We'll turn here.'

She was just pulling the horse around when she heard a young voice call out her name.

She turned Sherbert back again and sure enough, it was Abigail running towards them in a wetsuit. 'Whatever are you doing? It's miserable out today!' Hazel laughed and lifted a hand to wave at Gus who wasn't far behind his daughter.

'I haven't been to the beach yet. I couldn't wait any longer to go in the sea.'

'And I didn't want her getting hypothermia,' Gus grinned as he reached them, a sweatshirt on his top half, checked shorts that showed off tanned legs, his trainers paired and in one hand. He put a hand on his daughter's head briefly, but Abigail was more interested in Sherbert, who was curious about her too.

'Which one's this?' Gus asked.

Abigail tutted. 'This is Sherbert, Dad. He got his name because he's fizzy like the dip.'

'That's right,' Hazel chuckled.

'Not riding Cinnamon?'

'I'm hesitant to push him. I'll leave it this week, but next Saturday I expect I'll be out on him again.' She stroked Sherbert's neck. When she'd seen Gus at the stables yesterday, he'd asked about Cinnamon and she'd told him their vet had done the ultrasound and that there was no more damage. 'It's good to give this one a turn on a long ride. You appreciate it, don't you, Sherbert?'

The horse's ears twitched in response.

Abigail might love horses but when she saw another girl heading down their way, she dashed over to join her. 'Careful!' Gus called over loud enough for her to hear but not so loud he startled the horse.

'She's making friends.' It was good to see them settling in. 'The cove is a beautiful place to swim, no matter the weather. And the water is nice and calm today.' The waves at the water's edge beside them rolled in gently, the foam frothing on the shore before the water receded again.

'We came down from The Street, down what Abigail calls "the secret track".'

Hazel laughed. 'It stops too many tourists, we locals love it.'

'It's truly beautiful down here.'

'It gets my vote.' Despite the drizzle that had just started, it didn't detract from the beauty of this part of the coast.

When Gus heard squealing behind him, he ran a hand across his face. 'I told her not to climb on those rocks.' He sounded exasperated.

'The kids around here love the rocks. And it keeps them out of our way, doesn't it, Sherbert?'

'Did you get a good run along here?' Gus asked with one eye still on his daughter and the friend she was with.

Those rocks could be slippery, she didn't tell Gus she'd seen more than one kid hurt themselves. But then she'd also seen countless others have a whale of a time. 'It's a great run. With the tide out a bit further, I can see if anyone is around, I wouldn't want to go at speed if they were.'

'Very wise.' He looked up at her and added, 'I meant what I said, you know.'

Her hands steadied the reins as Sherbert moved his head, keen to appraise himself of his surroundings while they were stationary. 'What was that?'

'When I said that you did everything right for Cinnamon after he was hurt. You had the first aid kit, you comforted him most importantly.'

'Thank you.' She leaned to rub Sherbert's neck to keep him content. 'I was panicking inside but doing my best not to let Cinnamon feel my anxiety. It's just the blood, you know.'

'I know.' His soft voice whispered towards her on the breeze.

'Good to have a vet in the village, though, in case I can't get hold of our regular next time.'

'Happy to lend a hand whenever you need.' He took a few steps away from the horse and waved over to Abigail. 'That's far enough,' he called through open hands. They were climbing on the higher rocks now. 'Abigail, off please!' He turned back and rolled his eyes Hazel's way.

She wondered if he wanted to stay here the way she did. But he had other priorities at the moment. 'I'll leave you to it, you've got your hands full.'

He looked about to protest but then puffed air from between his cheeks, accepting there was no way around it other than to divert his attentions.

* * *

Hazel had been organised and full of energy today, especially since seeing Gus down on the beach. It had been an unexpected surprise and one she wouldn't mind repeating sometime soon. Since returning from her ride on Sherbert, she'd taken another hay delivery, mucked out stables, refilled hay nets, swept the yard and the middle of the stable block, reordered stock and returned phone calls, including one to her mum, who wanted to know how Cinnamon was doing. And now, as early evening descended, she and Arnold had already finished grilled tuna for dinner and with the horses in the paddocks, it was time to kick back for a while.

'Hard day?' she asked Arnold, pouring him a glass of wine. Sometimes she hated asking that question, but she was more relaxed than she'd been in a long while. She blamed the sea air for her blurting out the question before she could filter.

Thankfully Arnold seemed as relaxed as she was tonight. Perhaps, like her, it was the relief of no more dramas, no injured horses or riders. It was a good day. 'Not a bad day, as it happens, although Mum's phone calls to check up on us get a bit much.'

'She had you checking the fence again?'

'Yup,' he laughed. Both of them knew it wasn't that she doubted her children, it was more that these horses were hers and their dad's, or at least they belonged to all of them, and Hazel knew while the paperwork and the admin were one thing to let go of, their parents would never let go of caring for the animals they'd loved over the years.

'I suppose it's nice Mum and Dad are still invested in Heritage View,' said Hazel. 'It's nice we have the support.'

Arnold sipped his wine but then looked at her. 'Don't tell me you're going to bring up that guy James brought in, are you?'

'The proposed hired help, you mean? No, wasn't going to say a thing.'

'What's going on with you? You look... happy, relaxed.'

'And that's a bad thing?' She sipped her glass of red. 'I had a good morning on Sherbert, that's all.' She wasn't going to tell him she'd also bumped into Gus on the beach. She saw him a lot at the stables but seeing him elsewhere always felt that bit more exhilarating.

'You haven't hired someone without me knowing?' Arnold was suspicious, especially when he added, 'Don't tell me, you're back with James, you're in love all over again.'

Another sip of wine. 'Now you're being crazy. And stop trying to read too much into me not being miserable.'

'He's desperate for you to get back with him, you know. You must see that.'

'How would you feel if we got back together?' she wondered.

'Not up to me,' he shrugged.

'Don't you like him?'

'I don't mind him, if he makes you happy.'

'He did, once. And since when have either of us confided in the other about our love lives?'

He sipped his wine. 'That's a good point.' He patted his stomach as though they hadn't already had dinner and he looked heavenward when he saw the oven timer and realised he still had fifteen minutes to wait for dessert, the apple crumble still warming. 'But while we're on the subject, should we talk about the other man in your life, then?'

'What other man?'

'A certain village vet.'

'Arnold, seriously.' She picked up her glass of wine, mostly to hide her reaction, lest it gave something away. 'He's a client, a very important one for our finances. And a bit of a knight in shining armour for Cinnamon.'

'He did a good job with Cinnamon. I won't deny that. And I wouldn't like to be in his shoes if he hadn't.' He ducked out of the way when Hazel went to swipe him around the ear at his teasing. 'He's keen, I'm telling you.'

'He's only interested in me because Denby lives here and he wants me to teach Abigail.'

'Let me guess, you still won't.' He held up his hands as he pushed his chair back from the table and went to get the bowls ready for the dessert.

'I'm trying.'

'How, Hazel?' She tried to gauge whether he was as irritated as he sounded. One minute they were okay, the next he remembered how she was making life difficult around here. 'We're losing business and I'm worried James is going to persuade you that you're so helpless you need this outsider to step in. Which is not what I want, and I know you don't deep down.'

Her brow creased in confusion. 'What do you mean, James will persuade me I'm helpless?' The question reminded her of Gus's kindness, his belief in her and that she'd done everything right for Cinnamon when he was hurt. Gus had a faith in her that James didn't seem to have, despite the years they'd known one another.

'Nothing.' He found the ice-cream and the scoop and dropped them on the table. 'I shouldn't have said it.'

'You shouldn't, but you did. Do you think James makes me feel like I can't get back to how I was before?'

'Hey, I never said that.'

He hadn't, but now she thought it herself. 'Do you think he's holding me back?'

Arnold looked to be considering his words carefully. 'He's always been there for you, I can't deny that, but I don't think he sees how important it is for you to overcome your fears. I think he's helping by providing practical solutions like taking on help, which might well be sound business answers, but he doesn't necessarily factor in what you really want.' He shrugged. 'This place, full time, doing everything you once did. That's what you want.'

Arnold had inherited the same patience and understanding as their dad, who was level-headed even under the most trying circumstances. And now Arnold, who had spent very little time with her ex, had summed up exactly the way James was. He wasn't unsupportive, he wasn't absent, he just didn't get it. And Hazel had to wonder if he ever would.

'I do want that, you're right, but I can't get over my worry that something may happen if I'm teaching a young or an inexperienced rider, like it did before. I still remember that boy falling, the way his body contorted on the ground, Arnold. That memory haunts me.' Although not as much as his furious parent coming at her with a pitchfork, telling her it was all her fault, blaming her, making threats. 'And then what if I agree to teach Abigail and she wants to go out on hacks? That'll make it so much harder out and about, I'll be even less in control.'

'From what I've seen, she's capable.'

'Most are, right up until they're not,' said Hazel. 'Remember I told you about the young lad – must've been four or so years ago now – Mum and I were with six riders on a familiar path and all of a sudden there was a car in the ditch. It was unexpected, out of the ordinary, it startled Mum's horse, which frightened the one behind and the one behind that.'

'The domino rally,' he grinned. 'Not funny, but it's exactly like that.'

When one horse got spooked, the others very easily picked up on it and soon became out of sorts. It was fine if you were confident as a rider to reassure them but if you weren't, it made things so much more difficult.

'The boy at the back closest to me had obviously never been on horseback when a horse was agitated,' said Hazel. 'He had a couple of years' experience under his belt, but he'd never been in that situation before. I could see the fear in his eyes, the terror mounting in his horse. In the end, I dismounted, took charge of his horse, and he begged to dismount too. It took me forever to coax him back on the horse because he was terrified it would buck like the one at the front had.'

'And you're worried you'll be out on a hack with Abigail and something similar will happen?' Arnold had been using his hands around the ice-cream tub to warm the insides, getting it ready for scooping out. But now he looked at his sister and asked, 'What would you do if it did?'

Fear flooded her insides and Arnold, looking much like their dad, sat there with all the patience in the world until she said, 'I'd get off my horse and find something nearby to secure him. Then I'd calm the other horse with my voice, with my touch, the rider too.' As she spoke, she could hear Gus's voice in her head telling her she was capable, that she was able to do all the right things, the way he'd told her the day Cinnamon was injured. The memory of him putting his arm around her too drifted back and she wished she could feel that same way again: believed in, safe.

Arnold smiled. 'Remember how as kids we called Dad the horse whisperer? Well, you and I are both just as good as he was. You did it with Cinnamon when he was hurt, you did it in the last lot of storms when plenty of the horses were unsettled, not knowing what was going on.' He opened up the ice-cream and pushed the sides of the tub to assess its softness. 'If I were you, I wouldn't worry about a hack for now; agree to a lesson providing it's in the school. Do a few of those first and you'll know how Abigail and Denby are together, you'll know how you feel. Take it from there.'

She put her head in her hands. 'I wish I had your level of belief in me.' Or Gus's, even.

'Your confidence will come back, I know it will. What happened happened. It wasn't your fault, you know that, but you lost your nerve. I think it's high time you got—'

She sniggered. 'Do not say, "Got back on the horse!"'

And then they both began to laugh. 'It's an expression and a good one. We practise it here, we did as kids. We fell off, we got back on again. And you won't get your confidence back unless you take a chance. And Abigail likes you.'

'I like her. She's brave, she knows a lot about horses, she isn't daft.'

'Then she's the perfect young rider to start with.' He pulled on the oven mitts ready to pull out the dessert, courtesy of Celeste at the Twist and Turn Bakery. 'I've got waiting lists for teaching, that's money we could be earning. You don't have to leap back in and teach every kid who comes our way. Start with one. Abigail.'

And the oven timer pinged as if to put a full stop on his demands. Fait accompli.

Now it was up to her to take the next step.

* * *

It took Hazel a few days to think through what Arnold had suggested, what she knew to be true, and along with memories of the way Gus had encouraged her, she knew she could do it. She also had a breather from James and his business suggestions too, as he'd gone away for a few days, playing golf with clients.

By Monday, she finally felt ready to tackle her nemesis. She was really going to do it. She was going to offer to teach Abigail, in the school at first, take it from there. And the thought of it made her happier, despite the trepidation.

Hazel finished her morning jobs – the turnout to the paddocks, grooming, mucking out, tacking up horses, and preparing young riders for Arnold's lesson – and come mid-morning, she grabbed the list off the fridge of the few things they needed from the convenience store. She wouldn't have time to walk there and back today with a lesson looming at midday, but she had time to drive, park up in the village and get everything they needed. And she'd have just enough time to drop in on Gus too.

With her shopping on the front seat of the car, Hazel parked on the street outside the veterinary practice. She brushed her pale-blue T-shirt and the thighs of her jodhpurs to make sure she wasn't covered in straw or anything worse and she made her way up the path towards the main door.

But she stopped when she raised her hand to knock and heard voices coming through the open window at the front.

Was Gus with a client? She waited, unsure whether to go inside or not. But when the voices became raised, she left the porch and went over to the window. She recognised Gus's voice but any warmth she felt at hearing his velvety tones faded when she saw him mid argument with a tall, slim woman with the same pale skin tone as Abigail. It had to be her mum, still in their lives, after all. And she looked pretty upset.

Hazel knew she should go. But something kept her feet rooted to the spot.

She looked again and could see fury in Gus's expression. The woman was backing away, perhaps having had enough, maybe because she was scared?

This man was the same man she'd seen that night after art class, not the one who'd watched her and his daughter as they bathed Denby, not the man who'd talked with her about his feelings and worries over his daughter, the man who'd cared for Cinnamon professionally and with that little bit of extra attention horses needed to feel at ease. She knew from their own family business that that sort of personality trait wasn't taught; it was intrinsic. And the man before her now certainly wasn't the one who'd enforced her self-belief when he put an arm around her.

Hazel stood rooted to the spot, her heart beating hard, her palms clammy, terrified that if she walked back to her car, Gus might see her, and she didn't want to have to hear him try to explain away what she'd seen and heard. Not that she could make out the words; the tone and the fury were enough. Just as it had been the night of the art class.

And she knew then that she couldn't teach his daughter. Not when she'd been reminded, yet again, that when you taught a kid, you answered to their parents.

And those parents could be unpredictable, spiteful, and almost ruin you.

11

Gus's Monday morning had started early as usual and he was looking forward to a full day at the practice. He was expecting his first patients today and he had a good feeling that this would be the beginning of a client base he could steadily build on. What he hadn't expected today was a knock at the front door of his house before he'd even left for the day, announcing his ex-wife's arrival.

He opened the door to find Julie standing on the other side. 'What are you doing here?' He had one hand on the door frame, another on his hip, already sensing this wouldn't go well.

'Charming. May I come in?' Dressed in skinny jeans and a beige linen top, overly big glasses on top of her head despite the sun hiding behind the clouds and not making any attempt to peek out, she didn't wait for a response and came in, regardless of whether she was invited or not.

'This is nice, cosy. Did you buy?' she asked when he closed the door behind her.

'It's rented. I told you that.'

'So you're going to move again?'

'Not areas, but we'll move when we buy.' Obviously. 'It takes time finding the right home,' he justified. He'd never been like her, moving from place to place without hesitation.

'Coffee?' he asked. He should at least make her feel a bit welcome, even though this was classic Julie, turning up whenever she felt like it. And at least if he made her a drink, they'd be in the kitchen and she might stop inspecting his home. She'd already peeked around the door to the right, which was the lounge, and then the one to the left of the hallway, which was the study. All of them still had boxes in them, whether empty, half-empty, or ready to be collapsed and got rid of.

'Please.' She followed him into the kitchen.

Gus would rather not alert Abigail to her mum's presence just yet because getting her out of the door in the mornings was hard enough. Back in the Peak District, she'd always gone to say good morning to Denby so had been up way before most schoolkids, but here she didn't have that incentive, with Denby being a bit further from her front door.

He made her a mug of coffee – black, a splash of milk, one and a half sugars. 'You do know Abigail has school today, right?'

'I'm not stupid, Gus.' She was leaning against the bench so she could see out of the window to the side of the house.

'She'll have to go in.' That got her attention. 'It's school, it's the law.' He might have kept Abigail at home on the odd occasion after the accident but only because she was so fragile and he was too. But this move was about normality for them both as well as change, which meant their daughter doing the same as the other kids. And that meant no extra time off unless it was absolutely necessary. Besides, if he let it go once, Julie would do it time and time again.

'I thought it would be a lovely surprise, me turning up. I thought we might walk to a local café and spend the day together.'

This was typical of Julie, who tended to do things on her own schedule rather than factoring in anyone else's.

She sat down and clonked her cup in front of her to make a point. 'It's almost the summer holidays, they won't be doing much at school apart from watching movies or playing games, I bet.'

'It doesn't matter. She has another couple of weeks, and I'd like her to be more settled in school so that she knows kids her own age for the holidays.'

'Is she making friends?'

He lost the edge in his voice. 'She is, actually, faster than I thought possible.' As much as Julie was absent and inconsiderate a lot of the time, Gus had never doubted her love for their daughter. The problem was that her guilt over the accident had driven her first to almost fall apart, unable to pick up the pieces, and then to overcompensate by showering Abigail with expensive gifts when all the kid really wanted and needed was her mother's time.

'I don't see why she can't spend the day with me and go in every other day after today.' She tapped her long, nude-painted fingernails against her cup.

The edge in his voice was back already. 'For the reasons I just said. That's why.'

She responded to his firmer tone with a harrumph. 'All right, I get it. The answer is no.'

'Maybe a bit of planning on your part wouldn't go amiss.'

She opened her mouth to answer back but their conversation was stopped short with a shriek of delight from Abigail, who came tearing down the hallway upon hearing her mother's voice. 'I can't believe you're here!' She ran into her arms.

'I'm here to see you.' She put her hands on either side of Abigail's face and kissed the tip of her nose. 'I'm sorry I missed our last weekend together.' She took out a gift from her bag, wrapped in shiny blue paper.

'That's okay.'

It wasn't. But Gus turned away to make Abigail some toast with strawberry jam. Better that than keep looking at his ex-wife. It was unbelievable how she could keep doing this – let Abigail down, upset her, and then pick up as though it was no big deal. Well, it was a big deal to Abigail, she just didn't show it. The kid was just grateful her mum turned up and she forgot everything when a shiny present came her way.

'What is it?' Abigail cried, tearing at the wrapping paper, with Julie holding an arm around her waist. Gus almost wished one of Abigail's enthusiastic elbows would see its way to slipping and smack Julie in the face, but he knew that wasn't very kind of him. He kept picturing it, though.

'I love it!' Abigail threw her arms around her mum all over again. She turned the turquoise cardigan around to show Gus. It looked expensive, designer, and Abigail put it on to model for both of them.

'Handwash only,' Julie told Gus.

Of course it was. Nothing practical like a T-shirt he could throw in with the usual wash.

As he watched the pair, Gus knew it wasn't that he didn't want Julie to be in her daughter's life. On the contrary, he wanted her to be a constant part of it. But she messed her daughter around and didn't see the effect it had on her when Abigail insisted everything was fine. The last time Julie had cancelled their weekend plans, Abigail had taken to her room crying and then refused to get out of bed in the morning. It had taken a visit from Joan to coax her out and over to the stables, the perfect distraction from everything else, and by dinner time, she was at least talking to her dad. With Julie not around, Abigail didn't have anyone to take it out on except him. He'd got hold of Julie in the end and she'd told him she'd gone to bed with one of her headaches, that was why she'd had to cancel. She told him it wasn't safe for her to drive, not with the strong painkillers she'd taken. But he knew it was just what

Julie did; she hid herself away from the guilt, the way she'd done right after the accident and before the disintegration of their marriage.

Since those days, he'd always willed her to try to make more of an effort to be in Abigail's life but clearly she'd taken any suggestion that she might not be doing so as a cue to turn up unexpectedly, like she had now. And he was about to become the bad guy as Abigail gave him a look when her mum told her that she still had to go to school, that they wouldn't be spending the day together. His refusal to let her take the day off would be the problem, never her mum's lack of planning or inability to consider other people.

Gus passed the toast to Abigail, who was sitting right up close to her mum as she ate, admiring the new earrings Julie had on and telling her how she was going to get her ears pierced one day. Surprisingly she mentioned Hazel in their conversation, telling her mum how nice the lady at the stables was, and maybe that was why he waited a good twenty minutes, more than he should, before he knew they really had to leave if Abigail wasn't going to be late for school.

'Go get your bag, Abigail.' He picked up Julie's empty mug and rinsed it under the tap. 'We need to go.'

'Do I really have to?' She'd clearly hoped he'd change his mind right at the last minute.

'You know the deal. You can see your mum after school.'

'Well, actually...' Julie pulled a face. 'I have to get back on the road by three.'

'Dad, pleeeeeeease,' Abigail begged.

Sometimes he wondered if he dug his heels in because Abigail's accident had happened while she was under Julie's care. He sometimes questioned himself, asking whether he might be trying to punish Julie in some way for letting it happen. He'd said as much to Joan, who had helped him to see that he wasn't doing that at all. All he was doing was giving Abigail the stability she so desperately needed.

'I really would like to spend time with Abigail,' said Julie, hackles rising a little more. He wished she wouldn't do that in front of their daughter, not when they'd already been through this.

'Dad, just this once, please. We can get ice-cream.' Abigail's eyes lit up. 'I could take you to see Denby.'

'And Denby will be here at the weekend and every weekend after.' He looked to Julie. 'You're welcome to come back any weekend you like. Or one evening.'

'Evenings are difficult,' she said sharply, 'it's quite a distance.'

And there it was, the dig he'd always expected he'd get. 'Heritage Cove is good for us, Julie.'

'It does seem lovely,' she said, although, knowing her, she wanted to add so much more. 'Why don't I visit this weekend, Abigail? I could come Friday and be here when you finish school if you like. If it's all right with your dad?'

Gus nodded. 'Fine by me.' If she turned up.

'I have to be in Peterborough at seven o'clock, but we'll have a few hours.'

Gus tried not to harrumph that she was combining it with another commitment. He should focus on the fact she was coming and if she had somewhere else to be afterwards, perhaps it meant she would be more likely to turn up when she promised.

'Can't wait,' Abigail smiled.

Gus picked up his car keys, but Julie had other ideas.

'How about I take you to school?' At her suggestion, Abigail gleefully went to get her bag before he'd even said it was okay.

'Straight there or she'll be late,' he told Julie. She'd better not take any detours.

'Yes, sir.'

She was childish when she wanted to be, but he ignored his ex-wife's remark and instead enveloped his daughter in a hug when she came downstairs into the hallway. 'Do you have your reading book?' She'd forgotten it yesterday and although the teacher hadn't told her off, Abigail had been angry with herself. Unlike her mother, she was organised; she liked things on schedule, she liked planning.

'Got it,' Abigail smiled, her mother's arm around her shoulders. 'And my lunch.'

'I'll pick you up later then,' he called as she stepped out of the front door.

Julie turned to face him as she pulled down her sunglasses, car keys in hand as she left the house. 'She'll get there on time, I'm not that useless.'

Gus cleared the breakfast things and, after brushing his teeth, locked up and took the short walk to the veterinary practice, calm coming over him as he let himself in the front door. The inside of the bungalow he'd made his new premises still smelt of fresh paint, but that would soon be replaced by the usual aroma of disinfectant and animals.

Gus was pleased to find he had a handful of online queries which he answered first. He was just starting out, so it was a good sign. Yesterday he'd done a letterbox drop of flyers to get word out. He'd bumped into Barney, who'd taken a handful for him and covered a whole heap of back streets to save Gus some time and, of course, with Barney on his side, the word of mouth should help too.

Finishing his online queries, Gus looked around the reception area, doing his best not to obsess about whether Abigail had got to school on time, whether Julie might have tried to sneak her off somewhere first. But he hadn't had a text or email from the school noting an absence or lateness and so he supposed Julie had done what she'd promised and most likely gone on her way to lick her wounds. Hopefully she'd turn up as agreed on Friday.

He unpacked a small box that had been delivered yesterday and put the feeding bowls, dog leads, and dog chews on the shelving display fixed to the wall along with the other pet supplies – collars, cat litter, a couple of pet carriers, and a few cosy cat baskets, bedding for a hamster cage.

In time, as he expanded the patient database, he'd get a second practice room set up, but for now there was only one, and although he'd already done a check, he did a second once-over to ensure everything was ready. He wanted everything to go smoothly with his first appointment. He didn't want to be looking for what he needed when his attention should be on the patient and the client. The exam and procedure table was already set up – a hard-wearing piece of equipment that would withstand constant cleaning and disinfecting, and which had plenty of room on either side for him to stand and the owner to be with their pet to calm them and help with the exam.

The practice room had cabinets on either side housing equipment beneath, with everything from smaller pieces to an ultrasound scanner. One side of the cabinetry had a built-in sink, next to which were the soaps he needed, paper towels in a dispenser, and he switched on the overhead lights. He'd had nice bright lights put in so that he could see his patients better and in one corner was a mobile light he could position at will to exam a patient.

Gus hadn't thought he'd see Julie again today given he'd refused to let Abigail have the day off, but mid-morning, she waltzed into the practice. 'You're still here?' He finished tidying some bandages, dressings, and gauze in one of the widest drawers.

'Aren't you going to check with me that Abigail made it to school?' she asked with more than a hint of sarcasm. 'Call the teacher, the headmaster?'

He ignored the barb. 'What have you been doing since you dropped her off?'

'I thought I'd take a walk around the local area to see where you've brought our daughter.'

'It's a small village on the east coast, it's not a ghetto.'

'All right, Gus. You're pissed off I turned up unannounced, but can't you try talking to me normally? I merely said I walked around the village. I like it, the locals seem friendly. And I approve of the scones at the tearooms, stopped for those too. I thought you'd be glad I was taking an interest.'

He righted himself. 'I apologise, I'm being a jerk. Thank you for taking an interest.'

'In our daughter?'

'In the area,' he said quickly before their conversation dissolved into a fight. 'Abigail will look forward to seeing you at the weekend.' He smiled at her because he didn't want her to get agitated at his suggestion she might well not turn up.

'I'm looking forward to it as well. I'll come Friday and now I know where the school is, I can pick her up. I'll let her choose what we do.'

'You won't have much time together, I'm afraid. School finishes after three o'clock.'

'I know, but it makes sense to have a quick visit with Abigail if I'm not all that far away.'

She had a point and he tried not to clench his fists at the thought she might not turn up to collect Abigail and that his daughter would be waiting outside the gate, getting more and more upset.

'I'll be there, Gus,' she said as though she could sense his worry.

'Just call me if you're going to be late.' He checked his watch and explained, 'First client due in thirty minutes.'

'I'm really pleased it's working out for you. I know this is something you've wanted for a long time.' She looked around at the white walls, the clinical space, the sparseness that would undoubtably take no time to fill over the coming months. At least, that's what Gus was hoping.

'It's about time,' he said. 'Going off to different veterinary practices, filling in where I was needed, was good for a while but it's great to finally have the permanence and the stability of my own business. Particularly for Abigail. And it's good for us to be in a small village where she'll be able to walk to things, see friends, get out a bit. She's already been to the ice-creamery to meet friends.' When Julie shot him a look, he said, 'Yeah, it took a bit of persuading.'

'Well, she seems really happy.' But she was smiling, the same smile that was full of mischief, the smile he'd loved at one time.

'Why are you looking at me like that?'

'It's just that... well, I know how protective you are over her.' She held up a hand. 'I'm not for one minute criticising that.' It seemed both of them were wary of upsetting the other with remarks that could be taken a multitude of ways. 'I know how hard it is for you to let her go. But she would've enjoyed the ice-creamery. And she's certainly loving having a nice stables for Denby. I almost thought she wasn't going to get out of the car by the school, she talked about him all the way there.'

'I'm sure she did.'

Gus's solidity and stability was one of the big differences between them both. With Julie's wild side, he knew that their opposite personalities might well have been what drew them to one another in the first place. Julie had always moved from place to place and admitted to him once that in the early days, part of what she loved about Gus was that he made her see that sometimes not having constant change could be just as exciting. Clearly the novelty had worn off, though, because soon after Abigail was born, Julie got restless. At first, Gus thought it was because she'd gone from travelling for work – Italy, Paris, Milan – to being a stay-at-home mother, which had to be a shock to anyone's system. But even when she'd gone back to her job, she never did quite get used to it. She kept wanting more – more responsibilities at her work, more associated travel, more social nights out with colleagues.

He couldn't blame her for being a certain way, she'd always been like it, but they'd started the journey of marriage together and met a fork in the road, her taking one way, him the other. He'd waited for it to happen, for them to finally meet up again, but it never had. It didn't make her a bad person, but it had made it difficult to predict what their future held. Gus had waited for Abigail to get older, for their careers to be established, and he'd hoped his and Julie's problems would sort themselves out, he'd thought she might at last realise she wanted their family and didn't need everything else. But Julie's nights out turned into weekends away from her family and she turned into a party girl he'd never seen before. And with the partying came the drinking, the lack of responsibility, the promotions and bonuses at work, all of which she became slowly addicted to and didn't want to give up. Those things had become her priority. And then, after the accident, she turned to those things even more to make herself feel better and erase the guilt.

'I thought that in a few weeks, in the summer holidays, I could take Abigail for a trip up to North Norfolk to my parents' beach house,' Julie announced.

He stilled. Because Abigail would love it. 'I'd like her to settle in a bit more here before she heads off anywhere else.' What he worried about was that Abigail would leave here, have such a great time with Julie that it made it harder for her to be in this village, which was a fair distance from her mum. He wanted her to feel that this was her home before she flitted off anywhere else.

'It's a trip to the beach, not a way of luring her away from you.' Julie rolled her eyes expertly. 'Honestly, Gus, you can be so paranoid.' She stood up rather than resting against the cabinet at the

side of the room, which was situated at the front of the old bungalow, where a breeze brought with it the scent of summer flowers.

He had an idea. 'There's an inn on the corner as you come into
the village, perhaps come for a night or two on your next visit.'

'What's wrong with my plan to go to the beach house?'

'Nothing's wrong with it. Did you not hear what I said about
having her settled? It's a bit too soon, that's all.'

'We always have to do things your way.'

'Single parenting was never *my way*. But it's what happened.
Don't you see how much she needs to feel settled?'

'Sometimes I think this is more about your issues than hers.'

He felt his chest rise in frustration. 'It's not. I want her to feel she
has a home here. It's important, Julie.'

'I'm her mother, I love her, and I know it's important. But you're
making out whatever I do will put her off course.' When he said
nothing, she went on. 'That's your whole problem, isn't it? Anything
I do, you find it hard to trust.'

'Calm down, Julie.' Clearly he'd flipped a switch with his words
– whether a guilt switch or a frustration button, he wasn't sure –
and ignited her fury.

'You're so self-righteous, you treat me like—'

'Oh, come on!' He hadn't meant to raise his voice but settling
into a new home, a new business, a new village was a challenge in
itself. 'You show up unannounced and want her to skip school,
last time you promised to take her out for dinner you cancelled
last minute, the time before that when you were due to visit you
had a work crisis, and numerous times before that you've let her
down!'

It was all coming out now, fuelled by the frustration that she'd
come here today, unannounced, and got Abigail's hopes up and
he'd had to be the baddie by making their daughter go to school as
planned.

'Abigail should understand that work is important,' she said, so calmly it riled him all the more.

'It's never more important than family, motherhood!'

'Abigail will grow up learning she can have a career if she works hard.'

'And you think I don't teach her that?' He took a deep breath before he said, 'I've only ever got Abigail's best interests at heart. Someone has to.' As soon as he'd added the last few words, he regretted it because she exploded.

Gus stood and listened to Julie yell, tell him how he moved here to keep her from her daughter – he didn't have the energy to argue with her when they both knew that wasn't the case – she shrieked that he wanted to keep Abigail to himself. And then she added, 'I made one mistake and you will never let me forget it!'

Me, me, me, it was all about her.

Her accusation was one step too far and he roared, 'Never let *you* forget it? How do you think Abigail feels every time she looks in the damn mirror? Do you not think that those scars are a permanent reminder of what happened? She won't *ever* forget it, so why the hell should you?'

'I can't talk to you when you're like this. I came here thinking I could see my daughter, but you ruined that.'

'Your daughter is *at school!*' He yelled the last two words to try to get through to her. 'It's the law, it's what she needs, stop trying to do things on your schedule and not giving a toss what it means to anyone else. When you don't show up for Abigail, who do you think picks up the pieces? Who do you think has to try to comfort her when she's sobbing into her pillow at night?' His heart was pounding, his palms clammy, he could barely catch a breath.

'Well, obviously you!' she yelled, picking up her bag and car keys from the top of the cabinet where she'd left them. 'Because you are God, you are such a fucking saint!'

'Don't even get me started.' His voice lower, he hoped she'd go before he reminded her of what had happened with every painful detail.

She finished the visit by swearing at him again and reminding him she'd be at school on Friday to collect Abigail and with a slam of his freshly painted front door, she stormed out.

* * *

Gus stood with a big mug of coffee in his hand and leaned against the door jamb at the back door to the veterinary practice. He looked out over the compact lawn that didn't have much character and wondered whether he'd make it a bit neater in time, add some flowerbeds, or whether he'd use the area to expand the bungalow. He had no idea, but the future was exciting for him and Abigail, and he wasn't going to let Julie barrelling in today and arguing with him to take that feeling away, not when this had been his dream for so long.

He hoped that in the same way he was calming down, Julie was doing likewise as she left the Cove behind. But more than that, he hoped she'd keep her promise and come back to see her daughter at the weekend. Abigail had never asked too much about custody arrangements apart from initially, when she told him she'd assumed the child always went with the mother. Gus had told her that her mum did a lot of travelling with her job and that, while they both wanted their daughter, it made more sense for Abigail to stay with him for the time being. Abigail had put her arms around him and told him that she loved him. Truth be told, when the custody arrangements were settled, he'd wondered how it was all going to work out. It was what he wanted, of course, and he'd have fought to the bitter end for it to happen. He'd be forever grateful, though, that Julie hadn't challenged the decision in the courts. He'd have hated to have to stand up and say anything against his ex-wife. She wasn't a bad person, he never wanted to hurt her. And without the additional confrontation, things had been a lot calmer for Abigail too.

Gus watched a bumblebee duck into the centre of a pink flower growing near the wall behind the veterinary practice. It wiggled and either got what it wanted or didn't, and flew on to wherever it intended to go next.

Gus experienced a momentary pang of guilt standing here, guilt that he hadn't let Julie take Abigail out for the day instead of sending her to school. Her mother was here in the Cove and it was a big deal that she'd turned up. If he'd let them see one another today, then he wouldn't have to stress that Julie wouldn't show up on Friday. But deep down, as he finished his coffee, he knew he'd done the right thing. Allowing it wouldn't teach Julie anything, it would only reinforce the idea that she could turn up whenever she felt like it and expect everyone else to fall in line.

His thoughts drifted to Abigail and he wondered whether she was at school stewing and would be upset when he collected her later, angry he hadn't let her spend time with her mum, or whether her excitement at the impending visit from her mum would overshadow her frustrations today. Perhaps he should be turning his focus to managing her expectations if Julie cancelled.

Gus inhaled the summer air, sure he could smell the sea out here, even though it was some way away. Perhaps it was wishful thinking, or maybe with the breeze it was possible. Time for him to stop stressing over things he couldn't control. And thinking about the sea reminded him of Hazel and she was a distraction he didn't need when he had to keep his mind on the business. He retreated inside and closed the back door before rinsing his coffee mug in the kitchen sink. The kitchen was still functional, although old, but it would do for his needs at the practice.

He checked his watch. Fifteen minutes to go until his first appointment of the day. His first appointment ever. And he let himself smile because this was how it started, first one client, then a second, a third, a fourth and so on until you had a practice so busy you couldn't imagine it any other way.

A knock made him jump to attention and he went to the front door to find a big bunch of flowers and a woman who introduced herself as Valerie. 'We're business neighbours,' she beamed, 'these are to say welcome to the Cove.'

'Wow, thank you.' He took the flowers and gestured for her to come in.

'No can do, I've dashed out quickly. Honestly, the flower business is hectic 24/7, all year.'

He laughed. 'Good for you. Hopefully I'll be that way soon.'

'I'm sure you will be. Folks are very happy you're here.' She bent down and picked up something else. 'You'll be needing this, doubt you've got a vase.'

He had to laugh as he took the box with a picture of a glass vase on the front and held it beneath one arm. 'Quite right, the last thing on my mind in a veterinary practice.'

'Thought as much.' With a wave, she was about to dash away.

'Quick question, if I may.' His voice stopped her. 'Barney handed me a card for someone called Sandy, said to call on her if I need her for childminding.'

Valerie swished her hand through the air. 'Don't even hesitate. Wonderful girl, responsible, trustworthy. And she's not one of those teens who just sit and watch reality TV with your kids either. She'll have them cooking, playing games if they like; she earns her money.'

'Appreciate the recommendation,' he smiled as she went on her way. When he'd been in the pub with Joan and Abigail, he'd discreetly asked Terry the landlord about Sandy too and Terry, much like Valerie, was very complimentary.

Gus had only just set the flowers in water in the vase and placed them on the desk out in the reception area when the door opened and in came his first appointment: Lucy. And it was the same Lucy who'd been at the art class with Hazel and seen him naked, but he did his best to omit the association from his mind and focus on what this was today. His first patient.

'Come in,' he smiled. 'Welcome.'

'Am I the first?' she beamed. 'Ooh, nice flowers.'

'Thanks. And you're not the first, but whoever is in there is.' He dipped his head down towards the cat carrier she was holding and more importantly the slate-grey cat cowering inside, as though it suspected nothing good could come of this outing.

'Shadow, you're honoured,' she told her cat, setting the carrier down. 'Took me ages to get him into the carrier, he knows it means it's time for the vet.'

'Cats aren't daft, are they?'

'It's brilliant having you so close, much better than heading out of the village.'

'That's good to know. And I'm so close that you can nip out during work hours.'

'Caught me,' she smiled, hands wafting down from the top of her khaki dungarees to the bottom. Looking around, she said, 'I feel a bit guilty, it's so clean in here and now I've lowered the tone.'

'No need to apologise at all. I understand you are the Lucy from Lucy's Blacksmithing?'

'That's right. Did you get the local run-down from Barney?'

'How did you know?'

She began to laugh, her blue eyes dancing. 'Barney welcomed me to the village when I was new too, everyone has been wonderful.

Once you're here, you do realise we'll make it hard for you to leave, don't you?'

'I wouldn't want it any other way. And while I did get a good run-down from Barney, lots of which I've forgotten, this mention of you came from Arnold. We're stabling our horse at Heritage View and Arnold showed me the little name plaques in the tack room. Denby only has hand-written name signs for now.'

'And you want to upgrade?'

'My daughter would love it. I thought I might get some special signs made in time to give her for her birthday which is coming up soon.'

'Pop in whenever you pass by. I'm there early on until late most days, when the girls aren't persuading me to knock off early. I've got plenty of examples of other work I've done that I can show you.'

'Great, thanks. Now, if you follow me we'll take Shadow into the examination room.'

Gus closed the door behind them in case Shadow tried to make a run for it. Lucy scooped her cat out of his carrier and hugged her to him before setting him onto the table, where she continued to make a fuss of the feline.

'Don't worry, we'll take our time,' said Gus, knowing that sometimes clients were more nervous than the animals. 'I appreciate I'm new to both of you but I'm patient, I don't need to rush, I'll be gentle.'

'I'm a bit overprotective, I'm afraid.' Although she did relax a little bit now Shadow didn't seem too put out.

Gus fussed over Shadow, stroking him head to tail, and the cat purred as he faced away from Gus to lift his head at the sight of a bird out of the window, perching on the branch of a tree.

Gus let the cat choose his position, moving about on the table, and worked around him. With a stethoscope in one hand, he used his other to stroke Shadow beneath his chin. Lucy moved so she was in front of her cat and put her hands either side of his face, making him purr all the more as Gus felt Shadow's stomach, checking for swelling or abnormalities. He and Lucy swapped positions so he could inspect Shadow's eyes and ears. Gus checked his limbs, his paws, weighed him, and with Lucy's assistance, did everything else he needed to do.

'You have a healthy, happy cat here, Lucy,' Gus concluded, leaving Shadow's owner to cuddle him as he updated Shadow's online records using the laptop on the counter.

'He might not be happy in a minute,' said Lucy, when she saw Gus finish typing and begin getting ready for the main purpose of the visit: the booster shot.

'Let's get this over with,' said Gus, coming closer again. 'If you hold Shadow against your chest while he's on the table, that's the easiest way.' She did so and while Lucy cuddled her cat and reassured him this would be over soon, Gus administered the shot quickly and efficiently.

'You were very good with him.' Lucy pressed her face against Shadow's fur while Gus added the information to the online patient record.

Gus smiled at them both. 'I'm honoured I had such a well-behaved first patient.'

'How does it feel? Having your own practice here?'

'Amazing. It's good to be in the Cove.'

'We're making a local of you already,' she said, hearing the shortened name he and all the others in the village tended to use.

'Take your time putting him in the carrier,' Gus urged as he wiped down and disinfected the exam table and Shadow seemed unsure when he was lifted up again. Even if Gus was busy with patients, he didn't want people to feel as though they were on a conveyor belt. In some of his workplaces, that was how it had seemed, but what he wanted for this practice was for it to be a real part of the village, for clients and their animals to feel like more than a number.

'Thanks, but look, he's happy to get in, he knows we're going home.' Shadow had voluntarily gone inside the second he was put on the floor and he'd curled up at the end as if to say it was time to leave.

'Good for him.' Gus opened the door for Lucy to go through first.

'May I ask you a question?' Lucy, cat carrier in hand, turned to face him when they reached the reception area.

'Go ahead.' He expected her to ask about Shadow and whether he might have a reaction to the vaccination or enquire as to when to bring him for the next or whether there were any others he needed. But she didn't ask anything about Shadow.

'What made you volunteer to sit naked and be drawn?' She realised her question had shocked him. 'I'm just wondering, I mean you don't seem like the sort of guy who would do it. Not that it takes a certain type.' She began to smile. 'I'm blabbering on now. But I'm only curious. I was there to draw, but I'm pretty sure I'd never have the guts to pose.'

'I did it as a favour for someone who I'm very close to. I didn't feel I could say no. She's done a lot for me over the years.'

'Well, now she owes you, I'd say,' smiled Lucy.

When the front door opened, Barney came in and Gus joked, 'Have you brought me a chicken to look at?'

'No, the chickens are all good.' He didn't have to explain any further because Harvey followed him inside soon after, along with his dog Winnie, who trotted straight over to Barney for a fuss. When Barney had given Gus the run-down of the people in the Cove, he'd talked a lot about Harvey, who Gus remembered was like a son to Barney. And by his recollection, Harvey was married to

Melissa, and his brother Daniel owned the Little Waffle Shack and was Lucy's other half.

'Here's the patient,' Barney went on. 'I'm just here because I was at Harvey's anyway – Lois is baking and wanted me out of her way at home.'

'I don't have an appointment,' said Harvey and added hopefully, 'I thought I'd come in on the off chance.'

Gus looked around at the empty waiting room. 'Not enough people know about me yet, so turning up without an appointment is no problem at all.' He crouched down to fuss over Winnie, a golden Labrador with a glossy coat that showed she was just as well cared for as Shadow. Gus had a sense that he'd find that theme of animal lovers ran amongst the people of the village, and it made him feel grounded, as though he already knew a bit about everyone, whether he could put all the faces to names or not.

'Winnie's all right, isn't she?' Lucy settled her carrier down on the floor while she fished out her car keys.

'She's good, just has a nasty tick on her ear which needs to come off,' Harvey told her as she stroked Winnie and the dog wagged its tail.

'That's a relief. I'd better get Shadow home and go back to work. Thanks so much for today, Gus.'

'You're welcome, it was good to meet you, and you, Shadow. And I'll come in, look at those signs when I get a moment.'

'Please do,' she smiled. 'Listen, I was wondering, I'm having a birthday party on Friday evening, would you like to come? Barney will be there, Harvey, lots of people, Hazel…'

He wondered if she read the change in his expression, but he shrugged. 'Some adult company sounds great, but I have Abigail.' Unless he asked Sandy to look after her.

But before that thought went any further, she said, 'Bring her, honestly, kids are welcome. The more the merrier. It's at the Little

Waffle Shack so it's pretty informal and we'll have the outdoor area reserved and to ourselves. I'd love it if you could both join us. And Peter will be there too – he's ten – nearly eleven, as he loves to remind Daniel, who was like a dad to him for years and still is really. So Abigail will have company her own age.'

'I knew there was someone I hadn't told you about,' Barney admonished himself. 'How could I forget young Peter, he's in the Cove often enough.'

'You told me plenty,' Gus assured him, 'the rest I'll have to learn as I go along.'

'So you'll ask Abigail?' Lucy asked, blue eyes hopeful. 'You'll think about it?'

'I will.' He bent down to fuss the top of Winnie's head. 'Come on, you, let's have a look at that tick.'

He would ask Abigail, and if waffles were involved, he was pretty sure she wouldn't need much convincing. She was seeing her mum on Friday too so if that didn't go to plan, he'd at least have a treat in store for her to take her mind off it. The only hesitancy he had was putting Abigail into a crowd of strangers who might make her feel uncomfortable. But at the same time, he had Joan's voice in his ear telling him not to let his fears be Abigail's and if she was scared, it was up to him to be the stronger one and help her to move forwards.

And that was exactly what he wanted for his beautiful daughter. He didn't want to hold her back because he was scared of what may or may not happen.

Adjusting his thinking, however, was a big challenge and one that for now, with Winnie waiting for his attention, he had to push to one side.

12

Gus couldn't be happier that Heritage Cove had a local pub and secondly that the pub was as welcoming as it was traditional, with dark timber beams it was necessary to duck beneath in some places, and a brass rail that curved around the bar. Plenty of village pubs were run-down, others it was hard to enter when they were filled with locals who didn't like anyone new or any hint of a change, but the Copper Plough had been as welcoming as the tearooms. Recognised as someone new straight away the day he brought Joan and Abigail in here for lunch, landlord Terry had introduced himself and his wife Nola, as well as head chef, Benjamin, and Gus had left that day certain this pub would become his escape whenever he needed it.

And he needed it tonight. Not that anything terrible had happened today – Abigail had had a good day at school, Julie hadn't shown up unexpectedly and had assured him yet again via text that she would definitely turn up on Friday, he'd had three new patients today and he had bookings for another three. But what he really needed was some adult company. He hadn't realised how much he'd miss Joan's daily chats, especially in the evenings, and so this morning, between patients, he'd gone over to the Heritage Inn and met Sandy. After chatting with her for less than five minutes, he could already tell she'd be good with Abigail.

In fact, when he picked up his daughter from school and told her he was going out, she was almost more excited about that than going to the stables first. She'd ridden Denby in the outdoor school with her dad watching, although he'd been keeping one eye out for Hazel too, and Abigail had been ready to leave at the time Gus had said they'd have to go. Usually she stalled, but not today. And when she and Sandy had got stuck in with making cupcakes while he was still getting ready in jeans and a casual navy-blue shirt, he left them laughing and chatting away as though they'd known one another for months rather than minutes. The sight of the pair of them had been enough to propel him out the door, confident that even though he'd almost cancelled the childminder more than once, this was a good thing to do for both him and Abigail.

And now, Gus was here at the Copper Plough again, alone this time, and he'd spent the last half an hour talking to Benjamin, who had just come off shift. Benjamin filled him in about Heritage Cove. Gus knew it was going to take some time to get to know the locals properly in this way, their histories, what led them each here, but he was in this for the long haul.

It turned out Benjamin's family owned the local Christmas tree farm, which Gus had seen signs for but hadn't yet had the opportunity to explore. There wasn't much incentive out of season and with his hands full with Abigail, their horse, and the business, it was something he hadn't got to.

'My sister will eventually take it on,' Benjamin explained. 'Charlotte has always wanted it. She's not local at the moment, she's still working full time elsewhere, but you'll meet her at some point. She'll be here this winter for sure, she's got lots to learn about the tree farm.'

'I'm sure she has.' Gus sipped his pint of Guinness. It was summer and the beer garden was packed, so he'd chosen to stay inside by the bar. But it had its perks; he wouldn't have bumped into Benjamin when he came off shift otherwise. 'Abigail was pretty excited when she heard there was a tree farm around here. We've always had the same artificial tree and to be honest, it's on its last legs.'

'Can't beat a real tree,' Benjamin assured him, a smile behind well-trimmed stubble. 'Just head on down to the farm when the season starts, bring your daughter, you'll never look back.'

Gus laughed. 'I don't doubt it.'

Benjamin smiled at the group of women who'd just filed in. 'Here comes trouble.' But his claim was said in good humour and Tilly came over to plant a kiss on his lips. 'You two have met already, am I right?'

Gus nodded and smiled at Tilly. 'We have, good to see you.'

'How did your daughter like the bottle you bought?'

'Loved it, of course.' It was hard to keep his focus because one of the women who'd come in was Hazel. And he hadn't seen her, not properly, since that day on the beach. She was always busy, never had much time to stop. Although he was a bit put out she hadn't made much effort to chat with him, he'd thought they were on better terms than proprietor and horse owner. He'd even begun to feel as though they might be heading towards something more than friendship, but she seemed to be avoiding him.

The women Tilly was with, including Hazel, had headed over to a spare table next to a window and with Hazel facing his way as Gus chatted with Benjamin and Tilly, he could tell Hazel had seen him. But he was also pretty sure she was doing her level best not to make eye contact. He couldn't help glancing her way, though. She usually had her hair wound in an obedient plait at the nape of her neck with wisps escaping the second they could, but tonight, she'd let her wavy shock of blonde hair hang loose and he wondered if Benjamin or Tilly could tell he'd had to almost pick his jaw up off the floor when he saw her. This was a different Hazel compared to the in-order businesswoman who ran the stables. All he wanted was for her to look over, to smile and acknowledge him, but she still hadn't by the time Benjamin left for home and Tilly went to join her friends.

It was a good half an hour later and after a conversation with Barney and Lois and then local teacher Linc, who told Gus that Abigail was enjoying music at school, that Hazel came over to the bar. It wasn't the biggest space, so she couldn't do much to avoid him, and Tilly had already had a turn buying drinks, so had Lucy, so now it looked like it was Hazel's round. And call it timely, but there was suddenly a decent gap as well as a spare stool next to Gus.

'Sit down while you wait,' he suggested. She was dressed in a simple pair of jeans and a T-shirt that was fitted at the top and flared out at the waist. Her outfit suggested relaxed, yet she seemed anything but.

'Thirsty people over there, better not.' She placed her order with Nola and exchanged a lot more friendliness with her. She gave him nothing but a curt smile.

'Forgive me asking, but have I done something?' He was glad he wasn't talking with anyone now she was here. He was certain she'd been avoiding him. 'I haven't seen you since that day on the beach and I'm pretty sure I haven't done anything to upset you, but correct me if I'm wrong.'

She faced him and her chest rose as she considered his question. But then she let it go. 'No, you haven't done anything.'

He wasn't convinced but he sensed accusations would get him nowhere. 'Abigail has been asking after you.'

This time she found a smile. 'Say hello to her for me. I'm sorry

I've been so busy at the stables. Where is she tonight? With her mum?'

He shook his head before his pint glass made it all the way to his mouth. 'No, why do you ask that?'

She shrugged. 'No reason, just that you're usually together.'

'Sandy is childminding. I left them making cupcakes.'

She at least didn't pick up the drinks straight away. 'Sandy is a legend around here for those with kids. She works hard at the inn but doesn't let up when she's childminding.'

'So I'd heard. I wouldn't leave Abigail with a stranger usually but...' He ordered an orange juice next. He'd decided that with his business so new he wasn't ready to have more than one drink on a weeknight. He had a clientele to build, after all.

'You and Abigail will both be happy with Sandy.' She almost looked as though she was going to hang around but with all her drinks ready, she picked up a couple and Lucy came to collect the others.

Before Hazel could go back to her friends, his voice followed her. 'I wanted to ask again about the lessons for Abigail.' He saw her shoulders tense and she turned around. 'I thought perhaps seeing as I sorted out Cinnamon, maybe you could teach her once, fit her in.'

In her eyes he saw regret; she looked torn, like a part of her wanted to say yes but the rest of her, for some reason, couldn't.

But when Harvey joined him at the bar, Hazel made her escape. Clearly the answer was still no and as much as she insisted he hadn't done anything, he knew there was something she wasn't telling him.

With it being the pub quiz tonight, Gus was persuaded to join Harvey, his brother Daniel, and Linc, who had been playing his guitar out in the beer garden. Gus had been tempted to slope off home early but actually he enjoyed himself. Their team came in second place and Melissa's team – the team Hazel was on – won the quiz.

'Better luck next time,' Melissa giggled as she came over to console her husband with a kiss and a hug.

'Gus here got us second place,' Daniel declared. 'Without his answers about Japan, we would've been third.'

'I got those,' Gus admitted, 'but there were plenty of others I had no idea about.' And he hadn't been to Japan either, it was just that as luck would have it, he'd read an article about the country and so knew that the name of the bullet train was the Shinkansen and that Osaka was nicknamed the 'kitchen of Japan'.

Gus checked his watch. He'd told Sandy he'd be home around 11.30 p.m. and as it wasn't that long until closing time, he knocked back the remains of his second orange juice as he heard Harvey asking, 'Is she all right? Do you think we should call Arnold?'

Gus turned to see Hazel, who he'd had his back to for most of the quiz – he thought it would be less of a distraction – weaving between tables on her way towards the bar. Melissa went to intercept her, and it didn't take a genius to see that Hazel had had way too much to drink and Melissa, as predicted, steered her away from the bar and back to their table, nodding to Nola's offer of water.

Melissa came over to Harvey and explained what Gus could already see for himself. 'Can we walk her home? Or we could call Arnold.'

Harvey finished his drink and picked up his keys. 'We'll walk her home...' He looked more closely. 'Or perhaps carry her by the looks of things. We won't wake Arnold, no need.'

'Is this a regular thing?' Gus asked Lucy, who had taken the empties up to the bar for Nola.

'Actually, no, it's not. I mean, she enjoys a drink or two, she'll drink and complain of a headache the next day, but she's never like this.'

'Listen, why don't I run and get my car, I'm only around the corner,' Gus suggested. She was what you'd describe as legless, and it would take two to carry her home. 'You don't want to be stumbling down those country lanes in the dark, the three of you. I'll have her home in a couple of minutes, not a problem.'

'Is that okay, Hazel?' Lucy asked her friend, who only giggled. 'Is it all right if Gus takes you home in his car?'

Hazel seemed to focus on him. 'Gus!' And then in something nowhere bordering on a whisper, behind a cupped hand, she told Melissa, 'I've seen him naked, you know.'

'I'll go get the car.' Gus left the pub and ran back to the house, quickly told Sandy what was going on, and drove back to the pub, by which time Melissa and Lucy were waiting at the end of the path and helped their friend into the passenger seat of his car.

'He looks good naked,' Hazel told her friends through the window Gus had already wound down. 'I mean, *really* good.' She was speaking as though he wasn't there, and he gave the others a wave.

'Let's get you home.'

As he drove down The Street and indicated, he stole a look at Hazel. She'd already closed her eyes and was smiling away, humming to herself.

He eventually turned off and drove along the driveway, pulling up in the area right in front of Heritage View House. He tried to encourage her out of the car but with her eyes closed, she seemed to have forgotten where they were and so he got out and went around to her side.

When he opened the door, she'd obviously lolled against it because her body fell into his. 'Whoa, come on, let's get you into the house.'

She managed to step out of the car with a bit of help but flopped against him, unable to go any further. Her soft cheek rested against the top of his chest, and she was murmuring something about people hiding things. She looked confused, as though since getting out of the car, she'd forgotten where they were. She looked up at him, her hands against his chest. 'Why can't art show people's insides?' she asked bizarrely.

'Um... that's likely a different kind of art. Anatomy. I don't know, not something I've ever wanted to know about. Unless it's to do with animals, that is.' God, shut up, Gus. He sounded like a total idiot, although he was pretty sure Hazel wouldn't be remembering much about this by the morning.

'I saw you, you know.'

'I'm well aware of that. You drew me too.'

'I saw you after.'

'Yes, I live here in the village, that's why.' Reasoning with a drunk person was always difficult, although he didn't mind holding her while she did it.

'I saw you after the class.' She wiped the side of her mouth before putting her hand back on his chest. 'You were angry.'

She'd seen him? For some reason, he felt more exposed now than he had been posing naked, like she'd seen every last detail of him, his fury at its worst the night he was protecting his daughter.

Hazel pulled away and opened her purse, looked inside as though it was a very large handbag rather than a small item that would reveal its contents in one go. 'I'm sure I put my key in here somewhere...' She groaned. 'It's not here...' But in the next breath, she gasped and her eyes widened. 'Wait, we should go and say goodnight to all the horses!'

He grabbed her elbow before she could head over to the stable block. 'I think the horses are already tucked up in bed, the way you should be.'

'Are you offering to take me to bed?' She looked puzzled and he wasn't sure if their interaction was about to result in her slapping him or kissing him.

'That wasn't what I said.'

'You're funny.' She went back to looking for her key in a purse that really wasn't very big at all. 'Got it!' She held up a shiny key and promptly dropped it and groaned but made no attempt to bend down.

He did the honours. Probably safer that way, or she might well fall over. With the key in his hand, he was about to open the front door to Heritage View House when she stumbled into him again and went so weak he had to put an arm beneath her to support her.

'There's only one way to do this,' he declared when he saw a light come on the other side of the door. They'd obviously woken Arnold up already and they could be here all night trying to get her over the threshold with Hazel as legless as she was.

When he scooped her up, she put a hand to his cheek and laughed, oblivious to her brother opening the door to their home. 'You're trying to sweep me off my feet,' she told Gus and proceeded to bury her head in his chest and close her eyes.

Arnold simply shook his head and said, 'Up the stairs, first door on the right.'

Hazel didn't say another word to Gus, not until he'd pulled back the teal and white checked bedspread and laid her on the bed. He took off her shoes, which took a couple of attempts because they were strappy sandals; it was worse than trying to help Abigail off with her trainers when she'd managed to pull the laces into double knots. How women worked these things he'd never know. And at least with Abigail she wasn't trying to roll over and beneath the bed sheets while he was removing her footwear.

Gus set the shoes on the floor by the dressing table and lifted Hazel's legs onto the bed before pulling the bedspread over her. It was only when he reached the bedroom door to go that he heard her say, 'You're good naked but it's what underneath that counts.'

He almost asked whether that was meant to be a compliment but there wouldn't be any point trying to hold a conversation with her right now and he was pretty sure it wasn't anything good. All it told him was that his hunch had been right – he had done something to get under her skin. And if it was that she'd seen him angry outside the art class, then that didn't make sense. She'd been funny with him when he first saw her at the stables, and now he knew the reason why if she'd seen him having a go at those teenagers. But since then, they'd moved forwards and enjoyed one another's company. At least, he thought they did.

But it was no use trying to get answers now. It was going to take a much more sober Hazel to give him any kind of explanation.

'Apologies for the wake-up call,' he told Arnold when he reached the foot of the stairs.

'No worries, I'd only just headed upstairs. She's all right?'

'Nothing a good sleep and a lot of water won't fix.'

'It's not like her to get wasted.'

'It happens to the best of us.'

Gus had opened the door and was about to step out into the night air when Arnold told him, 'Be patient with her. Don't give up.'

He wasn't entirely sure what he was supposed to be patient with, but he turned and waved before he got in the car and told Arnold, 'I'm trying not to.'

It felt like the right thing to say.

13

It was almost the weekend and since the night at the Copper Plough, Hazel had yet again tried to avoid Gus, this time because she'd made a total fool of herself. The man had carried her to bed! Something Arnold had taken great delight in informing her of. Hazel had woken the morning after and when she remembered what had happened, she'd stayed in bed, eyes closed, thinking about Gus, how he had the two different sides to his personality. On the one hand, he was Gus, father, friendly, kind and approachable, dependable and strong. And on the other, he was this man who flew into a temper. She'd asked herself whether everyone had the ability to do that, for their moods to slip, and told herself that of course they did. But still, it didn't mean it was something she ever wanted to witness, something she ever wanted to have directed at her. She and Gus had been getting on well, really well, but after she'd seen him so angry at his practice, she couldn't get it out of her head. So when she got to the pub and he kept looking over at her, she'd distracted herself by drinking more and more. She was disappointed he wasn't the man she thought he was, sad that there would be nothing between them now.

The rain from this morning had cleared and the sun was set to shine all weekend, starting tonight in time for Lucy's party outside at the waffle shack. Hazel and Arnold had already done turnout for the horses, she'd mucked out the stables, and with lesson time fast approaching, Hazel got Pebbles from the paddock and brought him to the concrete area outside the stable block ready to tack up.

'I thought you had three in this lesson?' she queried with her brother, who had already tacked up Jigsaw.

'One of the riders wanted a private lesson, so I've moved them to this afternoon.'

'Private is a nice earner,' she smiled. Since they'd spoken about her starting with Abigail to get back into teaching, neither of them had said anything more. Perhaps Arnold didn't need to ask. The state she'd come home in after the pub, with Gus having to take her upstairs, said that that particular conversation either hadn't gone well or hadn't happened at all. When Gus had asked her yet again, in the pub, about giving Abigail lessons it had been on the tip of her tongue to say she didn't teach kids. But how could she say that to him? She didn't want anyone in the Cove to know, she wanted everyone to think it was business as usual.

'I've got two private sessions today,' she told her brother, anxious to prove she was pulling her weight on many levels. 'One at five o'clock, the other at six.' Hazel worked out she'd have just enough time to finish up here after the private lessons and get ready for Lucy's party. She'd wondered whether she should make her excuses when she heard from Barney that Gus had been invited, but she couldn't avoid him forever. She could get away with it here at the stables, as there was always so much to do, so much space to escape into, but the waffle shack wouldn't provide much opportunity to get away.

Hazel buckled the bridle on Pebbles and checked its fit using her fingers to ensure it wasn't too tight, particularly across his brow.

The two kids in the lesson showed up, both already wearing their own hats, and Hazel gave them a brief look over to ensure they were dressed appropriately. She needed to see that they both had a boot with a bit of a heel so the foot didn't slip through the stirrups, comfortable bottoms, and not too many layers on top, given the summer temperature. These were the real basics, or so you'd think, but some riders turned up in kit not fit for purpose – a few weeks ago, one girl had turned up in boots that did have a heel but were fashion boots and therefore totally unsuitable. Hazel had had visions of her foot slipping through the stirrup which brought with it dangers that didn't even bear thinking about. The same girl had also been wearing a very long and baggy sweater over the top of a polo-neck, and loose clothing was yet another hazard – if the rider fell, it could get caught in the saddle and the repercussions of that were equally frightening.

Arnold took over from Hazel. He was great with kids, they both were, or at least she had been once upon a time, but he'd never lost his touch. He already had the young riders laughing at some joke about a horse she'd heard a hundred times before. It wasn't the joke that made her smile, but the way Arnold could coax a kid out of their shell with a little bit of harmless banter, giving them a lift and a confidence for the lesson.

While Arnold got the session in the outdoor school underway, Hazel grabbed the wheelbarrow from inside the stable block and turned to go towards the indoor school, but not before she saw James pull up in the parking area. At least he hadn't pulled up in front of the house this time.

'Can't stop, I'm afraid, got poop to pick up,' she called over to him.

He jogged over, seeing she was in the middle of something. 'I wanted to catch you, wondered if you could have lunch today. I've got something I want to show you.' With another grin, he added, 'Something you're going to like.'

'You know what I'm going to say, don't you?' She lifted the handles of the wheelbarrow and proceeded to turn and make her way towards the indoor school where she needed to go through shavings and clear up any wet patches or dung.

'You're too busy.' She didn't miss the sigh accompanying his words.

Hazel had asked James for time and space, but the more of that they had, the more she was able to take a step back and look at their relationship from a different angle. She'd never made her dedication to this place a secret, but she knew James would have no problem if she walked away tomorrow. And if he thought that way, he obviously didn't understand how much Heritage View was a part of her. It didn't matter that it was harder than before, that she'd come up against a challenge so huge it sometimes seemed insurmountable, it didn't matter that she was struggling to be a fully operational part of this business like her brother, she couldn't give it up. Not ever.

'How are you?' James asked, his voice loaded with enough concern for her to query the question.

'I'm fine. Why do you ask?' She set the wheelbarrow down and found the pitchfork that was leaning against the wall.

'Arnold said you weren't well a few days ago. I sent a few text messages and then called the office phone when you didn't answer. Your brother told me you had a bug and you were staying in your room so you didn't pass it on.'

'Right.' She remembered the text messages – she'd ignored them and then hadn't had the energy to reply, and then not replying had been nice because he'd left her alone. She'd also picked up each of those texts wondering whether they were from Gus, disap-

pointed when they weren't. 'I'm feeling much better, thank you. And
no longer contagious, don't worry.' She'd have to thank Arnold later.
He tolerated James, but he wasn't her ex-boyfriend's biggest fan, and
she appreciated that he picked up on something happening with
her. Arnold also knew his sister well enough to know that if she
wasn't talking about the specifics, it meant she didn't want to.

'If you can't do lunch today, how about dinner tonight?' James
persisted. 'Your local or we could head out to a restaurant.' He kept
his smart loafers away from the sawdust in the school or anything
more sinister.

She pushed the pitchfork beneath a pile of damp sawdust and
threw it into the wheelbarrow, leaving the patch clear for now so it
could dry. 'I can't. I'm out tonight for a friend's birthday.'

'I'm away tomorrow,' he said, 'looking at that house I told you
about down in Essex. The one with the paddocks attached,' he
added, when it was clear she had no idea what he was talking
about. 'That was what I was going to show you.'

'I'm sorry.' He sounded so disappointed, but she knew where his
mind was going with this house and that wasn't on the agenda. He
had given her time and space and was now trying to leap three
steps forward in their relationship when she wasn't sure there was
even a relationship to salvage. 'I'm sure it's beautiful, but we have
been through this, James.'

'Just see it, you might change your mind. This place is getting
too much for you. You might well find that being away from
Heritage View is exactly what it takes to turn things around. A fresh
start.'

'Running away, you mean.'

'I'd describe it as moving forwards.'

'This is my home.' She jabbed the prongs of the pitchfork into
the sawdust beneath her feet and leaned on the handle. 'This is my
life.'

'This is your business and it's doing you in. You never get sick, like never. And now you're getting tummy bugs. It doesn't take a genius to work out that it's stress.'

More like the untold amount of alcohol.

'I worry about you, you know that. I've seen guys at work burn out under stress and I don't want it to happen to you.'

She reached out and squeezed his hand. 'I promise I won't let it.'

Hazel knew, however, that sometimes the stress did get to her. It had in the early days too. She and Arnold had been excited to take over the Heritage View Stables and although they'd seen their parents run it and helped out often enough, they'd both been shocked at how much work it was when it was just the two of them and ownership transferred. There was a great deal more that went on behind the scenes. The first year Hazel and Arnold had been totally in charge, they'd had to refer to their parents plenty of times – what did they do if an invoice for lessons was unpaid? What happened if a delivery wasn't up to scratch or failed to turn up? What were all the various insurance covers they needed, what happened when weather battered Heritage View Stables and the house itself? It was like growing up to a whole new level overnight and Hazel had been exhausted with it all but willing to ride it out with the reward so worth it. Things ran a lot smoother now, apart from her reluctance to teach, the one jump she hadn't quite been able to make.

'We'll catch up in a few days instead then.' James realised she wasn't going to budge, not on this, at least not now. But still he didn't give up. 'I'll take lots of photos of the house. And you still have Tate's number.'

Hazel was about to launch into another spiel about how this was a family business, tell James how if she got someone in to help, she might lose any impetus to get back to normal and she and Arnold wouldn't have what they'd always wanted to build. However, her spiel didn't even get off the starting blocks because she heard a scream that saw her darting out of the indoor school and around to where Arnold was taking his lesson.

Hazel's gaze fell on a child lying on the ground, yelling. She felt her legs wobble, James's hand on her back as he swore at the scene playing out in front of them. Her mind had already catapulted her back to a similar instance, a boy lying motionless in the riding school, his body twisted, and then the screams of pain, the ambulance and sirens and flashing lights, the nightmare playing out here and then in the days and weeks to come when his father confronted her in the stables and made threats she'd never forget.

Hazel almost melted into James's arms but something inside her snapped and instead she hot-footed it over to the school.

'Is she all right?' Hazel couldn't take her eyes off the young girl lying there, her pink top soiled with dirt, her blonde hair dishevelled, Arnold crouched beside her. 'I'll call an ambulance!'

But before she could turn on her heel, the girl had got up with Arnold's help and between them, they were brushing the dirt from her leggings. Her tear-stained cheeks were bright pink, but the young girl had actually begun to smile at Arnold's attentions.

'She's fine,' Arnold told his sister and in one look, conveyed to Hazel that she needed to stop panicking and thinking the worst and stop scaring this girl and the other rider in the lesson.

'Are you sure you're really all right?' Hazel bent down to talk to the little girl. 'Your name is Megan, that's right, isn't it?' Her dirty hands and clothes were the only sign now that she'd fallen. 'Do you want to come with me, take a break?'

'Hazel, she's fine.' Arnold was not impressed with her intervention. But it was better to be careful, act fast if they needed to.

'Are you?' Hazel asked Megan.

Megan nodded and Arnold encouraged her back onto Pebbles and continued the lesson.

'The more fuss you make,' he told Hazel once Megan was in the saddle, 'the more she will panic and likely never get on again. Is that what you want?' And when she shook her head, he told her, 'I assessed her when I was down there, I've got quite good at it, even have more than one certificate in first aid.'

'I know.' They both did, as did their parents.

Arnold encouraged the riders who were trotting around the edge of the school, Megan looking as though nothing had even happened. 'I'll talk to her mum when she collects her, Hazel. I'll explain what happened, but she's fine. Look at her.'

With a nod of relief, she left him to it. If she'd had her way, Megan would be having a drink and some cake in the kitchen right about now, but she knew Arnold's way was better. Not only had Hazel lost her confidence teaching, she'd stopped seeing horse riding for what it was, an activity that was fun, rewarding, a challenge that sometimes came with a few knocks. And she knew her brother; he'd never risk it if the kid had fallen awkwardly or really didn't want to keep on going. It came from years of experience, and she'd lost her ability to assess situations, to see that tears and wailing were sometimes a good sign. It was when the rider lay there still and quiet that was more terrifying.

'Arnold didn't seem too happy with you.' James was waiting for her as she closed the gate to the school.

She was about to point out that he might well be annoyed but she'd reacted that way because what had happened before had left its mark. But James hadn't totally understood it then and it seemed he still didn't get it. 'I need to get on. Enjoy the house viewing tomorrow. Tell me about it another time.' And she walked off, leaving him in no doubt it was time to go.

Hazel finished her chores and at lunchtime went inside to make a sandwich. And when Arnold came in for a break too, scraping the heels of his boots against the back step to get them to come off, she handed him the first ham, cheese, and pickle sandwich on rye. 'Peace offering?'

'Hmm. Thanks.' But he was too hungry to say much else and for that she was glad.

Sandwich finished, he went to the fridge, took out the orange juice, and poured a generous glass of it for himself. He put the carton back into the fridge and closed the door. 'You know you overreacted today, right?'

With a sigh, she told him, 'I felt it better to be safe than sorry.'

He took a swig of juice. 'And you don't think I'm safe?'

'Of course I do.' And she really did. But her reaction had been just that, a reaction, not something she'd felt in control of.

'You came running over in a flap and you scared both of those kids with your yelling and face of doom.'

Face of doom? That sounded worse than she'd realised. 'Arnold, I—'

'No, enough is enough, Hazel. It's one thing if you won't teach as much as you could, therefore impacting the business and me, but to interfere in my lessons?'

'I was trying to help.'

'And I had it all under control.'

She shook her head. 'You're right, I was in a flap. Mum and Dad always kept their cool.' When he made a face that suggested she wasn't telling him anything new, she asked, 'What happened today?'

'Does it matter?' But more calmly, he sat opposite her at the kitchen table. 'Megan was having a great time, both of the riders were, they were trotting in circles and the horses were behaving themselves. Megan turned to wave at the other rider, the momentum of her turn put her off balance and she fell.'

'I just heard the scream, I saw her lying on the ground...'

'Riders fall off, you know that. You've done it enough times yourself.' He reached over and gave her hand a squeeze. 'You more than me.'

'As if.' She managed a smile as he got up to go over to the back door and pull on his boots.

'Just try not to assume the worst next time – you can still stay safe and be careful without flying into a panic. Ninety-nine per cent of the time, all is well and the rider will get back on the horse straight away.'

'I know.' He had one boot on. 'By the way, thanks for telling James I wasn't well.'

With a smile, he pushed his foot into his other boot. 'I figured you could use the break.' But he didn't miss his opportunity. 'I thought you were going to ask Gus's daughter to be your first student. What happened to that idea?'

'Long story.'

And one he didn't have time for. And so he left her to it.

* * *

Come late afternoon, Hazel had finished both of her lessons and felt much more positive. One of her riders had actually fallen today – two in one day was pretty unusual, especially when they were as experienced as those in her group. But there hadn't been tears, there'd been laughter after Pearl, the lady who'd fallen, got straight out of the way of Franklin and stood up tall. 'That'll teach me to be a cougar,' she'd said, and Hazel had wondered what on earth she was talking about until she admitted she'd been looking over at Arnold when he walked past.

When the lesson was over and Hazel began to untack Franklin, she saw James parking up again. 'You're back.' She had the horse's saddle, girth, and saddle pad over her arm and his bridle on her shoulder.

'I came to see if you were okay after earlier, you know, the girl, the fall.'

She began to make her way to the tack room after saying goodbye to her students. 'I remember.' She didn't turn to face him, he spoke while she walked, and in the tack room, she put Franklin's tack away in the relevant places before picking up a cloth to give the saddle a good wipe.

'Hazel, I know you think I didn't understand you when we were together.' He was in the tack room with her but stepped aside when she moved to clean Franklin's bridle next. 'I wasn't there for you. Well, I was. I tried to be.' He ran a hand across his smoothly shaven jaw.

'There for me when? Say it.' Her voice rose as she ushered him out of the tack room after she'd put the girth away.

'When the kid fell and his dad blamed you.'

'You're right, you were there for me.'

'As I said, I tried to be,' he went on, as she strode back to get the other set of tack. He followed after her while she marched that lot to the tack room too. 'The kid recovered fine,' he added as she headed for the house this time. 'Nobody died, nobody was left permanently incapacitated—'

She turned suddenly, causing James to almost crash into her. 'Nice, James. Really nice.'

'I don't know what you want from me.' He sounded exasperated.

'I don't know!' She never yelled at him, but all the emotions had built up for so long she could no longer control herself. She was losing a sense of who she was, and he still didn't see it. 'I'm going out, please just let me do that.'

'I want to help you, don't you see that?' He put a hand to her cheek. 'All I want is for you to be happy.'

She felt tears welling in her eyes. He cared, in his own way, he thought he understood her. 'I know,' was all she could manage before she went in through the front door, boots still on and clumps of dirt depositing themselves onto the hall floor as she went to sit on the bottom stair. And she stayed there until she heard James tread the gravel to go over to his car, the sound of the engine and the rumble as he pulled away from Heritage View House. Seeing James wasn't just infuriating because he didn't understand what she wanted and needed, how this was her life and she didn't want to give up on it, it was also because with his sympathy and his support; it reminded her of how he'd held her up when she'd fallen apart, and with him still doing it, it only showed her how little progress she'd made. She was in just as much of a mess now as she had been back then. And that wasn't his fault; it was hers. And it was the most depressing, frustrating thing of all.

She swept up the dirt after removing her boots and headed straight for the shower. Tonight she wanted to forget about everything and have a nice time with her friends. But as she dried her hair, she knew she had to see Gus at the party too, and thinking about the way she'd behaved at the pub, how he'd taken care of her, she wondered: had she judged this man too harshly? She wasn't sure but what she did know what that she had to apologise for the way she'd acted and the sooner she did it, the sooner they could go back to the way things had been before: talking and joking at the stables, comfortable in each other's company. That was what she wanted most of all and yet it made her sad, knowing they'd never be more than friends. Because Hazel could still remember the smell of his shirt as she buried her head against his chest and he carried her inside the house up to her bedroom. And she remembered how it felt to be in his arms.

It had felt good.

14

Julie had not only turned up on time for Abigail today to collect her from school; she'd given their daughter a wonderful end to the week. Gus tried to ignore the fact Julie had given Abigail what looked like a pricey pair of earrings she'd bought on a trip to Milan, telling her to keep them safe and that she could wear them when she eventually got her ears pierced.

Julie had come into the house briefly when she dropped Abigail home at the time they'd agreed. And when Abigail went to have a shower, Julie asked Gus if they could talk.

He showed her into the kitchen and closed the door while she made small talk, asking him about business.

'It's going well?' she smiled, clearly nervous, the way she was wringing her hands.

'I had a steady flow of patients today.' He'd go with it, although he wondered what bombshell she was going to drop. 'News of the practice is already getting around, thanks to local word of mouth from Barney.'

'People trust him?'

'He's a local favourite, yes.' He checked his watch. 'Julie, what's going on? We're off out soon.'

'I know.' She fiddled with the pendant on her necklace as they sat at the table. 'Abigail told me.' It was another moment before she thanked him for letting her collect Abigail from school today.

'No need to thank me, she's our daughter. And she looked really happy when she got home.'

Her eyes glazed over. 'I've made a lot of mistakes, but having Abigail was never one of them.' She pulled herself together enough to tell him, 'I blamed myself so much for what happened because it was my fault, but our daughter, our beautiful girl, sat there today with an ice-cream cone in her hand and told me she forgives me.' Her voice broke.

Gus found a tissue from the box beside the fridge. 'She said that?'

'It was as though she was talking about ice-cream, not scars she will have to live with forever.'

He clasped his hands together on the table in front of him. 'As much as you think I've tried to take Abigail away or that I blame you for what happened, she and I have never had a conversation along those lines, I swear to you. We've never really talked about what happened, all our focus goes on moving forwards. In the early days, she'd cry, she'd get angry at the scars, but she never once got angry at you.'

'She didn't?'

'She sees it as an accident – which it was,' he added, because he knew that. An accident was by definition something unintentional and Julie would never hurt Abigail on purpose.

Julie took a deep breath. 'I think she knows about the tension between you and me, and this is her way to try to help.'

'That makes me feel terrible.'

She let out a little laugh. 'A child sorting out the parents, not right, is it?'

'It's not.'

'I'm sorry for all the times I didn't turn up. Sometimes my excuses were real, sometimes I made something up because the guilt was swallowing me whole.'

'I saw your pain and, contrary to belief, I didn't like it.'

'I'm sorry for the way things worked out,' Julie sniffed.

'All that matters is that the three of us move forwards. Abigail, me, you.'

She nodded. 'I'm getting there.'

'Good.'

When they heard the water in the bathroom stop, Julie smoothed down her top and stood. 'Right, I'll leave you both to it. I just wanted to catch you before you went out. I'll be in touch in a few days to arrange when I can next see Abigail.'

'Thanks for telling me what Abigail said to you. I appreciate it.' He followed her along the corridor. 'And about the beach house—'

'Gus, it's fine, let's keep our meet-ups here in the village until you're more comfortable.' She'd reached the front door and faced him as she stood on the front step.

'This isn't about me,' said Gus. 'It's about Abigail.'

She said no more about it, just smiled. And then when she reached the end of the path, she gave him a brief wave.

Gus closed the door behind her and headed straight up the stairs for the bathroom. 'We're leaving in half an hour,' he called out to Abigail as he passed by her bedroom.

Gus made his shower a quick one, although he couldn't help but think about Julie and the way she'd been today compared to the way she was the last time she'd shown up in Heritage Cove. And as he switched off the water and wrapped a towel around the bottom half of his body, he wondered whether all the yelling at the practice the other day had initiated a shift between them. Perhaps it was a good thing, them hurling accusations at one another. They'd aired what they'd both been keeping quiet and now they might be able to move on from it.

He wiped the condensation from the bathroom mirror and ran a hand over his chin, smooth enough for tonight, not much stubble poking through at all. He splashed on some aftershave and got dressed before knocking on his daughter's bedroom door. 'You ready yet? There are waffles, remember.' Perhaps that would entice her to speed up.

'Duh, I kind of figured that, Dad,' came a voice with the sarcasm he thought was reserved for someone at least three years older than she was. It was a reminder that she was growing up much faster than he sometimes appreciated.

'You can come home if you don't like it,' he called through the closed door as it dawned on him that she might not want to go to a place where a bunch of strangers were gathered and might stare, ask questions.

The door clicked open. 'Why wouldn't I like it?'

'They might not have any fresh cream or strawberries,' he said, when he saw how happy she looked. She didn't look uneasy or nervous and Joan's voice in his head told him to go with it.

Gus picked his daughter up in a hug, her legs dangling as she squealed and laughed. 'Da-ad!' When he set her down, he could see she'd put on a bit of foundation to take some of the redness away from the scars. It was never going to hide them, something that had upset her at first as she tried brand after brand to find the magic make-up that would. Over time, however, she'd begun to come to terms with it and looking at her now, dressed in denim shorts with a pale blue top, he wondered whether he was the one who was struggling with what happened more than she was. She didn't like looks or questions, but since coming here to Heritage

Cove, she'd taken everything in her stride, and he hoped it would continue.

'You look lovely,' he told her as she picked up the lightweight cardigan Julie had bought her, its sequins sparkling.

'You do too, Dad.'

'Ready for waffles?' He decided to make more of the food than the company, even though what he was really looking forward to was seeing Hazel.

Because the way she'd felt in his arms that night as he carried her inside was a feeling he didn't want to forget, no matter how she felt about him right now, given she'd seen him at his worst after the art class.

* * *

It was a pleasant walk to the waffle shack and Abigail was more animated than she usually was after a visit from her mum. Gus still couldn't believe that Abigail had come right out and tackled Julie's guilt, just like that, to her face, saying she didn't blame her for what happened. His little girl was growing up, but she wasn't too mature to hold his hand as they made their way along The Street and past the bus stop towards the Little Waffle Shack that looked more like a log cabin than an eatery.

'Would you look at this place, Abigail?' The shack was a treasure, at the top of a wide-open green space where plenty of people sat, some eating waffles from small containers, others enjoying an ice-cream or simply sitting there to make the most of the long evening. 'Ready to find everyone else?'

'I wonder if Hazel will be here.'

'I'm sure she'll be here soon.' He was about to tell Abigail to be brave, but he stopped himself. It was time to let his daughter judge new situations for herself. 'Now, let's get in there before all the waffles are gone, what do you say?' Gus thanked the person who stood aside to let them inside the waffle shack and held his arm out for Abigail to go first.

She answered with a smile and Lucy soon rushed over. 'You came!' Glass of champagne in hand, she extended her free hand for Abigail to shake. 'It's a pleasure to meet you at long last.'

'Lucy is the blacksmith,' Gus told his daughter as he handed Lucy a bottle of Prosecco with a big pink bow tied around the top. 'Happy birthday.'

'You didn't have to bring a thing, but thank you.'

'Do you make horseshoes?' Abigail asked, more interested in horses than bottles of booze.

'I don't, I'm afraid, I'm not a farrier, but I make lots of cool stuff, decorative things like...' She looked around. 'See those coat hooks over there? I made those. And the sign outside, did you see that?'

'We did,' said Gus. 'I'm impressed.'

Lucy turned her attention back to Abigail. 'I hear you have a horse at the Heritage View Stables.'

'Denby.'

'Great name. And if you've been near the office, I made the boot scraper outside. Check it out next time you're there.'

'I've seen it, it looks too fancy to scrape mud on.'

Lucy laughed and as her boyfriend Daniel came out of the kitchen and welcomed Abigail, gesturing for her to follow him, Gus lowered his voice. 'Thanks for not mentioning the plaques I requested for Denby and the tack room.'

'When's her birthday?'

'Monday,' he said, as they lurked at the entrance to the kitchen but stood well out of the way as Daniel talked to Abigail about all the kinds of waffles they did here.

'Then I will keep it quiet until then.' Lucy put a finger across her lips.

Once Daniel and Abigail had talked shop, Daniel led them outside and around the back to the dedicated party area, Lucy alongside them to make the introductions. Gus knew a lot of people already. Abigail stuck close to his side and took a hold of his hand.

'It's impressive out here,' Gus told Lucy, who filled him in on Daniel opening this place up, how the back area behind the shack had been badly overgrown and looking nothing like it did now, with people gathered on a raised paved area surrounded by bushes with a built-in outdoor fireplace at one end, which Gus bet would create a real atmosphere come winter.

Lucy smiled. 'You need a drink... Daniel is licensed to sell alcohol so there's beer, wine, champagne, lots of soft drinks, too – fizzy and juices.'

'You're the birthday girl,' said Gus, 'other people should be waiting on you.'

She chuckled at the same time as another arrival had her look over his shoulder. 'Hazel, you made it!' She went over and hugged her, although Hazel's eyes were on Gus, he was sure of it. Or was that big-headed of him?

'I'm sorting drinks for Gus and Abigail,' said Lucy. 'What can I get you, Hazel?'

'You shouldn't be a waitress, not tonight, it's your birthday.'

'Exactly what I just said.' Gus did his best not to stare as he thought back to the way Hazel had felt in his arms that night as he carried her inside, the feel of silky soft skin as she put her cheek against his chest. She looked beautiful tonight, hair loose, relaxed despite their last encounter, which had to be on her mind, as it was on his. And his senses leapt into life when, with her this close, he inhaled the same lavender scent he remembered coming from her hair.

'I'll get the drinks,' Hazel offered and posed the question first to Abigail and then Gus.

'I'll grab a beer, if I may?' said Gus.

Abigail, comfortable with Hazel, went to help with the drinks and Gus changed his focus and began chatting with Melissa and Barney, thanking Barney for sending clients his way.

'He's like a personal assistant,' Gus laughed with Melissa. 'Not sure I really needed any flyers to advertise.'

Abigail came back holding a small mason jar with a straw and a green and white chequered lid, holding what looked like colourful juice. 'It's mango and peach,' she informed him before her mouth searched for the straw so she could enjoy it.

Hazel handed him his beer. 'She put the order in for waffles with strawberries and cream, times two.'

Gus laughed. 'Thank you, Abigail, my tummy is rumbling.'

While Abigail and Barney talked mason jars – he had one too containing something equally colourful – Gus stood to the side with Hazel. 'I haven't seen you much lately.'

She opened her mouth and then closed it quickly again before looking at him. 'I'm really embarrassed about the other night.'

'Is it because of what you saw after the art class?' When she seemed taken aback, he added, 'You blurted it out the night I carried you into your house.'

She briefly closed her eyes in embarrassment but then looked at him. 'I can't believe I said anything.'

'I can. You didn't like what you saw.' His words hovered between them.

'I honestly have been busy at the stables too.' She stumbled over her claim a little. 'I'm also embarrassed at my behaviour at the pub. It was terrible and, with you a client, unprofessional. I really am very sorry.'

'You don't need to apologise. We all behave out of character from time to time.'

'Yeah.'

'And I like to think I'm more than a client.' When her head jerked round, he added, 'I like to think I can be a friend like everyone else here tonight.' Despite what she might think of him now.

'I'd like that.' Her voice came out small and he didn't let on that he'd enjoyed taking her home and would do it any day of the week.

Abigail, having had enough of talking drinks, came back over to ask Hazel whether anyone else had ridden Denby yet.

'Both Arnold and I have ridden him a couple of times, getting to know him. And we have a young girl having a lesson with Arnold on Wednesday morning. We are happy to put her on Denby – she's ridden with us before but broke her arm, so she hasn't been able to come to Heritage View for a while.'

'Did she break her arm falling off a horse?' Gus asked.

Hazel shook her head. 'She broke it doing a leapfrog over another girl at school and landing awkwardly.'

'Leapfrogging, eh?' he grinned. 'Dangerous sport.'

Barney called over to them. 'Abigail, could I borrow you again? Lois would like to know a bit more about Denby.'

Gus's heart lifted at his daughter's confidence as she went straight back over. Barney really was doing a good job of making them feel welcome. Everyone was.

Hazel followed his eyeline. 'She's settling in so well.'

'She really is.'

'And she didn't seem too put out about the other girl riding Denby.'

'She's been preparing herself. She knew it was going to happen and she's had a particularly good day today. Her mum came to visit,' he added, to explain why that might be. 'She actually showed up when she was supposed to.' The words came out before he realised they might have been better staying in his head.

'Doesn't she usually?'

He sipped his beer. 'It can be hit and miss. She turned up the other day and wanted me to take Abigail out of school. I was annoyed and we argued. It wasn't pleasant. But today we actually talked, and I think the row we had that day might well have helped us both to see a way forward that will be good for us and, more importantly, Abigail.'

Hazel was looking at him but not saying anything.

He picked up the conversation with an admission. 'Abigail has had a lot to contend with. You must be wondering how exactly she got those scars?'

Hazel's glass fell from her lips. 'It was never my place to ask.'

As Abigail was otherwise occupied, he gave Hazel the abridged version. 'When Abigail was seven, I was away for a few days on a course. While I was away, Julie found out that she'd got the promotion at work she'd been working so hard towards. She was over the moon, took Abigail out for dinner to celebrate, and the celebrations carried on the next night with friends at the house. When Julie's friends left, Julie realised Abigail must have sneaked downstairs at some point during the evening while they were all in the back garden because her pink beaker was out and the lid was off the bottle of vodka. Julie tried the contents of the beaker and realised it was vodka and orange juice. Julie was livid, she called Abigail downstairs and yelled at her. I think she was scared, it could've been so much worse, but it looked as though Abigail hadn't liked the taste at least and had left the drink.

'It was one of those hot, sticky summer nights and Abigail assumed the patio door was open, the way Julie would've had it all evening until she went to bed herself. And when Julie continued to yell at Abigail, Abigail ran. Outside. She ran straight through the glass of the closed patio door.'

'No.' Hazel's eyes widened, and she covered her mouth with her hand as though to silence what had happened to his daughter.

'No safety glass in our property, it was a really old house, we were going to do it up and never got around to it. I never even thought about the windows or doors and whether they needed replacing.' He shook his head. 'I wish we had. But we were lucky. It could've been so much worse.' He remembered Julie's panicked phone call, her sobbing uncontrollably as she told him she was at the hospital. 'Abigail has surprisingly little scarring on her torso but landed on a piece of glass that left her with scars on her face. Those scars will fade but never go completely.

'Julie didn't cope with the aftermath of what happened. She felt guilty, and I was furious that she'd let Abigail get her hands on the vodka. After that, and once Abigail was home and on the mend, Julie threw herself into her promotion. She'd stay away with work even more, spend longer hours at the office, row with me whenever she got the chance, and told me she was unhappy with her life, that it wasn't what she wanted.

'I knew she'd never fallen into the family and wife role and had always wondered what she was missing. I didn't expect her to pull away quite so much, but she was a mess. She partied hard with work colleagues, saw less and less of Abigail and me, and so eventually the marriage didn't survive.'

'I saw you,' Hazel told him, and when he looked at her, she added, 'that day at the practice. I came to see you and I heard shouting.'

'You saw Julie and me arguing?' And when she nodded, it all began to make sense: the way she'd barely looked at him in the pub, how she'd avoided him. At least now he knew the truth. He hadn't been imagining that he'd done something to upset her. Not only had she seen his fury outside the art class, she had also seen him rowing with Julie.

'You must think I'm an ogre.' He wasn't saying it to gain sympathy; he was trying to work out whether she could ever see him differently again.

'You've all been through so much,' said Hazel, in a way that suggested she might know that it wasn't simple at all. 'You were protecting Abigail, by the sounds of it.' And then, a little softer, she told him, 'Protecting those you love is an admirable quality.'

He hoped so, but who knew what she really thought deep down? 'The argument aired a few things for Julie and me, and I think we'll be all right from now on as long as I stop doubting her and she keeps her end of the bargain by showing up.' He looked over at his daughter. 'Abigail's love of horses has been a salvation since it happened. She'd ridden before the accident but afterwards horses became friends in a way I never predicted. She'd talk to them, offload about her day. She had friends, good ones, but the love of animals was where she got most comfort.'

'Must be in her genes,' Hazel smiled gently.

'Yeah.' He enjoyed sharing a smile with her, like they both understood something on a deeper level. And he hoped she could start to see he was more than a man who occasionally lost his temper in defence of those he loved the most. 'When the scars were new, when they were at their angriest, Abigail was angry too. I count my blessings that we had Joan next door for her support and for the horses, and that was when I decided to buy Denby. It was a big gift, but Denby has played a major part in Abigail's recovery. Horses were what got Abigail out of bed on a lot of mornings, and once Denby was hers, Abigail took on the responsibility as much as she could. She'd get up early before school to go to him and help Joan, she was there every day after school. It took a long while, but it helped her to come out of her shell again.'

'Horses can be your best friends,' Hazel agreed.

'Julie's guilt almost ate her up; it's why she didn't fight for custody. She doubted herself, she felt she couldn't parent, and I let her think that.' When he felt her questioning him without words, he told her, 'It was the best thing for Abigail and Julie acknowledges that she was too much of a mess to be a full-time parent. But I hope in time she and Abigail see much more of each other. Do you know, Abigail actually told her not to feel guilty?'

'Really? That sounds wiser than any ten-year-old should be.'

'You're telling me. But hearing Julie tell me about her talk with Abigail made me see how much frustration and resentment I've been holding onto as well. How I've let the accident influence the way I behave.' He swigged his beer before his daughter came back over as she spotted their waffles arriving on a tray carried by a young girl who worked there.

'Time to stop being so serious for a while,' Gus grinned at Hazel. 'Waffles!' he said, nudging his little girl as they found a spare seat at the nearest table. He looked back at Hazel. 'Join us?'

She sat down and looked at their treats. 'Perhaps I'll get some for myself, that topping looks very tempting.'

He cut off a piece of golden waffle and topped it with the slice of strawberry that had fallen off and added a bit of the cream to make it complete before he offered it to her.

'I couldn't.' But his look told her she could and so she leant forwards, opened her mouth, and took the treat from his fork, her eyes not leaving his for a second.

Their intimate moment was interrupted when a boy appeared at Hazel's side.

Hazel finished her mouthful before introducing the boy, Peter, to Abigail and Gus. She told Peter, 'Your dad has done Lucy proud with this party and all these waffles.'

'I had maple syrup on mine,' he beamed. But he was looking at Abigail, and Gus almost leapt in with a comment about it being rude to stare until the boy stepped closer to his daughter.

'Would you like a game of swing ball?' Peter asked Abigail.

'There's a pole over there.' He pointed beyond the seating area. 'And there's nobody using it, as we're the only kids up this late.'

The conspiracy seemed to please Abigail, but she shook her head. It was the first time tonight that Gus had seen her confidence wane.

'That's too bad.' The boy was disappointed, Gus could tell.

Usually Gus would've let Abigail shy away, but he knew that needed to change. He had to be there to support her but part of that was pushing her a little bit out of her comfort zone in times like this when he felt sure she'd love to play but wasn't sure about this stranger. 'Why don't I give you a game?' Gus offered. 'Hazel and Abigail could come watch.'

'Cool.' Peter seemed pleased with that.

'I'm pretty good, I warn you now,' Gus called after him as he ran off to get the rackets.

Swing ball was much as Gus remembered from years ago, but he hadn't reckoned on the energy levels of a youngster and after a few games, he was desperate for a break. Abigail had started to look as though she was enjoying watching and every time Peter looked at her when Gus missed the ball, they shared a laugh.

Gus took a chance and held out the racket. 'Your turn, Abigail, I'm going to pass out.'

'Bit dramatic,' Hazel laughed.

'Girls against boys,' Abigail leapt in.

'It's a two-person game,' he pointed out.

Peter had an idea. 'I could play Abigail and if I win, it's one point to the boys, if she wins, one point to the girls. We play five games, then you and Hazel play five games.'

'What's the prize?' Hazel wondered.

'How about the losers buy the winners ice-creams tomorrow?' Gus suggested. 'Peter, will you be around?'

He nodded. 'I'm sleeping over.'

'That's settled, then,' said Hazel. 'Let's do this,' she grinned at Abigail, a hand on her shoulder in encouragement.

Abigail gave Peter a challenge by winning the first two games but then Peter won the next three in a row. Rather than being annoyed, Abigail collapsed in fits of laughter because she'd lost the final game when her bat flew out of her hand, almost cracking Hazel on the head.

'That's three-two to the boys.' Gus picked up a racket and went over to the swing ball set. 'Come on Hazel, me and you now. Peter, I've got this, don't worry.'

But Hazel had already started, much to Abigail and Peter's amusement, and the ball flew past his head.

'I wasn't ready!' But he managed to whack it back clockwise, sending the ball in the right direction on the coil of the post to secure his win.

Hazel gave it some welly and back the ball came anticlockwise. 'You were too cocky for my liking,' she laughed, the sound so pleasant it almost made him stop to listen.

He hit it back again, laughing when she air-swiped and missed her shot, although he did exactly the same straight afterwards.

They finished with Gus winning two games and Hazel winning three.

'Call it a draw?' Hazel asked, out of breath as the kids discussed carrying the match on for longer.

'Light's starting to fade,' Gus told Peter and Abigail.

Hazel came close enough that he could see a mischievous glint in her eyes. 'So that's your excuse, is it?'

'Fact, not an excuse.' He liked how close they were, how he could see the amusement on her mouth while he argued back.

'Are we going to the ice-creamery for our ice-creams?' Abigail's question pulled him out of his daydream.

'There's no better place,' Hazel smiled. 'And we'll go just before midday, if that suits everyone.'

'Good for me,' said Peter. 'Mum is collecting me late afternoon. I'm working in the waffle shack at lunchtime.'

'Isn't that illegal?' Hazel said quietly to Gus as they all sat down on the ground near the swing ball set and got their breath back.

Peter had good hearing. 'It's not a proper job, I'm too young to work but I get some extra pocket money if I wipe down tables or do some washing up.'

'Daniel sounds a bit like a dad,' said Abigail. 'Why?'

Gus almost leapt in to point out that she didn't like people asking her personal questions, but Peter didn't seem to mind the query.

'Daniel is kind of a stepdad. He married my mum once, but they were only friends really, like they are now. Then I have my biological dad who isn't around, ever. And now there's Stu, who is married to my mum.'

'What's he like?'

'He's nice, I like him.' It was his turn to ask a question now. 'I heard you telling Barney and Lois about a horse. Is it your horse?'

'His name's Denby and he's staying with Hazel at the Heritage View Stables.'

Hazel nodded in acknowledgement and glanced over at Gus, who realised he'd been staring her while the kids carried on their banter. He cleared his throat. 'Denby likes his new home.'

'Do you ride him every day?' Peter asked Abigail.

'I try to see him once a day,' Abigail explained. 'I didn't ride today, my mum came to visit. But I saw him before school.'

'I'm scared of horses,' said Peter, seemingly unaware or unbothered he was admitting that to a girl.

'Why?' Abigail wanted to know.

'I got bitten by one once, all I did was stroke it.' He explained he'd been in a field and his friends wouldn't dare touch any of the horses. He went up behind one and tried to pat it.

'He didn't see you coming,' said Hazel softly. 'Horses like to know what's going on, so you probably frightened him and he turned and bit.'

Peter thought about what she'd told him. 'That sounds about right. He had a bit of a scowl on his face.'

This amused Gus more than anything else, imagining a horse with an extra-long face or a perturbed expression.

'Did it hurt?' Abigail asked Peter.

Peter hesitated and then admitted, 'I cried.'

'I would've cried too,' said Abigail. 'Denby stood on my toes once, I screamed and I think I scared him.'

'Do you still have all your toes?' Peter asked the question so innocently Abigail began to giggle.

'I still have ten toes. And he didn't mean to do it. I'm extra careful now.'

'What do you wear?'

As the kids talked about horses, Gus leaned back on his elbows and Hazel did the same next to him. 'Get her on the subject of horses and she'll be talking for hours,' he said quietly.

'It's a good focus.' She sounded as though she was talking from experience. But she changed the subject. 'Are you enjoying having your own practice?'

'It's early days, but it's been a long time coming and I know it'll be worth it.' He looked around them, not that you could see much now the sun had had enough for another day. 'This all helps: the village, the beautiful surrounds with the cove, finding the stables, the eateries we have to choose from, all within walking distance of home.' *You*, he wanted to say but didn't because he suspected she'd run a mile.

'Are you getting a steady flow of patients?'

'I am. I have quiet times because I'm so new, but I need those at the moment. Eventually I'll have to employ a receptionist, but for now the admin is manageable with such a gap between appointments. I could advertise the position, or I could just tell Barney and have him do the honours.' He explained how a few clients had already come his way because of Barney.

'Barney will make sure anyone coming here to live soon feels a part of it, you'll wonder how you ever got by without any of us.' She met his gaze and the moment between them hung in the air until she began to laugh.

'What's so funny?'

'I bet you couldn't believe it, when you posed naked for the art class, that two of the students would be living in the village you were moving to.'

A deep laugh rumbled through him. 'No, I couldn't. I didn't think I'd see any of those art lovers again.' He waited until she looked at him. 'I'm glad I did, though.'

Coyly she didn't reply, just watched the kids as they attempted swing ball in the fading light, laughing that they couldn't see the ball properly.

Without Hazel focusing on him, Gus felt able to carry on talking and share more about himself. 'The night of the art class, Abigail went outside to the car before I did. She wasn't gone for long, but by the time I got outside, there were some teenagers hanging around and one of them was asking about her scars. He wasn't asking in an interested way, either.' When Hazel's eyes begged the question, he added, 'He was insulting her and calling her names. I don't even know why kids have to do that. What do they get out of it?'

Hazel shook her head. 'I really don't know. They probably do it to look big in front of their friends, try to get a bit of a laugh, some do it when they're jealous, others might do it if they've been bullied themselves.' She shrugged. 'You'd think they'd know how it feels, but sometimes it makes a victim feel better to be the antagonist.'

'Joan is always telling me to lead by example, but that night, I lost my temper. I think the summer heat, the exhaustion of the move and then the art class all got to me, and I was so angry for Abigail. That night was the beginning of our fresh start and there they were putting a dampener on it by being spiteful.'

'You're a good dad.'

He looked at her then. 'I like to think so, but that night? You saw me. I'm ashamed of how furious I was. The teenagers looked afraid at least and who knows, maybe it'll make them think twice about doing it to someone else, but I couldn't sleep that night, thinking I might have scared them witless.'

Hazel didn't speak straight away but when she did, she told him, 'They deserved to see repercussions for their tormenting. And you're right, it could make them think twice. It might not, but hopefully something of what you said to them might have got through.'

They were interrupted when someone called out that it was cake time. 'I guess that's our cue to move.' He looked over to see Daniel emerge from the back door with an enormous yellow cake and too many candles to count from this distance.

'Jade from the bakery made that and it looks delicious,' smiled Hazel, taking Gus's hand to pull her up from sitting when he offered.

Gus hadn't really thought about his gesture until he was actually doing it and judging by her reaction now she was standing almost against him, neither had she.

'Grab the rackets, you two,' she said to the kids. 'Cake!'

Both Abigail and Peter came over and Hazel took the rackets from Peter.

As they walked over to rejoin the party, Peter queried, 'I know I said I was scared of horses, but Abigail says Denby is a nice horse, Hazel.'

'He's a beautiful horse.'

'Would I be able to have a lesson on him, do you think? If I ask my mum or Daniel?'

'I don't see why not. I'll talk with my brother, see when he has a space.'

'Or you could teach me,' Peter suggested.

It was as though her persona completely changed and already Gus missed the Hazel who had begun to let her guard down tonight. 'Arnold is the better teacher for you, Peter. I'll let him know you're interested.' Her tone friendly but firm, they walked on, and she left the rackets by the back door to the waffle shack before coming over to sing 'Happy Birthday' to Lucy.

Gus watched Hazel as everyone launched into the final line of the song. So it wasn't just Abigail she refused to teach. And yet she had a wonderful rapport with kids, an affinity with horses, so surely putting the two together worked.

As their eyes met over the candlelight from the birthday cake, Gus had to wonder what Hazel was hiding. What was it that made her so afraid?

15

The rain lashed at the windows of the ice-creamery as Hazel, Gus, Peter, and Abigail huddled inside on the largest table. It looked like they were among the very few to brave the downpour in their quest for ice-cream. Hazel, armed with an enormous golf umbrella, had walked over to the waffle shack to meet Peter and brought him down here to where Gus and Abigail were waiting. Though Hazel knew full well it wasn't, it felt a bit like a date.

Being in Gus's company, especially after hearing him tell her the full story of what had happened to Abigail, the emotion beneath his words and the harsh way he judged himself, had made her realise how much she'd come to care for him and feel comfortable in his company. Now she knew the truth, that he'd been protecting his daughter and hurting at the same time, Hazel didn't feel the need to run a mile; she wanted to get to know him even more. And as she lay in bed last night, she realised beyond a shadow of a doubt that there was no future for her and James. She was falling for another man and no matter whether anything came of it, it wasn't fair to keep him hanging on.

Zara, who owned the ice-creamery, brought over a tray filled with their orders – buttermilk and blueberry in a tub for Hazel, strawberry shortcake in a cone for Abigail, and Gus and Peter had both chosen a mixture of salted caramel and mint choc chip in a double waffle cone.

'That's huge,' Hazel laughed as Gus registered the size of his ice-cream. 'I did warn you that Zara is generous with her serving size.'

'No need to be stingy,' Zara laughed, hair swinging in her pony-tail as she left her happy customers and went back behind the glass serving counter.

Gus flexed his bicep and Peter followed suit as Gus announced, 'We won't be defeated, will we?'

Peter shook his head but asked, 'Abigail, do you want to sit over in the corner by the window?'

'It only has two seats,' said Gus, when the kids got up to move. 'Are the adults cramping your style?'

With the pair giggling, Gus told Hazel, 'Thank goodness I brought her to the party. She's making friends at school, one of them is coming for tea next week, but Peter is quite something. He's down to earth and I think that's what she needs right now.'

Hazel enjoyed another spoonful of the buttermilk and blue-berry and put her thumbs up to Zara, who'd been the one to suggest the flavour. 'From what I know of Peter, he's a great kid.'

'He sounds excited about learning to ride on Denby when Arnold can fit him in – he told me all about it while you were ordering the ice-creams. And Abigail's all for it; that shows she likes him.'

'I wonder if he's still wary?'

'You mean after he was bitten?' Gus licked around the bottom of his ice-cream so it didn't melt down the cone, and Hazel did her best to look away when she saw his tongue dart out.

'He's not the only kid to be wary. I see it a lot and it's not always a bad thing. I think Peter might like it once he has a go.'

'I heard Abigail on the phone to her mum this morning, telling her about Peter and how he'd been bitten. She said she's going to have to share all her advice on safety when it comes to horses. She sounded bossy.'

'Good for her,' Hazel laughed. 'She knows a great deal, she's sensible, and knows her limits. I can tell by the way she talks. And it's great she cares so much, not only about Denby's wellbeing, but the other horses at the stables. She doesn't ignore them, she always has time to fuss them or feed them a treat.'

'Don't all kids care about the horses?'

'Some are little monsters, believe me.'

Gus began to laugh but then, after another lick of his ice-cream, turned more serious. 'Is that why you won't teach kids?' And then he pulled a face. 'Sorry, I didn't mean to blurt that out.'

He'd bared a part of himself yesterday and she felt she owed him the same, or at least something. 'It's complicated,' was what she managed before she asked, 'What's with the smile?'

'That's the most you've ever said about it. Usually when I ask, you just refer me to Arnold and smile sweetly. You tell me it's not personal to Abigail or you drink so much I have to put you to bed.'

She felt colour flush her cheeks and scraped the last of her ice-cream out of the bottom of the tub.

He let her off the hook, and instead of focusing on her, told her how he'd agreed with Julie that she could take Abigail up the coast to a beach house. 'I said no originally, that I wanted Abigail to settle in more here first. But I need to let Julie make some of the decisions when it comes to our daughter, I need to stop assuming she'll let Abigail down and perhaps give her the benefit of the doubt.'

'Good for you, and I bet Abigail will love it.' She turned to watch Abigail draw what looked like a cat in the condensation on the windows, Zara egging her on to do it. 'The simplicity of being a kid, eh?'

He smiled as he looked over too. 'Yeah, I miss that. Adulting is way harder.'

'Yup.'

'So do you want to talk about it?' He smiled at her. 'You're very good at moving a conversation on but I'm moving it right back. You didn't give me much to work with by telling me "it's complicated".'

'I didn't, did I?' And as uncomfortable as it was, she liked that he cared enough to persist.

'So give me the short version, the way I did last night. We've got time.' He nodded over to the kids. 'They've got the rest of the front window to deface with their drawings yet.'

She looked into kind eyes, a face that said it would understand and that she didn't have to worry he'd think her incapable of keeping his daughter safe when another kid had been badly hurt in her care. But the choice of telling him was taken out of her hands when James came into the ice-creamery.

'Arnold pointed me in this direction,' James smiled, stopping short of leaning in for a kiss as he usually did when he saw the company she was in. 'Thought I'd give you a lift back to the stables, it's pouring out there.'

At the sight of this man who had the best intentions, Hazel felt terrible because she knew they needed to talk. She had to end things and she'd tried to call him before coming here, but he hadn't answered.

Gus picked up on the tension and more than a hint of awkwardness and rallied the kids, suggesting Peter go back to their house.

'We'll be up at the stables later on today to see Denby,' Gus told Hazel.

'See you both later on.' And Hazel left with James, who didn't say much at all as they drove back to the stables.

They pulled into Heritage View and the windscreen washers swiped angrily back and forth, clearing the rain as best they could.

When James parked up and switched off the engine, he turned to Hazel. 'What's going on with you and Doctor Dolittle?'

'You mean Gus?' She wondered how he knew that Gus was the local vet, but it didn't really matter.

'Whatever. So is he more than a client?'

'No.'

'But you want him to be.'

It wasn't a question. 'James, I don't want to answer that, but we do need to talk.' His actions came from a good place, but he was trying to be the knight in shining armour by taking her away from all of this rather than helping her work through it. And he was hanging on to a relationship that had run its course.

'I knew this was coming.' He sounded sad and she knew this man, who'd once been her fiancé, deserved so much more.

Heritage View House was barely visible beneath the heavy rain as James said, 'I made an offer on the house I viewed.'

She turned in her seat to look at him. 'Already?'

'When you know, you know. And it was accepted.' With a gulp, he turned to face her, and she knew by his expression that he'd realised that they were never going to fall back into the relationship they'd had before. It was probably the reason why he'd made a move so quickly on the property he'd viewed.

'You deserve to be happy,' she told him, moving across to kiss him only once, on the cheek. She wanted to offer friendship, but she couldn't. James would never let her go properly if she did. And that wouldn't be fair on him. 'Take care of yourself.'

He didn't say much in reply and the second she climbed out and popped up her umbrella, she heard the crunch of gravel as he pulled away. And all at once, Hazel felt an overwhelming sense of relief, an unburdening that made her feel as though this might well be the way forwards.

* * *

With the rain hammering down as though it was never going to give up, Hazel hunkered down in the office to get things done. She contacted the farrier to arrange for him to come out in a few weeks for the horses' foot trimming and shoeing as necessary. She returned two calls regarding lessons, telling each person that they were on a waiting list, and got lost in the mountain of paperwork as Tabitha moved from her lap into the little cat basket, having no interest in venturing outside. At a knock at the door, Hazel called out, 'Come in,' as she finished printing off her orders ready to file along with the expenses and keep their accounts up to date.

When nobody came in, she assumed it was likely Arnold, carrying something and unable to open the door. But she realised how much she was hoping it might be Gus and Abigail instead, that they were as disappointed as she'd been that their time together today was cut short.

She opened the door with a smile but immediately went hurtling back from the man on the other side, a man she recognised all too well even after all these years, as he sneered at her and advanced towards her, pressing her against the desk.

'We meet again,' he said, breath reeking of alcohol. 'Nobody here to help you now.'

16

'Peter's a character, isn't he?' Gus said to Abigail after they'd taken Peter up to the waffle shack on their way to the stables. Peter and Abigail had played Jenga over and over again, she'd shown him her room, and when the noise level increased, Gus went up the stairs to find them performing stunts in her bedroom, which involved leaping from the lowest chest of drawers to the bed, doing a forward roll and finishing standing up at the head of the bed. He'd wanted to let them keep doing it but his responsibility as a parent had him urging them to be careful and not climb on the furniture or worse, bang their heads on the wall at the finale of their move.

'I told him all about horses and keeping safe,' Abigail informed him as they got back into the car on The Street and carried on towards Heritage View.

Gus wondered whether that was why Peter had turned to stunts – Abigail was probably getting serious, the way she did about horses, and Peter wanted to swap the seriousness for fun. And who could blame him?

'I can't see Denby,' Abigail moaned as they pulled in at Heritage View.

'I can't see anything, it's raining too hard.'

Abigail climbed out of the car and popped up a bright yellow umbrella over her head. 'He might be in the far paddock. I'll go find Hazel.' She ran off before Gus had a chance to answer.

Gus was relieved he couldn't see Hazel's ex-boyfriend's car anywhere as he picked up the bag that Abigail had forgotten. It contained carrot and apple slices, enough for Denby and probably the rest of the horses here, she'd cut up so many. He'd told Abigail she'd have to ask Hazel's permission to feed the horses first and when he saw his daughter move from the stable block, clearly having had no luck finding Hazel and heading for the office, Gus was happy to see she must be doing just that. He popped up his umbrella and briefly hovered at the fence to say hello to dependable Franklin, sympathising at his location in a rain-soaked paddock.

But he didn't have much of a chance to pay the horse any attention because Abigail came running from the direction of the office, screaming.

Gus tore towards her as she yelled something about Hazel, a man, her office.

Gus made it past the stable block and around the side, and raced straight through the office door, where he pulled a stocky man off Hazel, who was pinned to the desk, terrified.

'What the hell are you doing?' he roared at the man, who seemed stunned at the intervention. 'Go find Arnold!' he urged Abigail. He needed the backup, but it was more that he didn't want Abigail to witness this.

Hazel didn't move; she was in shock, leaning against the desk, her breathing heavy. The man was still in Gus's clutches and Gus had no intention of letting go.

'I said, what are you doing here?' Gus demanded. The man, dressed in grubby jeans and an old sweatshirt, crumpled beneath Gus's fist and wouldn't look at him, only sneer at Hazel.

'She knows what she did,' he slurred and then, more spitefully, 'she's a monster.'

Gus manhandled him out of the office, well away from Hazel, just as Arnold came charging towards them.

'Look after Hazel,' Gus yelled to Abigail, who was crying but ran into the office and slammed the door shut behind her.

'She destroyed my family,' the man spat before he saw Arnold with his phone against his ear. 'What the fuck are you doing?'

'Calling the police.'

'Now look here...'

'Be quiet,' said Gus. 'Shut up and stop throwing your weight around.'

Gus kept a hold of the man, who was wittering on about Hazel and how she'd ruined him, and between him and Arnold, they shunted him away from the office and out in front of the paddocks.

The police were there in no time at all, and Gus gladly handed the man over to them before he charged back to the office. Arnold was already on the phone, calling their parents, by the sounds of it.

A female police officer had gone ahead of Gus and had already sat down beside Hazel. Gus opened his arms for Abigail, who was hugging Hazel, and she left one comfort for another.

'Has he gone?' Hazel asked, eyes glazed as though barely registering much at all.

'He's being taken away now,' Gus assured her. He went to her side, crouched down on his haunches and put a hand on her knee, his other hand holding Abigail's. 'You're safe. I promise you.' He wasn't sure she even heard him, but for now, he had to look after his daughter and Hazel had the female officer with her.

'You really are safe, love,' he heard the policewoman reiterate to Hazel before he closed the office door behind him and Abigail. He wanted to stay there with her, put his arms around her and hold her close, keep both of his girls at his side.

Arnold was on the phone again when Gus and Abigail came out of the office.

'I called our dad,' he explained, 'and I've cancelled lessons for the rest of the day so I can be with Hazel.'

Hazel had plenty of people in her corner. 'Can I do anything?'

Arnold shook his head. The rain had finally stopped. 'I'd just put the horses back into the paddock so everything is sorted.' He was about to go into the office when he registered how upset Abigail still was. Her bottom lip wobbled, and he crouched down to meet her at eye level. He put a hand against her cheek, his thumb brushing away a tear. 'Thank you for being there, for getting help.'

When Arnold went into the office, Gus hugged Abigail again. It seemed she didn't want to leave.

'I never got to ask if I could feed the treats to the horses.'

'We'll do it another time. How about we go and watch them in the paddocks?' Perhaps it would do her good not to be whisked away too quickly, to realise that this was a safe space now, the nightmare had finished.

They waited by the paddocks and fussed any horse that came their way and eventually Arnold emerged, having talked with the police officer. He immediately eyed the bag of treats cast aside on the floor. 'How about we feed the horses together?'

Minstrel was first over to the fence and Abigail giggled as she held out her hand flat with a piece of apple, and the horse's lips tickled her palm to claim her treat. Next up was Peony, then Milton, and Pebbles wasn't daft – not wanting to miss out, the dappled gelding trotted over to the fence where Abigail was in charge.

Gus saw Arnold look over to the remaining police car parked up, one having gone to take the man away. 'Who was he, Arnold? He wasn't a stranger, was he?'

Arnold shook his head, conscious of Abigail as she tried to get the attention of Sherbert before she'd let any of the horses have seconds. They moved a few steps away.

'It was close to three years ago now,' Arnold began. 'Hazel was teaching one day and at the last minute added another boy to her list of riders. That man here today was the boy's dad. He'd booked his son in and told us his son had plenty of experience. Turned out that experience was being led around on a rein on holiday once or twice. That wasn't a problem, but his behaviour was. Hazel kept telling him to take it slow, I heard her say it more than once, and I could see for myself that the boy needed to calm down and listen.'

'Don't tell me, he didn't.' Gus put a thumbs up at Abigail when Sherbert finally sensed something was going on at the fence and came to claim a piece of apple or carrot.

'He was all over the place, arms high, reins loose, looking in the other direction as though he was on a plastic horse at the funfair rather than on an animal with a mind of its own. My sister had to tell him three times to put his feet back in the stirrups. He just wasn't listening, at all. I knew Hazel had her work cut out for her, but my sister is very capable.'

Abigail's giggles as Sherbert nudged her for another treat had Arnold telling her to go ahead with seconds for all of them. 'The boy, Levi, wanted to skip the basics, he was all about going faster; he thought going around in a circle in the school was dull and didn't mind telling us. I couldn't wait for the lesson to end as I pushed a wheelbarrow past, it wasn't nice to listen to it. Usually you look over, you take pride in the progress riders are making, even give tips, but that was a lesson I wanted nothing to do with. And when Hazel rolled her eyes at me, I knew she was thinking the same. I thought I'd empty out the wheelbarrow and then go and give her a hand. But as I was emptying it out, I heard Hazel yelling for help. I knew then that something had gone horribly wrong.

'Levi had fallen off. He'd got cocky, was messing about, he'd dug his heels in to make his horse move and he'd called out to another rider, "Look, no hands!" as he dropped the reins. His horse took exception to the chaos and got annoyed, turned suddenly, and off Levi came. He collided with a fence, knocked his shoulder badly. By the time I got over there, he was lying on the ground, breathing but not moving. And his hat had come off, he must've played with the straps – Hazel said he kept moaning about having to wear it, how he wanted to have a cowboy hat like they did in the movies.'

'Bad idea,' said Gus, smiling over at Abigail, thankful she was laughing as the horses all wanted to know her this afternoon, rather than thinking about what she'd just seen.

'Very bad idea. There was some blood at the side of his head, and one look at his twisted form and it was clear his shoulder was out and his leg too. Hazel had already called an ambulance, we covered him with a blanket, and waited. It was terrifying. I went with Levi in the ambulance and his mother met us at the hospital. They rushed him into surgery, and I came home. The hospital wouldn't give me any updates after that, but we got one from his dad a few days later.'

'The man just now.'

'He showed up one day and cornered Hazel when she was mucking out one of the stables. She was distraught at what had happened, but she couldn't fall apart, not when we had a business to run. He confronted her much in the charming way he did today. With a lot of yelling and accusations. Told her he'd lost earnings having to care for his boy, might lose his job and never work again if his boy needed further treatment, which I don't think he ever did. I heard the commotion and found the man in the stables, a pitchfork in one hand, the other arm pinning Hazel against the wall.'

Gus swore. 'Good job you were there.'

'He was vile. Shrieking at my sister, telling her she wasn't fit to be in charge of kids, accusing her of negligence, that he was going to sue and finish her for good. He called her plenty of choice names too, which I won't repeat. That's why Hazel has shied away from teaching kids or anyone inexperienced. She was beginning to improve, she was starting to think she'd try again. She even thought she might try with Abigail – my sister is a brilliant rider and teacher, it's not her capabilities that have taken a knock but rather her confidence.' He shrugged. 'She must've changed her mind though, I've no idea why. One minute, I thought she'd come and see you, and the next, she was getting drunk at the pub and didn't say another word about it.'

Now Gus had seen what she'd gone through with that man, it made sense. She'd been strange with him after the art class, which he now knew had more to do with his anger afterwards than any nakedness. Then they'd begun to bond a bit, he'd even thought it might go further, but then she'd seen him and Julie arguing. She must have thought he was yet another parent who had anger issues and after knowing what had happened with that man today and before, it was no wonder she hadn't wanted to teach Abigail. She hadn't wanted to put herself in that position again.

'So the man never took it any further?' Gus asked.

'He didn't. But clearly he never let it go, given his reappearance.'

When Abigail came back over, treats all gone, she and Gus left Arnold, Hazel, and the police officer to it and headed for home.

The first thing Gus did when he got back to the house was call Julie. Not something he often did if Abigail had a problem, but he wanted today's events to come from him, for her to know that their daughter was fine, she was safe. It was a fresh start for them in the village, but he also needed to respect that it was a new chapter for Julie too.

After talking to his ex-wife, he passed the phone over to his daughter so they could talk, and when she was at last happily telling her mum about the horses and the treats she'd fed them, he retreated into the kitchen and made a mug of coffee.

As he sat listening to the happy sounds of Abigail chattering away, he thought about Hazel. He finally had answers as to why she was reluctant to teach his daughter or any other child, for fear the same might happen. She'd lost confidence after that man had scared her half to death and told her she was such a terrible human being. Gus hoped that Hazel might someday be able to see what happened for what it actually was. An accident. Just like Abigail's had been. And he hoped that rather than looking behind her all the time, at ways it could've been avoided, Hazel could now begin to move forwards.

But he was also worried that today's incident might put her right back to square one.

17

Hazel had gone up to her bedroom on Arnold's orders after the policewoman left. She'd run herself a warm bath, sank into the water, and tried to let her worries float away. If only it were that easy.

Now, curled up on the sofa in the lounge at the front of Heritage View House, she had a mug of tea clasped between her palms but when she took a sip, she pulled a face. It had gone cold. Arnold had made it for her the last time he popped his head in before going back out to the stables to take care of the necessary tasks – the horses' care couldn't wait.

Hazel knew that horrible man was in police custody now and so the sound of a vehicle pulling up wouldn't be him. She assumed it was someone who had come for a lesson, even though she was sure Arnold had cancelled any that were scheduled for the rest of that day. But when she looked outside and saw her dad's car, she ran from her place in the lounge and straight to the front door, which she flung open.

Barefoot, she ran out to him. She fell into his arms, felt his strong hold and presence and soothing voice.

And right now, there was no need to say anything. He was here. She was safe.

* * *

Thomas had always been a patient man. When Hazel was little and struggled to ride a bike, something her friends took to with ease, he hadn't forced her to keep trying when she didn't want to, when she'd rather get onto a horse and do all the things she knew she could do. He'd known that over time it would come, and the best thing he could do was stand back and bide his time, that his daughter would soon sort it out for herself. It wasn't all that different today as her dad waited for Hazel to tell him everything, cry out her feelings, let her fears of failure and frustration be fully aired at long last. He let her ramble on about how seeing Levi fall that day had made her doubt her ability to keep anyone safe, let alone a minor. She went on and on about how she missed teaching, how she loved to see a beginner's progress, but how big a leap it was to try again. He listened while she told him about Abigail, a girl she would love to teach but had refused to up until now out of fear she'd not keep her safe, out of worry that she couldn't be supportive when she didn't feel strong enough herself.

The sun began to set. The rain had stopped, puddles pooled outside in any part of the ground that wasn't entirely even, but the horses in the paddocks looked happy enough as Hazel gazed out of the window. She'd cried all the tears she needed to now, blurted out everything she'd been holding back for so long. And with her eyes red and sore, she asked about her mum. Her dad had apparently come straight here, and with her mum out for the day on a hack with a friend, there was no time to wait behind and explain.

'I called her on the way up here to tell her what was going on. She'll be worried, but she knows I've got you.'

'I'll call her in a bit.'

'She'll want an update,' Thomas smiled. 'But only when you're ready.'

She'd thought she was done talking about it, but the words tumbled out again. 'It was horrible, Dad. That man.'

'I know, love.' He put an arm around her, let her lean her head on his dependable shoulder.

'I didn't expect it; he's not shown his face in years. I never forgot him or Levi, but I never thought I'd have to see him ever again.' She toyed with an almost-disintegrated tissue between her fingers.

He let her words sink in before he offered to make them a cup of tea each.

She followed him to the kitchen. 'I happen to know that there's a box of clotted cream shortbread at the back of the larder cupboard.'

He rubbed his stomach before picking up the kettle to fill. 'That is music to my ears. From the Twist and Turn Bakery?'

'Good guess.' She took out two mugs while her dad filled the kettle and set it to boil. 'They were a gift to me from one of the ladies I teach. She dropped them off yesterday and I thought I'd save them for something special. And you being here *is* special, no matter the circumstances.'

'I'm sorry we don't visit more often.'

'Dad, you've got your own lives.' Hazel found the shortbread. 'Arnold and I are the same here, we have our own business and lives, so we don't get a chance to come down to you either. But it's nice to know you're only a phone call away.' She proffered the box of shortbread and as Thomas took one, she left the cardboard box open on the table for them both to help themselves.

'When Arnold called, he sounded distraught.' Thomas filled the mugs with water on top of the tea bags and added milk to each, no sugar. 'He talks to me a lot about you.'

'He does?'

'He worries about his little sister.' They sat at the kitchen table on chairs next to each other at an angle. 'What you went through was terrible back then and for it all to rear its ugly head now?' He shook his head, unable to find quite the right word to describe it. 'I'll go and see him in a bit. I texted him already, so he knows I'm in here with you. He'll be giving us space and seeing to the horses as a priority.'

'As it should be,' Hazel smiled. 'And he really has been brilliant through all of this, it's not often he lets his frustration show, even though he's been carrying the load, with me picking and choosing who I think I'm able to teach.' Tabitha gave Hazel a fright when she jumped up onto her lap. She stroked the cat from head to tail as the feline settled into position.

'You're a team, that's why.' He complimented the shortbread and reached for a second piece, but this time he didn't start eating it straight away. 'Hazel, I've a bit of a confession to make.'

Tabitha was dribbling on Hazel's knee as she jutted out her chin and Hazel continued to rub her fingers beneath. 'Go on,' she urged when her dad stayed quiet.

'It's about that man. Ewan.'

Hearing his name sent a shudder cascading through Hazel. Calling him 'that man' made it easier to dissociate herself from him.

With a deep breath, Thomas wound back more than a couple of years, to the aftermath of what happened. 'I wanted to help in any way I could after the accident.'

'And you did. I remember you taking on some of the lessons, you and Mum being here for me and Arnold, to support us and encourage us.' Their parents had allowed a good handover period for the business, staying in the Cove to ensure that their children knew the day-to-day running of the place before they moved further away.

'I also went over to Ewan's house,' Thomas admitted.

'When?' Tabitha picked up on the shift in tension and leapt off Hazel's lap to go and find a more comfortable surface that wouldn't move, most likely the cushion of the sofa.

'After Arnold told me Ewan had come for you at the stables.'

She would never forget it. She'd dulled the memory ever since and unfortunately now had a fresh one to keep it alive. 'What did you do?'

'Not a lot. I hadn't really worked out what I was going to say. I was mad at him coming at you, threatening you, but your mum and I talked, and we both knew it must've come from a place of sheer terror when he thought his son was seriously hurt. I don't know why we excused it, I suppose we wanted to give him the benefit of the doubt and assume he was like any other parent.

'I got to the house and I could see the young boy, Levi, through the window, slumped in front of the television but otherwise alive and hopefully getting better with every passing day.' Thomas set down his piece of shortbread. 'Ewan came to the door and I started off by saying how sorry I was that the accident had happened, thought I'd give him a chance to apologise for turning up at the stables and scaring you out of your wits, but there was no reasoning with the man. He told me that this accident would finish you for good. You'd never teach again, your stupid riding school – that's how he phrased it – would be as good as dead. He ran on and on about your neglect, that he was going to make an example of you.'

'I remember when he said the same to me.' Hazel gulped. 'Until today, I thought maybe he'd decided the biggest focus was that Levi was all right, that that was all that mattered.'

Thomas shook his head. 'I didn't know his game that day, but he had one for sure. He wasn't all about his kid's welfare, it was more about how much trouble he could make. I'm afraid I panicked.'

'You didn't hit him, did you?'

Thomas chuckled. 'Since when have I solved a problem with my fists?'

'Good point.' Her dad was far too gentle for that. 'So what *did* you do?'

'I always believed in you and Arnold when it came to this place. I knew you could both make it work.' He paused. 'But with his threats, I saw him making it difficult for the business, especially you. And my fatherly instincts came out to play, rightly or wrongly. I didn't want that man to take anything from you. I didn't want your name in the newspapers, as he was threatening to do. I didn't want you to have to go to court.'

'But we had insurance, so we were covered legally, and that cover would've seen to Ewan's bills too if they were genuine.' It hadn't been the first thing she'd thought of when the accident happened, far from it, but Arnold had taken charge to check the particulars.

'I wasn't thinking straight or practically, Hazel. All I was thinking about was keeping you from harm, protecting you. You and Arnold loved horses as kids – growing up here at Heritage View was quite a life.'

'You don't have to remind me...' She looked around the four walls of the kitchen, the place that was home.

'In all the years we'd run the stables and the riding school, all those horses and all those riders, we'd never come up against a man like Ewan who was out to cause trouble. I wasn't stupid in that respect, but I should've been stronger. I wanted to come to some agreement with him that would see him leave you and Arnold and the stables well alone. I listened to him rant about lost wages, physio bills, and compensation for stress. You name it, he listed it. I don't think it mattered to him whether it was true or not.'

It dawned on Hazel with painful clarity. 'You paid him off.'

'I gave him a sum, he asked for more, I told him I could do it in instalments as I didn't have cash lying around, not to mention I might have to explain it to others. He obviously realised if that were to happen, he might not get his money at all because others in my life might not be quite so stupid.' For the first time since he'd arrived today, her dad looked tired. Always strong, forever dependable, he showed his vulnerability in having to recount the story. 'There were twelve instalments in total, and I felt such relief when I made the last instalment. But then he showed up after I'd put the final cheque through his letterbox. He was drunk, he was angry, he was looking for you.'

'You never said anything.' Her voice came out small at the realisation of all the trouble behind the scenes when she hadn't thought anyone other than her was struggling to move forwards. 'How did you get rid of him? Don't tell me you gave him more money?'

Thomas shook his head. 'I knew that if I did, it would never end. And over those twelve months, I regretted my decision as it was. It felt deceitful, no matter whether I was protecting you or not.'

Hazel realised something else. 'You never did gamble that money away, did you?'

He shook his head. 'I made up an excuse when you questioned the invoices I had to use to cover my tracks. I hated the lies I told, but I admitted everything to Sally after we moved away. She understood, and I think she was just grateful that man had gone off the radar. Or at least that's what we assumed.'

'I wish he had.'

'Do you remember my fall?'

Thomas had been out on a hack with Franklin, taking the bridleways that bisected two of the largest fields beyond Barney's home and barn. It was quite a trek that way, but one he was used to. It hadn't even been dark or anywhere near bonfire night, but someone had launched fireworks across the bridleway in Franklin's path, causing Franklin to buck and Thomas to come off. Whoever the idiot had been had run off the second they'd done it, leaving Thomas lying on the ground, injured. A dog walker had found him and called an ambulance. And Franklin was by his side; he hadn't bolted, as though he knew his master was hurt.

'How could I ever forget? You were lucky, it could've been worse.' And then she gasped. 'You think it was Ewan who set off the fireworks.' His name left a sour taste in her mouth.

'I know it was him. I saw him about five minutes before the accident happened. I assumed he was going to head to the stables and so I was on my way back there to warn you.'

'Why did you never tell the police what he did? When they asked questions in the hospital, you said nothing.'

'I'd seen him that day, but I couldn't actually prove it was him. Believe me, I thought about letting the police go question him, but then I had to consider the ramifications for you if he tried to finish the business by mouthing off about Levi's accident the way he'd said he would.

'Anyway, as I lay there in that hospital bed, I had a visitor. Ewan's wife. She told me Ewan had been drunk and admitted everything to her. I thought she meant the fireworks, but then she produced a cheque for me. It was for the full amount of what I'd paid to him in instalments, to keep quiet about the accident and to leave you alone. She'd never known about what he was doing, the money he'd got from me, not until during divorce proceedings, anyway. She told me she'd never once blamed you or anyone else at the stables for the accident. She'd had no idea that her husband did either because at the time they were already in the process of separating. She looked devastated when she told me that one day she'd heard Levi boasting about how his dad had put the fear of God into the woman at the stables because she deserved it.

'I can understand the divorce,' Thomas went on. 'She told me she was furious with Ewan because the focus should have been on

Levi and his recovery, not on placing blame. She also said that she had no doubt that Levi would've been at fault that day because he'd inherited a lot of his father's attitude.' His eyes filled with tears when he admitted, 'She sat at my bedside and cried, sad for her son, that his role model wasn't helping him turn into the man that he should be.'

'I can't imagine being married to someone like that,' said Hazel.

'I expect she's better off out of it.'

'So you didn't mention you'd seen him to the police because of that woman, Levi's mother?'

He was unsure whether to answer but eventually told his daughter, 'I thought I'd give her and her son a chance to avoid more trouble. She was getting out, that was what mattered, and she wanted what was best for Levi.'

'Those fireworks could've killed you.'

'But they didn't.'

'They could've seriously injured Franklin.' Hazel felt panic rise, her whole body stiffen until her dad's hand covered her own.

'But they didn't,' he repeated.

'Why did he show up again now?'

'No idea. Not our business. Because now the police will charge him. And I will tell them everything that happened back then with the fireworks, everything.'

'I told the policewoman about the time he confronted me in the stables and made threats.'

'Then they will have all the facts. And they can take it from there. I should've gone to them in the first place.'

'Hindsight is a wonderful thing.'

'It sure is.' Thomas took a deep breath. 'Your fear of teaching breaks my heart, you know. I hate that you doubt yourself.'

'My visitor today didn't help.'

'I'm sure it didn't.' His face softening, he asked, 'Do you

remember how Barney used to bring over the odd basket of apples from his trees?'

She managed a smile at the memory. 'He brought them for the horses and I taught him how to put his hand flat to feed them. I remember his deep chuckle the first time he did it and the horse's lips tickled his palm.'

'And do you recall finding a bad apple one day and refusing to let any of the horses have it?'

'I don't.'

'You were adamant. You marched off and threw it on the compost where it could rot away and disappear.'

'Are you saying we should throw Ewan on the compost heap?' The thought of doing so was enough to dampen the emotion of using his name. Thinking of him covered in soiled sawdust, dung, and food remnants was strangely satisfying.

'If only we could. But don't you see? He's one bad apple in a bunch of apples that are perfectly fine. He's one parent, one person who crossed your path and made life hard.'

'He really did.'

'Arnold told me a little girl fell off her horse here the other day.'

Hazel finished her tea. 'It was terrifying.'

'I know it must have been. It's never easy to witness. But do you know what else? Arnold talked to the parent, explained what had happened, and that was it. The girl is perfectly fine. The parent accepts that horse riding is risky and has shown no sign they want to stop sending their child here for lessons. Let's face it, Ewan's problem wasn't really what happened to his son, it was that he was out for trouble. Forget the bad apple, focus on the good ones.'

'You're so wise.'

With a grin, plucking another shortbread from the tin, he said, 'I do my best.'

But Hazel's smile faded. 'I'm really trying, Dad. I want to get back to normal. Especially for Arnold.'

'Your brother knows you're trying too. I don't think my behaviour back then helped in the way I thought it would, unfortunately. And I'm glad I've finally told you the truth. But it was a misguided attempt to protect you.' He shook his head, frustrated with himself. 'I can't help thinking if I'd been upfront, not paid that man, let him do what he threatened then we would've dealt with it all and put it behind us. I think in doing that you might have been back to the teaching that you love by now.'

'No, Dad. Do not put any blame on yourself. Everything you did, you did for me and for Arnold. But I'm glad you told me everything. It makes me even more determined to make this work.'

The back door opened as though Arnold might want to assess the situation indoors before he braved coming in. He told Thomas, 'You know, Franklin is most put out that you bypassed him in the field.' As soon as his boots were off, he went to his dad for a father-son hug.

'I'll make a fuss of him later. Hazel needed me first.' He held a fresh mug aloft and Arnold nodded to accept the offer of tea before grabbing a piece of shortbread from the tin.

'How are you feeling?' Arnold looked at Hazel.

'Not too bad.'

'The police will take it from here. He'll likely be charged with assault.'

Hazel wondered when their dad was going to tell Arnold all about what he'd done, paying Ewan off, but he simply passed Arnold his mug of tea once it was made. She supposed it didn't really matter much anyway. The whole truth was something they could talk about in time. For now, a calmer home and her family by her side was all Hazel wanted.

'I might leave you kids to it for a bit,' said Thomas, setting his empty mug in the sink. 'Time I went to see Franklin and tell him that we'll go out on a long ride in the morning.'

When it was just the two of them, Hazel thanked Arnold for calling their dad. 'I didn't realise how much I needed to talk to him today. It's really helped.'

'You were attacked, twice. That's not a small thing to get over, Hazel. And I understand that. I'll try to be patient.'

'You're not doing a bad job so far.' Her smile faded. 'But I won't let that man define me any longer. His threats changed a part of me, made me doubt myself, gave me an overwhelming fear. But in a weird way, him turning up today has been a good thing. I'm not for one second saying I ever want to be confronted like that again, not by anyone, but for years, I've remembered his face, his words, and now, when he's saying the same thing years on, when it's all about him and his suffering without a word about Levi, it just tells me that this is more about him than me.' She looked at her brother. 'What's that smile for?'

'I'm just pleased,' said Arnold. 'Pleased that you are such a strong person you can see at last that this was always about more than you and what happened in your lesson.'

'I can't believe I've let him and his behaviour rule my life for so long.'

'But it stops now though, right?'

'It won't happen overnight, but I'll take it one step at a time.'

'Sounds wise. And Abigail would be a good start.'

'I think so too,' Hazel smiled, sure that if there hadn't been quite so much drama here today, he might drop in a bit of teasing about Gus too.

'Where are you going?' Arnold asked when she got up from the table.

'I'm going to get dressed and I'm going to see our horses.' A bit of normality would do her the world of good. 'And I'll go find Dad and ask what he wants for dinner.'

When the front door opened, they both looked along the hallway, expecting to see Thomas when instead it was Sally.

'Mum!' Hazel was first to run to their mother, hugging her madly in the hallway, an excited greeting rather than the one their dad had got, where she'd fallen against him and he'd had to hold her up.

'I couldn't stay where I was, not when I knew what was going on up here.' Sally hugged her son next.

'How did you even get here?' Arnold asked.

'I got a train, then another train, then a third train, and a taxi from the station.'

'You must be exhausted,' said Arnold.

'Not now I'm here with you two.' She looked around the walls of the house as they all went back into the kitchen. 'I texted your dad, he knew I was coming, I told him to keep it as a surprise. And we're both here for a week, thought we needed some family time.'

And just like that, all the pieces fell into place. And for Hazel, it was the best she'd felt in years.

18

Gus had found it difficult over the last couple of days to put what had happened up at the stables far enough to the back of his mind to focus on work, but focus was what he had to do. And not only with his veterinary practice: with Abigail, more importantly. He'd worried about his daughter and what she might take away from the whole confrontation she'd witnessed at Heritage View, something a ten-year-old should never have to see, with language reserved for 9 p.m. watershed television programmes.

Julie had been a surprise in all of this. Not only had she spent almost an hour talking on the phone with Abigail about what happened; she'd also called ahead the next evening and asked whether she could visit for a couple of hours after school on Monday, Abigail's birthday rather than doing what she might usually do and sending a gift to tell her daughter she was thinking of her and making her feel special. In previous years, she would've cited work as an excuse not to come all this way during the week. But not this time. She'd come to the Cove and after a birthday tea all together, cake included, she had taken Abigail to see Denby before she went on her way.

Gus saw his final client of the day, a woman who lived on the outskirts of the Cove and had been in the Twist and Turn Bakery one day when Barney had a pile of flyers in his hand and promptly handed her one before telling her all about the new practice in the village. Bubbles, the patient, was the woman's chocolate-coloured rabbit, with wide brown eyes, and it had an abscess on its neck that Gus drained before administering antibiotics. Before she left, the woman told him she also had three dogs and a cat as well as two guinea pigs, so she'd probably see him sooner rather than later.

Now, up at the Heritage View Stables with Abigail, the sun was shining and all Gus wanted to do was see Hazel. He hadn't wanted to crowd her if she needed space, but he was desperate for her to know he was thinking of her and the brief exchange of text messages between them over the last couple of days hadn't been enough. He wanted to put his arms around her to reassure her everything was going to be okay from now on, he wanted her to look up at him and smile in a way that showed him she believed it too. He might have turned up here to check on her had she not said in her message that her parents had decided to stay a whole week for some family time. He hadn't wanted to interfere with that because it was important for Hazel to move on from what had happened. There was a history he'd never known about, and he knew what a weight from the past could do to you, it had the power to overwhelm and change things beyond your control. He knew from painful experience that there wasn't a finite limit on how you coped with these things either. They took as long as they took. And he had a feeling he could wait for Hazel for a long while. She was worth it.

'Hello, handsome boy,' said Gus, as Denby sauntered over to them. Riding hat on, Abigail was raring to go. She knew he wouldn't be able to take much time off over the summer given that his practice was new, but Gus had promised they'd be up here at the stables every day the moment he finished work. And Sandy had agreed to accompany Abigail here a couple of mornings a week, which was a great help.

Gus hadn't realised Hazel had spotted them until he heard his daughter say her name and run over to greet her. He waited for Hazel to come closer. He loved the way her eyes met his but fell away, coy, unsure what to say.

Franklin came to the fence to see the three of them and Abigail told Denby it was his turn to have a fuss. She stroked the length of Franklin's nose and let him nuzzle her hand as she apologised for not bringing a treat today.

Hazel plucked a couple of pieces of parsnip from her pocket when Franklin put his nose over the fence, as though he knew someone had something hidden away. It took Gus back to the day outside his practice when Cinnamon had sussed out he had an apple and had claimed it for himself.

Hazel handed one of the treats to Abigail to feed Franklin. 'Does Denby like parsnips?' she asked, hanging onto the other piece.

'I'm not sure.'

'Shall we see?'

Abigail took the treat and went over to Denby, who seemed to know his owner would be back his way. She held her palm flat and he wasted no time in taking the vegetable from her. 'He likes it!' Abigail announced happily.

'Better add parsnips to my shopping list,' Gus told Abigail, although his eyes were on Hazel and hers on him by now.

'The sun is finally out,' she said.

'Yeah.' He didn't want to talk about the weather.

'I'll bet you were beginning to wonder whether this was really the start of the summer holidays with all that rain.'

'Didn't stop us coming up here,' he said. He meant he had come for her, and he knew she understood, although Abigail had no intention of being excluded from this conversation. He longed to get Hazel alone.

'Denby doesn't mind rain,' Abigail informed them, as if neither of them knew.

'Franklin here gets really funny about walking through puddles if he has a rider on his back.' Hazel's confidence came back, talking about her horses. And when Abigail giggled, she added, 'I'm serious. We've been out on hacks and reached a puddle and it's taken forever to get through. I've had to dismount and lead him through it before I get back on.'

They were all laughing when Hazel's parents Thomas and Sally came over to join them. Sally had the same smile and laugh as her daughter as she told an amusing anecdote to Abigail next, something about one of her horses – Gus didn't catch the name – having a habit of nipping her on the bottom every time she tried to clean out his hooves. Abigail liked that story the best.

Gus was pleased to be so close to Hazel after a long couple of days waiting to see her properly. 'How are you?' He kept his voice low, not wanting everyone to hear him quizzing her as they shared more horse stories.

'I'm good.' And then, more convincingly, 'Very good. I'm not magically mended, but for the first time, I can see more clearly.'

'I'm glad. You look well, happy.'

'Having the family around helps.' She said, a little quieter, 'So do you.'

His breath caught, not at the shock of what she was thinking, but that she'd been so honest about it. And her smile told him all he needed to know. She was moving forwards.

Abigail interrupted them again. Gus loved his daughter to pieces, but her timing left a lot to be desired, and when Hazel grinned at him, he knew she was thinking the same.

'Can I put up Denby's signs?' From her backpack, Abigail took out the signs Lucy had made for Denby's saddle place and bridle hook in the tack room.

'That sounds like a great idea.' Hazel admired the glossy, gold name plaques, both with Denby's name alongside the silhouette of a horse. 'These are beautiful. And happy birthday, Abigail. I have a little something for you as well, I'll give it to you after.'

Gus didn't know what to say but he knew this was what he'd wanted: to feel a part of something, the way he did already in this new village they called home.

'Do you need to make a hole in the sign?' Abigail sounded concerned.

Hazel shook her head. 'I have some super strong adhesive pads in the office that have worked well for other name plaques; we'll try those, shall we?'

In the office, Hazel began to laugh at herself when she couldn't find what she was looking for. 'I like to think I'm organised, but they're fairly small pads, they could literally be anywhere.'

'I'll help.' Abigail was already opening up the drawer to the left of the desk while Hazel hunted on the shelves in the corner and the tidy boxes kept on there.

'What do they look like?' Gus asked. 'White? Black? How big?'

Hazel explained they weren't very large at all. 'They're white and will be on a backing sheet like a piece of paper.'

Abigail kept hunting. Kneeling on the desk, before Gus could tell her not to do that, she plucked a piece of paper from a colourful notebook on the shelf. 'Nope, that's not them,' she declared, but about to put back the piece of paper, she began to giggle.

'What are you laughing at?' Gus wondered, but Hazel had already come forwards and she looked hot and bothered, despite it being reasonably cool in here. And when Abigail, still amused, held out the piece of paper, he realised exactly what it was.

'I can explain,' Hazel said awkwardly, unable to meet his gaze.

'Is this you, Dad?' Abigail asked her question with her hand across her eyes as she refused to look again.

'Lucy...' Hazel stumbled over her words. 'She drew it... I mean, she's good at art.'

'She is,' Gus agreed, enjoying this moment. 'She made the signs for Denby.'

'And she draws.'

Hazel's embarrassment made him want to pull her against him so they could laugh it off together. 'I know,' he batted back, rather enjoying the way her cheeks flushed and she held her breath high in her chest as though she might burst. 'She showed me drawings at her workshop, she's talented.'

At last Hazel looked at him. 'She gave me you... I mean, that... after the class.'

'And you kept it.' It wasn't a question but an observation that pleased him.

'Got them!' Abigail announced gleefully, waving a sheet with little white adhesives on it in the air.

'Then let's get those signs on,' declared Hazel, putting the drawing back inside the notebook and leaving it in the office without looking at Gus again.

In the tack room, with the adhesives on the signs, Hazel let Abigail do the honours for the bridle place and then saddle spot. Abigail admired them for all of a few seconds before she gathered Denby's tack together.

'She's excited,' Gus told Hazel as they left the tack room and went back around to the paddocks.

'I can see that.'

He really wanted a chance to keep on talking, but with Abigail ready to groom Denby and get him ready, he sensed he wouldn't get much chance, especially not with Cinnamon this side of the fence too. Sally must be taking him for a ride and now he could hear

Abigail guiding the woman in how to pick out the horse's feet, as though Sally hadn't done the same a thousand times before. Arnold was standing by, laughing at the exchange too.

Gus supposed he'd talk to Hazel later. And it was strangely nice to know she had that picture of him, albeit a bit uncomfortable. He might have sat there naked that night for the artists to draw, but to see the image floating around weeks after the class and the whole sorry experience was over with was strangely discombobulating.

'Would you like your present now?' Hazel asked Abigail. 'I hope you're not disappointed.' She pulled a face.

'What is it?' Abigail grew impatient but remembered to give Denby's rear end a wide berth, so she didn't risk being kicked when she came around to see Hazel.

'Your birthday present is me. Well, me and Cinnamon, for a session in the school, and then, if you're up to it and your dad says yes, we'll ride down the lane and around to the bridleways.'

Abigail ran to Hazel and almost knocked her flying with a hug she clearly didn't expect. 'Thank you! Thank you! A proper ride, Dad!'

'I know, that's amazing.' He smiled at his daughter, but his focus wandered over to Hazel, this confident, beautiful woman who had just made his daughter's day.

He watched as Abigail finished grooming Denby and Hazel did the same for Cinnamon, and when both horses were tacked up, Hazel reiterated that they'd start in the school. She most likely wanted to gauge Abigail's behaviour alongside her own confidence before they ventured out. And that was fine by him.

Gus went over to Hazel's side as she got ready to mount up. Sally was helping Abigail by holding Denby still. 'Thank you for doing this.'

'It's my pleasure.'

He put a hand on her arm. 'I hope it is. I hope you enjoy this as much as I know Abigail will.'

Hazel mounted her horse and, taking the reins, she looked down at him. 'Thank you for trusting me.'

But he waved away the gratitude that wasn't necessary. 'I was wondering... I know we went to the ice-creamery, but what do you say to meeting up again, just the two of us?'

Cinnamon tossed his head as though he thought it might be a good idea. 'You mean like a date?' she asked, seemingly happy at his suggestion.

'Yeah, like a date.' Just the word made him happy, especially when she smiled back at him.

'What do you have in mind?'

'Something simple, how about a picnic?'

'Ready!' came Abigail's voice.

'I would love a picnic,' she said so only Gus could hear, and as he watched them ride over to the school, he tried to come back down to earth.

Arnold came over to stand with him. 'You two coming here has been the answer to my prayers,' he confided. 'This moment has been a long time coming.'

'I can well believe that.' He could now that he knew everything that had happened to Hazel.

And as Gus stood back, watching the scene play out in front of him, he thought about what Arnold had said. He might appreciate their appearance in the Cove and what it had done for Hazel, but in the same way, Gus knew that Heritage Cove had brought him and his daughter something very special too. And he hoped this was only the beginning.

19

Hazel came downstairs to a wolf whistle from Arnold and told him to be quiet. 'You've seen me out of my horsey clothes before,' she said. She had on a floaty, pale-blue dress with tiny yellow flowers, her hair hung in loose waves, and she had a little bit of mascara on that made her blue eyes appear wide.

'I have,' he declared, 'but there's an air of something else about you...' He put both of his hands, one on top of the other, against his heart and did double rhythmic beats.

'Oh, stop it,' she told him. 'You're such a loser.'

But no matter the teasing, it was good to see her brother more laid back. Hazel was healing and it had started with the lesson for Abigail. Her progress would be a slow build, she wouldn't return to teaching youngsters and beginners right away, but she'd get there in the end. Baby steps, her brother had said to her after Abigail's lesson, and she'd smiled and repeated the same words to him.

With a picnic blanket rolled into its holder that she hooked over her shoulder, Hazel walked from Heritage View all the way into the village. She and Gus had arranged to meet today on their first official date. Abigail was at the waffle shack with Peter and so it would be just the two of them. As Hazel made her way to The Street, she smiled to herself. Now she'd taken the first step to return to teaching youngsters and novices, it was as though her mind had switched gears and she was able to fit more into her life from a personal side too.

After the day Hazel had given Abigail a riding lesson as her eleventh birthday present, Hazel would never forget the little girl's delight and the admiration from her dad. She'd tried to read Gus that day, wondered whether he'd be nervous of her teaching his daughter now he knew what had happened to make her shy away from teaching kids. But all she'd seen was what she hoped was happiness and adoration, and that had certainly been the case as they'd begun the lesson in the school. Abigail was a competent rider, but more than that, she didn't assume she knew it all; she listened and she was respectful, qualities Hazel suspected were learnt almost by osmosis from her dad.

And that lesson had been a start. They'd only been down to the quieter bridleway, it would be some time before Hazel wanted to take anyone up towards the village and more traffic, but that time would come, she felt sure of it. She'd not taught another child yet, but she had three separate individual lessons to do so this week. Arnold, Sally, and Thomas all agreed that one-on-one lessons were probably best at this stage: focus on a single student and take it from there. And rather than dreading it, Hazel was nervous but felt able to cope. Finally, it felt as though she was getting back a piece of herself.

Hazel crossed over at the corner towards the Twist and Turn Bakery, where she spotted Gus holding a couple of paper bags.

'You've already got the picnic for us?' she asked, trying to detract from him looking at her so intently. She surreptitiously took in his appearance in dark green shorts, muscular forearms in a white T-shirt. He looked good, and when she caught a waft of spicy sensual shower gel or aftershave, it was as though her nerves switched to high alert.

'I thought I'd go into the bakery alone so that we don't become local gossip just yet.' His fingertips grazed hers as he swapped the bakery bags to one hand and turned to walk around the bend as though heading out of the village.

Hazel almost began to laugh and said quietly, 'Too late.'

As Barney and Lois walked towards them, Barney winked and boomed a hello. Lois had her arm linked through her husband's and with a greeting of her own, she wouldn't let him stop.

'Do you think they know?' Gus murmured against Hazel's ear as they walked on.

She replied, 'I expect Barney knew before either of us did.' And this time, she slotted her hand beneath his, their fingers slipping between each other's and staying that way until they'd gone around the bend, through the gates, and out to the countryside. They were headed for a small area perfect for a cosy picnic, just beyond the bridleways. Not many people knew about the area because it was difficult to see, unless you were on horseback and could spot it from a distance.

Before Hazel could unroll the blanket, she caught sight of a rabbit in the longer grass near an upturned log. 'Did you see him?' It hopped into sight again briefly and this time stopped momentarily, looked at them both, its long ears stretched tall before it turned and flashed them its fluffy tail and disappeared once again.

Gus took the picnic blanket from her shoulder, flicked the carrier open, and laid it out on the ground. He set the paper bags from the bakery down and took both of Hazel's hands in his own. Hazel realised she was nervous. It had been easier to focus on the rabbit than Gus, as she'd never felt quite this jittery on a date before.

She gulped when Gus moved his hand beneath her chin, gently coaxing her to look up at him. 'Is this moving too fast?'

She shook her head.

'Tell me if it is. Although I suppose I have already put you to bed.'

With a grin, she replied, 'And I've already seen you naked.'

He took a step even closer so that their bodies were pressed together in the warmth of the sunshine from up above. 'No time to waste, then.'

'Aren't you hungry?' she breathed as he dipped his head.

'Not particularly.'

Her eyes fell to his mouth as she murmured, 'Me neither.'

And when Hazel kissed Gus, she wondered how it had ever taken them so long to find one another.

Because somehow the pieces just fit.

ACKNOWLEDGMENTS

I can't tell you how wonderful it's been to work with the magnificent team at Boldwood Books on this latest book in the Heritage Cove series. A huge thank you to everyone... I'm thrilled to be a part of Team Boldwood!

A big thank you to Tara Loder, my editor, who has guided me from conception of idea right through to publication and I'm so proud of what we've achieved together with this book. I love how supportive and involved Tara is when we discuss ideas, plots, characters and all the ingredients that go into a work of fiction. Thank you also to Claire Fenby and Jenna Houston for such wonderful graphics, advertising, and social media plans as well as timely advice - their knowledge and dedication is incredible. Thank you too to Nia Beynon who initially began discussions surrounding my backlist of books including my Heritage Cove series. And of course, none of this would be possible without the fabulous Jessica Redland, writing friend and a truly generous human being. It is Jessica who introduced me to Boldwood and I owe her a debt of gratitude for doing so. Thank you so very much Jessica!

When I wrote this book I thought all my knowledge about horses and horse riding would come flooding back, but it's surprising how much I'd forgotten. I spent a long time watching YouTube videos which were wonderful for helping me with horse terminology and knowing how to groom a horse, put on a bridle, put on a saddle, how to bath a horse. I'd like to thank Equine Helper on YouTube for so much informative and brilliant footage.

I'd also like to thank my bestie Amara Ugoji for answering all my questions about horse riding whether it was about grooming, what a rider should wear, terminology or horse feeding and care. Living in different hemispheres we don't get to chat as much as I'd like but Amara kept those answers flying back across the miles!

Thank you also to Emma Lambert and Helen Rasberry, two very generous readers who helped to answer a whole heap of horse questions too. I hope you love *Finding Happiness at Heritage View* and that I've done the stables and the world of horse riding justice.

YouTube and the internet were fabulous resources when it came to creating Gus's character and new veterinary practice and as well as online research I'd also like to thank my mum for giving me a rundown of what it's like to visit a veterinary surgery. All I could remember from my childhood was a smell of disinfectant but Mum helped me understand what goes on at an appointment and what to expect. Thanks Mum!

To my husband and my daughters who are always by my side and supporting me every step of the way – I love you all so very much. I hope you'll always be celebrating publication days with me.

And finally, to each and every reader who has picked up a copy of this book or listened to the audio version. I'm so pleased to have found you all and I hope you continue to enjoy my novels for many years to come.

Much love,

Helen x

MORE FROM HELEN ROLFE

We hope you enjoyed reading *Finding Happiness at Heritage View*. If you did, please leave a review.

If you'd like to gift a copy, this book is also available as an ebook, digital audio download and audiobook CD.

Sign up to Helen Rolfe's mailing list for news, competitions and updates on future books.

https://bit.ly/HelenRolfeNews

Coming Home to Heritage Cove, the first in the Heritage Cove series, is available now.

ABOUT THE AUTHOR

Helen Rolfe is the author of many bestselling contemporary women's fiction titles, set in different locations from the Cotswolds to New York. Most recently published by Orion, she is bringing sixteen titles to Boldwood - a mixture of new series and well- established backlist. She lives in Hertfordshire with her husband and children.

Follow Helen on social media:

 twitter.com/hjrolfe
 facebook.com/helenjrolfewriter
 instagram.com/helen_j_rolfe